THE L[...]

As far as Miss Caroline Wentworth was concerned, Mr. Robert Neville clearly had to be taught a lesson. And just as clearly, she was the only one to do it. . . .

Everyone else was at his beck and call. Gentlemen imitated his polished manners, elegant garb, and dissolute morals. Mothers with marriageable daughters used every design and device to win his favor. Young ladies' lashes fluttered wildly at his most casual glance. Even Caroline's beautiful but susceptible younger sister Julia was under his seductive spell.

It was up to Caroline alone to show this invulnerable egotist that he was just another man . . . even as he did his dazzling best to teach her she was very much a woman. . . .

A
Brilliant
Alliance

by

Elizabeth Jackson

A SIGNET BOOK

SIGNET
Published by the Penguin Group
Penguin Books USA Inc., 375 Hudson Street,
New York, New York 10014, U.S.A.
Penguin Books Ltd, 27 Wrights Lane,
London W8 5TZ, England
Penguin Books Australia Ltd, Ringwood,
Victoria, Australia
Penguin Books Canada Ltd, 10 Alcorn Avenue,
Toronto, Ontario, Canada M4V 3B2
Penguin Books (N.Z.) Ltd, 182-190 Wairau Road,
Auckland 10, New Zealand.

Penguin Books Ltd, Registered Offices:
Harmondsworth, Middlesex, England

First published by Signet, an imprint of New American Library,
a division of Penguin Books USA Inc.

First Printing, March, 1993
10 9 8 7 6 5 4 3 2 1

Ⓟ REGISTERED TRADEMARK—MARCA REGISTRADA

Printed in the United States of America

1

MISS CAROLINE WENTWORTH settled back into her chair, automatically positioning her hand so that it covered the worn spot in the brocade, and fetched up a deep sigh. To be sure, the Aubusson carpet was faded and the curtains so stitched and restitched as to alter their original pattern, but the shabbiness was of longstanding duration, and it was not the gloom of the library at Wyndham Priory that occasioned such a melancholy response. In fact, the Gothic windows overlooked a lovely prospect of informal gardens and a vast expanse of unscythed lawn, deep green in the cool sunshine, and it was this scene of familiar beauty that touched her with all the pain of impending loss.

She was not alone in her distress. Her mother, Lady Wentworth, was kept from swooning only by frequent application to her vinaigrette, as well as to the array of laudanum, tincture of valerian, Hungary water, and Godfrey's cordial arranged to buttress her exquisite sensibility. Beside her on the settee sat Caroline's younger sister Julia, her beautiful blue eyes glittering with unshed tears, and over them both hovered the black-coated figure of their man of business, Mr. Lambert, like some ill-omened bird of prey.

This comparison was perhaps unfair to Mr. Lambert, who had so far behaved with perfect propriety and was at this moment doing his best to calm the tempestuous feelings of her ladyship and the younger Miss Wentworth. "My dear madam, Miss Wentworth, I would have spared you this if I could, but we agreed—yes, yes, your ladyship's drops! We agreed, did we not, dear ma'am, that your only choice was to sell Wyndham Priory. When his lordship passed on—"

At the mention of her much-lamented spouse, her ladyship roused herself. "I never liked the idea, never!" she said, in threadlike tones. "Nothing will ever convince me that Wentworth could have left things in such a state as you represent! Why, he told me many times that he expected to bring the Priory back to its former glory, and I know he was hopeful of a number of transactions on the stock exchange. *You* were his man of business," she said, rounding on the unfortunate Mr. Lambert; "could not *you* have managed his affairs so that we need not have suffered this misfortune?"

Mr. Lambert, who had repeatedly advised his lordship against such unwise investments, and who had tried valiantly to stem the tide of mounting debts of honor, mortgages, and expenses (of which he profoundly hoped her ladyship was unaware) laid out for the muslin company, opened and closed his mouth several times in an attempt to frame a reply. He was saved from this necessity by the elder Miss Wentworth, who interjected, "Oh no, Mama, how can you say so? You know Mr. Lambert was not"—she gave him a slight smile, which showed him that she knew very well how matters stood—"wholly admitted into Papa's confidence, and it was his schemes upon the 'change that put paid to us once and for all. And it is Mr. Lambert, after all, who has kept the creditors away from our door for the last year, or we might have been turned out of the house while we were still in mourning."

Such plain speech caused Lady Wentworth to have recourse to her restoratives again and Julia to protest, "Caro, please! Remember Mama's nerves."

Caroline thought she was unlikely to be able to forget them, but said firmly, "I'm so sorry, Mama, but I shouldn't like Mr. Lambert to think we are ungrateful, when he has gone to so much trouble on our behalf."

Lady Wentworth gave her a pained look, but fluttered her fingers and murmured, "Of course. So very kind."

Mr. Lambert was sufficiently heartened to bow graciously and resume his seat behind his late lordship's desk. "Well, ahem! I assure your ladyship that I have taken as much care as possible to allay anxiety, because nothing could be more *fatal* than to have one's creditors scenting ruin, believe me. There would be no stopping the demands for payment *then*. That is why the utmost discretion had to be observed in soliciting a buyer for the estate, and, of course, a buyer whose pecuniary circumstances were in so felicitous a state as to be able to accommodate your ladyship's, ah, rather pressing need. I am pleased to say that I have located such a person and have concluded terms that are extremely favorable." He stopped, apparently expecting congratulations, got none, and hurried on. "A most respectable gentleman, of *very* great means. He plans to plow considerable brass—er, money into the estate. He says he would like to *transform* Wyndham Priory."

A horrid suspicion suggested itself to Lady Wentworth. "I knew it!" she exclaimed piteously, fanning herself frantically in an attempt to avert a spasm. "A cit! A mushroom! Some vulgarian who will pull out the wainscotting and the stone fireplaces and install gas lighting or some such thing! Transform Wyndham Priory indeed! When it's been good enough for the Wentworths for—oh, a thousand years!"

"Not quite, Mama," said Caroline with a wry smile, "and the monks did have it first."

"Yes, my love, but I don't doubt there were Wentworth monks as well. But what does it signify? I will not have some odious merchant putting shop-soiled hands on my house! I will not!"

Mr. Lambert, who perceived that he had taken the wrong tack, turned his bow to the wind at once. "No, ma'am, I beg you! It's no such thing. I assure you I have too much respect for his lordship's memory, and for your ladyship too, to approach such a person as you describe, however great his means. No, the buyer I have located is a member of one of the oldest families in England and is very good ton. As for *transforming* the Priory, I only meant that he plans to restore it to its former heights—much as Lord Wentworth himself hoped to do!" He stopped and mopped his brow apprehensively. "His name," he said, producing his last and best argument with a dramatic flourish, "is Robert Neville."

Julia gasped. "The Nonpareil?"

Mr. Lambert bowed triumphantly. The lengthy illness and subsequent death of Lord Wentworth, followed by the prescribed period of mourning, had buried his ladies in the country for nearly two years, but they were not so far removed from Society that they had not heard of Mr. Neville, the *rich* Mr. Neville, a Pink of the Ton, an Arbiter of Fashion, and, for a number of years, the biggest prize on the Matrimonial Mart.

"Why on earth would he want to buy Wyndham Priory?" asked Caroline. "He has his own estates, surely?"

Mr. Lambert nodded. "A London town house, a hunting box, and of course there is Chartleigh, the family estate. Mr. Neville *particularly* wishes to acquire the Priory. But you will appreciate, Miss Wentworth, that just as I must be diligent in maintaining the discretion of your family in this matter, something of the same sort is owed to the Nevilles, and I feel it incumbent on me to say no more of a personal nature about him. Suffice it to say that the terms are very generous, as you will see in these documents, and Mr. Neville wishes to accommodate your ladyship and the Misses Wentworth in every way possible as to your removal from the estate, items of furnishings you wish to retain, and the like."

"Well, I'm sure that's very handsome of him," said her ladyship reflectively, "but I fear I shall be so overset at the thought of moving that I don't know how I shall be able to manage it. In fact, I shouldn't be at all surprised if the blow was so shattering it carried me off altogether. I daresay that would be for the best in any event. I'm sure *I* don't wish to be a burden to anyone; anything in the nature of that sort of selfishness is quite unknown to me."

Some minutes after this were occupied with the remonstrations of Lady Wentworth's dear ones, so that it was a short while before Mr. Lambert was able to settle the details of the sale and obtain the necessary signatures on his documents. He then begged their indulgence in attending one other matter of a painful but unfortunately necessary nature. "In short, my lady, I have also found a buyer for the jewelry!"

Julia, who had not been privy to this scheme, started up, real alarm on her face. "Not the Wentworth diamonds!"

Mr. Lambert bowed his head sorrowfully. "Most particularly the Wentworth diamonds, I'm afraid."

"But Mama! I am to wear them when I am presented at Court. Caro did, and all the Wentworths! You *can't* sell them, Mama. They mean too much to me."

"That will do, Julia," said Lady Wentworth faintly. "Your distress can hardly rival mine, and as you see I am quite calm. I have become inured to disaster. Not only shall I have no roof over my head, but I shall have no clothes, no jewels, no coaches, nothing. Yet you do not see *me* complain."

"Oh, my lady!" exclaimed Mr. Lambert. "I trust it won't come to that!"

Julia looked at her sister through damp lashes. "Oh, Caro, I don't think I can bear it."

Caroline, seeing her eyes fill with tears again, addressed herself to Mr. Lambert in a voice of quiet composure. "Is there no way to put off the sale of the diamonds until after my sister has her London Season?"

Mr. Lambert, to whom plain speaking in such delicate matters was anathema, was tempted to present her with some of the soothing evasions he had been using on Lady Wentworth for the past year, but something about her manner overbore his instincts. Miss Caroline did not have the beauty of her bewitching younger sister, but her self-possession, and the intelligent expression in her wide gray eyes made her extremely attractive, and when she smiled at him he was even inclined to admit that she was very taking indeed.

"I am very much afraid, my dear Miss Wentworth ... well, the fact of the matter is that there are creditors who simply will not wait any longer to be paid, and then—ahem!—her ladyship's expenditures during the past year have not been trifling. It must be either the jewelry or the London house at once, and of course, you would not wish to sell the town house before your sister embarks upon her Season."

"Badly dipped," muttered Caroline, under the cover of her mother's audible rejection of any such notion.

"I am afraid so, yes."

She put her arms around her younger sister and said soothingly, "It *will* be all right, love, you'll see. *You* don't need diamonds to set off your beauty, at Court or anywhere else." It was quite true. Julia's golden curls, dazzling blue eyes and delicate features gave her the look of an angel, and at seventeen she bade fair to become the accredited beauty Lady Wentworth had been at the same age. It was only Caroline, with her gray eyes and darker coloring, who resembled their father.

"It won't be the *same*," Julia protested unarguably. "Oh pray, Mr. Lambert, don't ever tell me who shall have the diamonds in my stead. Hide it from me, please!"

"Well, now, Miss Julia, that's just the way I feel too," said Mr. Lambert, only too happy to concur in these sentiments. "It's quite usual in these matters for the buyer to remain anonymous, and in a case of such—delicacy—I can't but think that would be best."

"I don't care if a red Indian buys them, so long as he is discreet," said Lady Wentworth. "No doubt I will have to become accustomed to being treated as a person of secondary consequence, but I will *not* have anyone flaunting my jewels on the ton, and making sport of my misfortune!" Her ladyship, despite having become inured to disaster, showed alarming symptoms of requiring her vinaigrette and begged leave of her man of business to bring the interview to a close. "For I must go and rest now, while a measure of comfort is preserved to me!"

"Oh, Caro, wasn't he the most *odious* man?" Julia cried, when the room was empty of her mother and Mr. Lambert. "Prosing on and on in that *dolorous* way, when I'm quite sure we shall come about in the end. Not but that it's too late to save Wyndham Priory, but I've thought of a plan!

But, Caroline, you mustn't let Mama dispose of the jewels!"

Caroline looked at her with concern. "Julia, I beg you not to deceive yourself. We are 'in the basket,' as Bertie would say. Under the hatches! The truth is, Papa brought an abbey to a grange, and now we have to make the best of it."

"Caro!" cried Julia, shocked. "How can you speak so of poor Papa?"

"I say no more than the truth."

"But he is *dead*."

"You are quite right," Caroline said calmly. "And blaming him won't change matters in any event. But you must understand that we are at *point-non-plus*. What could be more foolish than clinging to our consequence when only the strictest economies will keep us out of debt? Mr. Lambert was most specific: we must sell either the town house or the jewelry at once, and you would *much* rather make your come-out in London this year, would you not?"

"But that is precisely why I need the diamonds. It's part of my plan to save us." She smiled radiantly. "I am going to contract a Brilliant Alliance! I know I can, if I set my mind to it."

"Julia—"

"Now don't scold, Caro! You know Mama will support me in this."

"Julia, you never said anything of this to Mama! She has scarcely forgiven me for being unmindful of my duty in that respect, and my come-out was two years ago!"

"Yes, but it's hardly fair of her, when we had to leave town because of Papa's illness only a month into the Season, and we've been here ever since. And you did make Lord Ridley fall in love with you, and it's not *your* fault he hadn't a feather to fly with so that he had to marry an heiress instead."

"You will oblige me," said her sister with a slight flush, "if you forget any romantical notions you might have about Viscount Ridley. We were scarcely acquainted long enough to form an attachment."

"Well, but the point is, if you could succeed on the ton,

so could I! In fact—" she broke off, biting her lip in embarrassment.

"In fact, you are likely to enjoy far greater success," Caro finished for her with a laugh, "if you can check the impulse to point that out yourself. But, seriously, Julia, you may depend upon it that word of our misfortunes will get out before the Season ever begins, and it will make a difference. We will no longer be the *Wentworths of Wyndham Priory*. I have had just enough experience to discover that where a fortune is nonexistent, a great many eligible gentlemen suddenly become quite impervious to one's other attractions."

"Well, that is true of *young* men, perhaps," Julia persisted, "but surely there are wealthy old men who wouldn't mind a young wife with no money."

"I daresay," Caroline said dryly, "but I think it is far better to let everything go than to sell yourself like that. I know you, Julia! You would be quite miserable if you didn't love your husband!"

"Mama says that to *esteem* one's husband is all that's required," Julia replied smugly, "and I'm sure I should be able to esteem anyone who rescues me from a life of counting out the coals in the grate and living on the charity of Aunt Needham in Bath. You don't understand, Caro, because you've resigned yourself to living as a prop to Mama or some such thing. I *can't* live that way. I'm not meant to!"

Caroline knew from experience that urging her sister against taking an action was the surest way to impel her into it, so she held her tongue. There was no real harm in Julia, but she had been petted and cossetted from an early age, and her striking beauty had made her the darling of everyone from the servants hall upward. Her mother had made little attempt to discourage her vanity, and in fact had abetted it. If she had an enlarged notion of her own consequence it was little to be wondered at, but she also had a tender heart and a passionate nature which made her lapses more forgivable. Caroline hoped that her impulsiveness would not lead her into lack of conduct in London, where the consequence to her sister's reputation could be so much more injurious than in the country.

The two sisters had lapsed into silence, the one mulish and the other pensive, and both welcomed the interruption when Fenwick, the butler, opened the door to announce Mr. Bertram Lacey, who, upon being told that her ladyship was not to be disturbed, wondered if the Misses Wentworth were at home to him. One look at Fenwick's exceptionally lugubrious countenance told Caroline that the true nature of Mr. Lambert's visit was at least in some degree already known to the servants, but that was only to be expected. "Please show him in here, Fenwick," she said promptly, "you know we don't stand on ceremony with Mr. Lacey."

Mr. Bertram Lacey, whose cockfighting cant Caroline had already invoked, was the son of Lord Wentworth's nearest neighbor and old friend. He was a year younger than Caroline, and one older than Julia. The senior Mr. Lacey, while of less exalted rank than his noble friend, was considerably plumper in the pocket, and his son would come into a handsome estate some day. At one time it was his parents' fond hope that their Bertram might make a match with one of the Wentworth girls, and indeed they had stood godparents to Julia, but of late there was little talk on such a subject. Nevertheless, the young Mr. Lacey had run tame at the Priory for years, and the family there regarded him in the light of a sort of honorary brother.

He was also, on this day, an aspiring Tulip of Fashion. His buckskin breeches set off a pair of very good legs, and the fit of his coat, while not eloquent of Weston or Stultz, had little need of enhancement by buckram wadding. But his shirt points were so stiff and high he could scarcely turn his head, and his disordered locks, which he supposed made him look Byronic, but which Caroline secretly thought made him look worried, affected a modishness beyond that of a country gentleman. His one regret was that his father, whose sole purpose in life seemed to be to blight his son's aspirations to Fashion, refused to supply him with the champagne necessary to exact a truly splendid shine from his top boots.

"Bertie, who do you think's bought Wyndham Priory?" cried Julia explosively when Fenwick had closed the door.

"Can't think," said Mr. Lacey succinctly.

"Mr. Robert Neville!"

"Oh, I say! Top of the trees! A real Corinthian!"

This unrestrained enthusiasm did not sit well with the Misses Wentworth, who were united in regarding him with a stricken look. "Oh, I didn't m-mean, well, he's all the crack and all that, but I had *much* liefer have you as neighbors," he backtracked, looking acutely uncomfortable. "Caro, Julia, you know I didn't mean it!"

"I daresay the idea takes some getting used to on all our parts," Caroline said compassionately, "and as long as *we* can't stay on here, I'm glad you'll have a neighbor you can be on good terms with."

"Be on good terms?" said Mr. Lacey with a laugh. "With the Nonpareil? He's above my touch, I can tell you. I shouldn't wonder at it if he's far too top-lofty to mix with the likes of us. Not at all the thing, you know!"

"Well, if he's a Neville, he's certainly no better than a *Wentworth*," protested Julia, "and I'm sure the neighborhood was quite good enough for us."

"Shouldn't wonder that you're both blue-deviled," Mr. Lacey said sagely. "Wish there was something I could do!"

"Well, there's something *I* intend to do," announced Julia grandly. "I am going to save the family fortune by forming an eligible connection. In fact," she added, as an idea occurred to her, "I don't see why it shouldn't be with Mr. Neville. Then none of us would have to leave the Priory!"

Mr. Lacey's mouth fell open. "Gammon! You're short a sheet, Julia! A man like that get leg-shackled to a chit from the schoolroom? When diamonds of the first water have been casting out lures for him for years? Not to mention all the high flyers he's had under his protection! You've got windmills in your head, my girl!"

"Well, of all the beastly things to say!" responded Julia. "You might as well call me an antidote and be done with it."

"And you needn't try to wheedle me into paying you

compliments," Mr. Lacey continued, in fine form. "Didn't say you won't take in London; you ain't a Homely Joan, even if you are bird-witted."

Julia's bosom heaved in indignation. "I am *not* bird-witted."

"Well, you are if you think you can land Neville," he said conclusively.

Julia was not her father's daughter for nothing. "Lay you a pony!"

"Done!"

"Julia! Bertie! Will you two stop pulling caps?" cried Caroline. "Julia, I'm sure Mr. Neville would find you delightful in every way, but I'm inclined to agree with Bertie that men of his age, particularly men of what can only be charitably called experience, do not generally make suitable husbands for girls of seventeen. Moreover," she added with a smile, because she did not take either her sister's scheme or her bet very seriously, "under the rather *delicate* circumstance of his buying the Priory from us, any attempt on your part to attach Mr. Neville could only be seen as the grossest sort of mercenary behavior, and would probably ruin any chance you have of forming *any* kind of connection at all."

"Besides making you the *on-dit* of the ton," added Mr. Lacey.

"Oh, pooh!" said Julia sulkily. "I think you're both very poor-spirited, I must say. In any case," she added with a sigh, "I daresay I won't get the chance to cut any kind of a figure in London, because that horrid Mr. Lambert says we must sell the jewels, and Mama wants me to make do with some of Caro's hand-me-downs for day wear, because ball dresses and such are so shockingly expensive! And how I'm to get on without jewels or clothes I'm sure I don't know!"

Mr. Lacey and Miss Wentworth exchanged glances. "That reminds me," said he, clearing his throat. "Forgot to mention why I called. Brought Lady Wentworth a note from Mama. Wants you to come and spend a week or two with us before you go up to town. Thought it might make it easier for you to l-leave Wyndham Priory, and she wants to make a present to Julia of her Court dress. Godmama, and all that."

"Oh, Bertie," said Julia rapturously, "how very kind of her. I'm sure Mama will be happy to accept. She's quite overset by having to leave the Priory, and dear Mrs. Lacey will be such a comfort to her."

"I'm afraid I'm committed to visiting Lady Withering in town," said Caroline. "She's *my* godmother, you know, and I shouldn't like to disappoint her. She was expecting us all, but to be perfectly frank, while she and Mama were bosom-pieces when they were girls, three days in each other's company is more than sufficient to exhaust their mutual goodwill. I can go up with Fenwick and the servants, and oversee opening up the house, and I'm sure Lady Withering won't mind sending her coach back for Julia and Mama."

"Thing is," said Mr. Lacey, "I can escort them up myself. My father is sending me up to town on business, and I—he—thought I ought to visit my uncle while I'm there. Might as well take advantage of the Season, you know."

"Acquiring a little town bronze, Bertie?" asked Caroline.

He blushed and grinned. "Can't say my father would like that idea! Wants me to settle down, learn how to run the estate. Don't say that he's wrong, but dash it all! I mean to have a bang-up time and see all the sights before I'm too old to enjoy 'em. As long as my uncle's standing the huff, my father can't object. Besides, told him somebody ought to go up to London to keep an eye on the two of you!"

"I collect that was the deciding argument," said Caroline.

"Good God, Caro, you must know *your* behavior never puts one to the blush," he said at once. "But Julia . . ." He turned and favored her with a speaking glance, which prompted her to throw a book at him from across the room.

"Bertie, you are quite as odious as Mr. Lambert," Julia said with passion, "and that is saying a great deal. Besides which, it is very shabby of you to use me as an excuse for hoaxing your papa. But I *shall* make use of you in London. You are going to help me find a *suitable parti.*"

"Good God," said Mr. Lacey again.

2

18
had underta
not accor
dyshir
der

THE REMOVAL of the Wentworths from Wyndham Priory was accomplished in due course, and when the carriage that was to take her up to town at length rolled out the gates, Caroline thought that however long she lived she would never be called upon to endure a more trying fortnight than that preceding her departure. Mr. Neville had sent word through Mr. Lambert that his claim to the furnishings of the household extended only to those things that might properly be considered part of the house's history, and that in all other matters they should feel free to accommodate themselves. Accordingly, each item became a battle ground of sensibility, invested with a nostalgic power to cast Lady Wentworth into a fit of the dismals. Her ladyship, equally determined to think herself ill-used as well as to be a trouble to no one, worked herself into such a state that Caroline feared she really would become ill, and much of the work of directing the packing fell by necessity to her lot. Julia was of little more use; Caroline would daily find her in contemplation of a beloved prospect or marquetry table or picture or pottery jug, fixing it with a mournful glance, and audibly imagining, in the most melancholy accents, some woeful change in its condition to be brought about by a new master.

As Caroline was suffering from a certain oppression of spirits herself, she was scarcely able to maintain an air of cheerfulness, and the sorting and the wrapping and the dispensing of many of the household items to their—now Mr. Neville's—tenants were accomplished in an atmosphere of decided gloom. The only bright spot was that Mr. Neville

.en to maintain all of the servants who would
.pany them to the London town house or to her la-
s establishment in Bath, so the fate of their depen-
.s at least was assured. Caroline had to believe that the
.ay of their departure, hers to town, and her sister's and
mother's to the Laceys, could not come any too soon for
everyone's peace of mind.

The first part of her journey was performed in such a fu-
nereal disposition, dictated in part by the inclement weather
and in part by the stately pace mandated by Lady Withering's elderly coachman, as to render it tedious, giving her
ample time to indulge in a fit of apprehension about her
forthcoming visit to London and to reflect on the melancholy nature of her own abbreviated Season. This, as Julia
had suggested, had not been a success. Scarcely a few days
after her come-out Caroline had become the object of
Charles, Viscount Ridley's, most particular attentions. For
three weeks he called, took her for rides in the park, and
stood up with her for every dance propriety would permit.
Her godmother had tried to warn her that his financial affairs were such that his intentions could not be serious, but
his handsome face and his air of address caught her off
guard, and in a short while she was more than halfway to
being in love with him. She could not believe he would be
so persistent in distinguishing her if he had nothing more in
mind than a flirtation, or that he could be so callous as to
trifle with her feelings. So, when the sudden illness of Lord
Wentworth caused the abrupt departure of the family from
London, she expected very soon to see him at Wyndham
Priory. He did come, but his manner was so cool, his inquiries about her father's health and her own well-being of
so perfunctory a nature, that the announcement of his engagement to a considerable heiress, scarcely three weeks
after this event, did not come as quite the surprise to her it
might otherwise have been supposed.

She was too collected to parade her bruised feelings before her family, especially in such a time of stress for them
all, and after a short while even Julia ceased to tease her
about it. She told herself that inexperience had led her to

read more into the well-bred ease of a Man of Fashion than he intended, but she still could not quite forgive him. Moreover, while she would be perfectly happy to move in Society when the opportunity presented itself, she could not but regard it with a certain skepticism, and she vowed that she would never allow consideration of fortune to direct her choice of a husband, even if it meant that she ended her days as an ape-leader in Bath.

This unsatisfactory history, and the undoubted bleakness of her future in Bath, went a long way toward persuading her to eschew the probable slights and disappointments of another Season altogether, but her plans were fixed, and in time the leavening effects of natural good humor and liberation from the oppressive sensibilities of her mother and sister wrought a change in her spirits. When the traveling coach at length pulled up before her ladyship's front door in Park Street, Caroline was in a much better frame of mind than when she had left the Priory, and was able to look forward to her visit with tolerable composure, if not every anticipation of pleasure.

Lady Withering greeted her with kindness, clasping her to her ample bosom, bidding her shed her thick pelisse and change out of her traveling dress in time for dinner, which had been put back for her arrival. Her mother's friend was not a woman of particular sense, and the years had done more to broaden her waistline than her horizons, but she was very good-humored and was genuinely fond of her goddaughter. Her late husband was a man of breeding and considerable means, who had done her the good turn of sticking his spoon in the wall before he could grow tired of his silly wife, so that she had only the happiest memories of their time together. She was in general an indolent creature, but her passion was Society, and no amount of exertion was too great to secure the latest *on-dits*, discover the newest French milliner, or secure tickets to the performance of the diva who was the current favorite. As she moved in the First Circles, she had had high hopes of helping to launch her goddaughter and of seeing her settled in respectable, if not brilliant, circumstances by the end of her first Season, and no one could have been more disappointed at its lamentable outcome. She was outraged at the behavior of Lord Ridley and had even tried, without success, to hint him away after her rather plainer warnings to Caroline were disregarded. She perfectly understood, and sympathized with, his need to marry money, but he had taken pains to seriously engage the affections of a green girl when what he had in mind was a mild flirtation, and then he had trampled on those affections in a most ungentlemanly and unfeeling manner. She wondered if Caroline knew that Ridley's wife had died, leaving him considerably plumper in the pocket, about the same time as Lord Wentworth. She decided it would not matter much if she did, though she might drop just the tiniest hint so her goddaughter would not be taken unawares. She had far too good an opinion of Caroline's common sense to accuse her of nursing a *tendre* for someone who had treated her so shabbily. What she needed was diversion, and a chance to try her wings a little. The poor girl had been buried in the country for the last two years, and while all of Lady Wentworth's attentions would now be focused on Julia, Lady Withering intended to see that Caroline was not overlooked.

"My dear," she said that evening to Caroline when they sat before the fire in the small saloon drinking tea, "I have been thinking the best way to bring you out into Society again, after the—the misfortune that's befallen your family. I know you are too sensible a girl not to realize that word gets out about these things, and you should be introduced quietly, in a smaller way than we might otherwise have done. I know your dear mama plans a brilliant come-out for Julia, but I fear it's not at all the thing to call too much attention to oneself in these circumstances. Not that it wouldn't be equally fatal to seem to be *stricken* or to hide oneself away!"

Caroline looked startled. "Dear ma'am, I hope you won't tease yourself on my account! I have not the slightest interest in cutting a figure in Society, and will be happy to visit and receive those few acquaintances from two years back who can be counted on *not* to be overset by what you rightly name the family's misfortune. I might wish that the plans for Julia's Season were a little less costly and brilliant, but if you could see how much pleasure the prospect affords them both, you would not even attempt to dissuade them. I'm sure I wouldn't!"

"No, and you couldn't if you would," Lady Withering said candidly. "Besides, you need not scruple to tell me that your poor mama has little notion of economy, for I know it well enough!" She set the Sèvres cup delicately on the tray and sat back in her chair. "But my love, you must get out a little. You won't meet any eligible gentlemen otherwise, and then how will you ever get an offer?"

"I'm not perfectly sure I *want* to get any offers, at least not the sort I am likely to get under the circumstances," Caroline said calmly. "Someone excessively long in the tooth, no doubt, in need of a nursemaid or—worse!—a mama for his motherless brats."

"Nonsense, Caroline!" cried Lady Withering, much dismayed, although, if she were to acknowledge the truth to herself, which she would not, she had thought along these lines herself. "You are from a very old family, you have impeccable connections, and you are a charming, intelligent girl. I do not say it would do to aim too high—I am sure I need not warn you! But you don't want to end your days with Mrs. Needham in Bath, or dwindle into an aunt to Julia's children."

"No," said Caroline judiciously, "I must own that I do not. But I am a gamester's daughter in nearly penniless straits, and if I were a man I'm not sure I should want to marry into our 'very old family.' Never mind, ma'am, I don't mean to quarrel with you; I just don't want you to cut up your peace worrying about my prospects, because *I* don't intend to."

Lady Withering was so shocked by this speech that for some moments she could say nothing. She perceived that Caroline was going to be a more difficult case than she had previously imagined, and decided there was no time to lose. "Well, my love," she said hastily, "you are not at your last prayers yet, and you cannot object to a few amusements,

whatever the future holds for you. Now that those dreadful
riots are over, people will be entertaining again, and going
about. London is still a bit thin of company, as the Season
has not yet begun, but I think you might like to attend some
assemblies and rout parties. My dear friend Lady Bassett
will be having such an evening on Tuesday next, and when
I told her you were coming to me she made sure to press
me to invite you. Nothing formal; some music, and cards,
and perhaps enough couples for the young people to dance.
Just the thing for you, my dear Caroline! I'm sure there will
be a few familiar faces, and I should so hate to disoblige
Lady Bassett. Oh, and I hope you shall not mislike it very
much, but I have engaged to dine with Lady and General
Sir Mordred Frant tomorrow evening. I daresay it will be a
little dull for you, my dear, as there won't be a soul there
who will see thirty again, and I doubt if Sybil Frant will invite any gentleman for any other reason than to gratify the
general's passion for odiously long discussions of military
campaigns, so we can hardly expect to meet anyone really
eligible. Not but what—"

Seeing Caroline stiffen again, she cast her a look of entreaty which quite melted her goddaughter's resistance. "Indeed, ma'am, I am most grateful to you!" Caroline said, a
little ashamed of her own truculence, when so much was
being planned for her entertainment. "It sounds a most excellent scheme."

Lady Withering sighed in relief and hoped that Caroline
might not turn out to be an eccentric, after all.

Her godmother's excellent schemes for reintroducing a
girl of diminished expectations to the marital *Champs de
Mars* might not ordinarily be expected to comprehend a
dinner party in which most of the guests, in addition to having military inclinations, might be supposed to have the
liveliest interest in which of the various available plasters
and potions constituted the most effective cure for gout or
rheumatism, but the Frants were very good ton, and her ladyship, while not possessed of anything so blatantly useful
as a set of eligible nephews, kept an excellent table, and her

approval, if not her patronage, carried weight in the highest circles. Not for anything would Lady Withering have disclosed, before the dire eventually became real, that her greatest fear was that the Wentworth girls would not receive vouchers for Almack's. Wentworth had been a shockingly loose screw, and his exploits upon the town could not be palatable to such high sticklers as Sally Jersey. Two seasons ago, when the family name had still been buttressed by Wyndham Priory, and the extent of their financial embarrassment less widely known, it was another story, but now it would be foolish to remain complacent when a push in the right direction might secure all that was needed. Lady Withering found herself wishing that the stroke of Fate which had carried off Lord Wentworth might have been more precipitate, before he had had the chance to ruin his family altogether.

Caroline's determination not to disappoint her godmother suffered a check when, upon descending for the Frant dinner in an evening dress that had cost a staggering sum two years before and had been considered rather dashing besides, she discovered the good woman staring at her in frank disapprobation. "Is—is there something wrong?" she asked faintly, coloring a little.

Lady Withering was annoyed with herself for having forgotten that Caroline's clothes would quite naturally be out of style by now and determined that she would take her charge shopping at the first opportunity. "Oh, no," she said quickly, "you look most charmingly, and the color suits you. Only, Albany gauze is not *quite* the *dernier cri*, my love, and if you'll permit me to remove it, and just rearrange the lace *so*, all will be well."

Caroline received the news that she looked, if not a dowd, a trifle démodé, with admirable composure. "You must do as you think best, ma'am," she said with a smile. "I'm sorry to vex you!"

"Oh, it's no such thing. With just the smallest change we may hope no one will notice that you are not perfectly *à la mode*."

In fact, the amiability of the company in which Caroline

found herself in the Frant's drawing room gave her every reason to believe that Lady Withering's hopeful prophesy might be fulfilled. Lady Frant greeted her with kindness, and as she invited her guests more for their wit and accomplishment rather than their à la modality, Caroline began to regret her youth and inexperience more than her toilette. Her godmother, harboring no illusion that she was included for any other reason than being a schoolroom friend of Sybil Frant, made no attempt to join in the more interesting conversations with anything other than a fashionable commonplace, and seemed unself-consciously content. So Caroline was surprised, when the butler announced "Lady Buxton," to see her start and mutter, "oh no!"

"She is the veriest dragon," said Lady Withering in a whisper. "I pray you won't regard anything she says. She is very great, but very proud. She is Mr. Neville's aunt, you know, and Her Grace of Vernon's granddaughter!"

Caroline was naturally quite interested in this august personage, as much because her presence so discomfited Lady Withering as because of her relation to the famous Mr. Neville, about whom she harbored no little curiosity. As she knew the mere stateliness of money and rank were not enough to excite trepidation in her godmother's breast, she wondered what it was that could have put her ladyship so out of sorts.

Lady Buxton was a large woman with strongly marked features which might once have been handsome, except for a rather beaky nose. She wore black as if she had been born in it, and her manner was not conciliating. Caroline began to discover the source of Lady Withering's discomposure when Lady Buxton approached them and announced, in the stentorian tones of the hard of hearing, "Good evening, Amelia. I am pleased to see you here, as I particularly wished to speak to you. It won't do, Amelia, it really won't." She regarded her victim expectantly, as if she expected her immediate concurrence.

"M-Ma'am?" inquired Lady Withering, stammering like a schoolgirl.

"I need not hide my teeth with you, Amelia, as I am persuaded you will know exactly what it is I wish to warn you about."

"I do not, that is, how can I?" inquired poor Lady Withering piteously.

"You will recall that I am related by marriage to Carlton Killbride," said her ladyship, with the air of one explaining something to a stupid child, "so I know you won't take it amiss if I venture to give you a hint. It won't do, Amelia! To let him dangle after you like a schoolboy, and at your age too! He's quite a man of the town, you know! I can't think what you are about."

Lady Withering's reaction to this piece of gross impertinence was to color up and look confused, quite as if she had been guilty of something far more indiscreet than keeping occasional company with a "most respectable elderly gentleman—old enough to be my *father*," she later assured Caroline, "who only escorted me to the theater twice, and once or twice to the opera!"

"B-But, ma'am—"

"No, no, there is not the least need to thank me, Amelia," said her ladyship with awesome generosity. "I knew you would feel just as you ought, so let us say no more about it." She then passed on to Caroline, favoring her with a hard stare, two fingers, and a coldly civil greeting. Caroline just touched the fingers and made a slight curtsy, keeping her face a courteous mask.

Lady Buxton's presence at the dinner table might be expected to impair the pleasure of her immediate neighbors, but as Caroline was seated far from her, and hidden from view by a rather grand and elaborate epergne, she had no expectation of having further experience of her conversation. In this, however, she was soon proved wrong. Her Ladyship's authoritative pronouncements, hints, and judgments on a variety of topics were uttered in such audible tones as to intrude into all the other diners' conversations, and Caroline, while striving to attend to her own partner, soon formed the opinion that she was the proudest, most disagreeable lady of her acquaintance.

She began to be amused, but amusement changed to embarrassment when Lady Buxton began her animadversions on the subject of Wyndham Priory. "Oh, one of Neville's distempered freaks, as far as I can tell," said her ladyship, her voice cutting like a knife through the knowledgeable recitation of Wellington's activities in Europe that Caroline was receiving from her dinner partner. "I hear the place has grown quite *shabby*, and no wonder. They say Wentworth was quite done up. Ha! A Knight of the Elbow and a real here-and-thereian. Well, Neville's very well to pass and can indulge his whims as he likes, but why he wants to saddle himself with another expensive property is quite beyond me!"

Lady Frant, who was sitting close to Lady Buxton, cast a stricken glance of apology at Caroline and attempted to turn the conversation. But Lady Buxton, still big with her topic, affected not to hear her hostess's observation. The gentleman on her left murmured, in a low tone Caroline had to strain to catch, that perhaps Mr. Neville was thinking of marrying and setting up his nursery.

Lady Buxton's response was a nasal titter. "I begin to fear that will never happen. He appears to be wholly abandoned to the single state. I can't tell you how many eligible females I have tried to bring to his notice, but to no avail. I *can* tell you I have spared no exertion. He ought to be guided by me. He must and should be guided by me. But my natural partiality has not blinded me to the faults in his character which have led him to persist so selfishly in the unmarried state. He could look as high as he pleased, you know, but he has been much indulged and flattered, and females are always casting out lures for him. It is no wonder, with his face and fortune, that he has become quite cynical."

The effect of this remarkable speech on a party of well-bred persons might well be imagined. Several forks, laden with such delicacies as pork cutlets with Rober sauce or tenderones of veal and truffles, might have been momentarily suspended over the plates, but conversation resumed almost instantly in well-modulated tones, and Caroline's partner seamlessly picked up the thread of Arthur Wellesley's exploits on the Continent. Flushed with anger and embarrassment, Caroline scanned the table quickly, but as no one's eye was upon her or betrayed the least consciousness that anything was amiss, she began to recover her countenance. As she did so, she found herself grateful for the epergne which hid her from scrutiny, and by the time the servants removed the covers and the ladies retired, she had comforted herself with the notion that, in the face of so many introductions, few of her fellow guests could have remembered she was a *Wentworth* after all.

Someone, however, had evidently reminded Lady Buxton of it. She made her way over to Caroline with so much determination, and so little apology, that Caroline had to strive very hard to keep her tongue between her teeth.

"I am persuaded, my dear," she said with a small nod of condescension, "that you will not be offended by my speech just now. My character is everywhere celebrated for its frankness, and my words have no bark upon them."

Caroline could find little to say to this, and her ladyship continued without interruption. "You are but lately come up to town, I believe? And your mother is to bring your sister out as well? Well, I don't hold with the younger being out before the elder is married, but I suppose you must be on the scramble for a match. You see, I don't beat around the bush. I hold with plain speaking, and I certainly don't expect anyone to toad-eat *me*!"

"How—how very fortunate!" said Caroline, breathing fire. "And I assure you, ma'am, that neither my sister nor I will be 'on the scramble for a match,' as you put it!"

"Humdudgeon! Of course you are," said Lady Buxton, with unruffled equanimity. " A pretty pair of fools you would be if you were not. I daresay we will not meet again; I never make calls."

Since the gentlemen entered at just that moment and Lady Buxton turned away, she did not hear Caroline say that this intelligence had quite cast her down.

"Of all the disagreeable, insufferable—" Caroline began, when she was at last free to discharge her mind on the subject to her godmother.

"Yes, yes, but you should not cross swords with her," said Lady Withering. "She is famous for her bad manners, and indeed some hostesses invite her just for the sort of display you saw tonight. You must not mind what she said; no one pays the least attention."

It was on Caroline's lips to say that she thought everyone had paid a great deal of attention, but she remembered that Lady Withering had also suffered embarrassment, and so she held her peace. "To think of her being Neville's aunt! I fear I am sadly lacking in Christian charity, but I loathe the thought of that woman's being admitted at Wyndham Priory. The servants will all leave in a week! But—oh!" she said, as a thought occurred to her—"perhaps she doesn't stand on very good terms with her nephew? What a character she gives him!"

"As to that," said Lady Withering judiciously, "Mr. Neville's manners are everything that is correct in a man of rank and fortune. If he is a little cynical, as Lady Buxton suggests, it may be because he is so very sought after, you know. But there can be no question of *his* behaving with his aunt's impropriety, I assure you."

Caroline was inclined to think that his aunt's assessment, despite her expressed partiality, of her nephew as idle, vain, and spoiled was likely to be based on superior knowledge of his character, but as she had every hope of avoiding both of them in future, she let the subject drop.

3

HAPPILY UNAWARE of the salt being poured into the wounds of Wentworth self-consequence by Lady Buxton in London, Julia was determined to meet and dazzle Mr. Neville at the Priory. She had not been the reigning flirt for miles around without becoming confident of her power to attract, and if it occurred to her that a man of experience and address might not succumb to her charms as readily as the bashful schoolboys who made up her train, she dismissed such notions as poor-spirited pessimism.

To be able to cast out lures, however, one first had to meet the gentleman in whose breast she hoped to excite the warmest of feelings, and in this she was unexpectedly balked. Within a day or two of Mr. Neville's arrival at the Priory, the senior Mr. Lacey had paid a call on him and had been received (he said) with the utmost civility, and apologies for his household being, quite naturally, at sixes and sevens. Most unluckily, the family were out when Mr. Neville left his card at Ilcombe Hall, and since then there had been no intercourse between the two households. This led to such an oppression (albeit temporary) of spirits that she was moved to enlist the aid of the younger Mr. Lacey, by inducing him to drive her over to the Priory to visit the housekeeper, or even to call on the Nonpareil himself.

Mr. Lacey, dismayed, strove to the best of his ability to give a more proper direction to Miss Wentworth's thoughts. "Of all the cork-brained notions! Me, call on a man like that? His butler would laugh me out of the door, I can tell you. Tell you what, Julia: wait till he calls again, that's the thing."

29

"But he might go up to town again soon, and then it might be *weeks* before I can contrive to meet him. There isn't much time, Bertie! If I don't find a husband *this Season* I shall have to repair with mama to Bath, and think how dreadful that will be! Oh Bertie, please! You must help me think of some way to get into the Priory!"

"Well, I won't do it. Won't help you make a byword of yourself; shouldn't ask me to," replied Mr. Lacey with what Julia regarded as an unnatural lack of sympathy. "And if you want to behave as if you've no more notion of propriety than the kitchen cat, I wash my hands of you!"

But Mr. Lacey, despite this admonition, was moved to voice the concern to his mother, a woman of calm disposition and quiet good sense, that Julia, in one of her hey-go-mad moods, was about to do something excessively bird-witted.

Mrs. Lacey was fond of her goddaughter, but she had often regretted that Lady Wentworth's partiality had prevented her from placing a sufficient check on Julia's whims and high spirits, and that while no one would dare to go so far as to call her *brass-faced*, the word "coming" was not altogether inapt. Still, while Susan Wentworth was somewhat deficient in sense, she was never vulgar, and Mrs. Lacey had every hope that she would not permit her daughter to do anything so foolish or improper as throw herself at Mr. Neville's head. She said as much to her son, and reminded him that even if Julia did go so far as to forget herself, Mr. Neville was a gentleman and scarcely likely to take advantage of a miss just out of the schoolroom.

"No, very likely he would snub her," he said frankly. "Not that it wouldn't serve her right, but—"

"But?" his mother prompted.

"But it wouldn't do. Acts like a heartless minx, but it ain't true. You know that ma'am. If he was to snub her, or take her up and then drop her, it would break her heart. Thing is, she's all in a taking about finding a rich husband. Says she wants to restore the family fortunes, or some such hum as that. Can't blame her for being so scared. But the truth is, ma'am, I don't know what it may lead her to do."

Mrs. Lacey thought Bertram was rather more charitable toward Julia than she would have been herself, and a new suspicion planted itself like a tiny seed in her mind. She looked at him carefully, but his countenance was so open and he looked so absurdly young that she banished it almost at once. She said hastily, "Well, I daresay it will all resolve itself when she goes up to London. She's sure to take very well, you know, and as nothing could be worse for her chances than to be thought forward in such company, I feel sure she will settle down. Besides, she will have her sister to steady her, if her mother does not."

Mr. Lacey, knowing his childhood friend rather better than his mother did, could not wholly enter into her optimism on the subject, and resolved to keep a close eye on her until they went up to town.

Julia, meanwhile, though a great believer in Providence, had begun to feel that Providence was unaccountably slow in intervening on her behalf in the matter of Mr. Neville, and she determined to take matters into her own hands. Mr. Lacey had proven himself a scoffing addle-plot and could not be admitted to her counsels, and she feared that the half-formed plan which had taken shape in her brain would not be just what her mother would like. Still, she could not come up with a better attack on the Nonpareil's citadel and accordingly drew up her artillery. This consisted of a flowing riding habit of sapphire velvet, the color of her eyes, tied with lace about her neck and topped with the most dashing plumes she could contrive. She practiced a glittering smile before the mirror, discovered herself to look enchanting, and set off for the stables for the mare the Lacey's had provided for her use.

As a small girl Julia had been accustomed to ride at will all over Wyndham Priory and the surrounding countryside, and in consequence she was irked, as a young lady, by chaperonage and often dispensed with her groom. That this habit would not be acceptable under the present circumstances she knew very well, but she was an old friend in the Lacey stables, and it was not difficult to decline an escort, on the grounds that she intended only a short ride to the manor stream.

She soon came to this, and crossed it, and plunged into the park that belonged to the Priory. She rode on some way till she judged she had gone far enough, reined in, looked about her, and quickly dismounted. The ground was rather wet from the spring rains, and she slipped a little, turning her ankle, but she chose to disregard it. She dropped the mare's reins and sent it off with a pat on the flank. Then she sat down on the damp rise beside the lane to wait.

An hour later it had begun to drizzle again, and her ankle was throbbing. She had meant to present a pitiful scene, but did not at all care for supplying it with this degree of authenticity. Her plumes were drooping, and her habit was stained with splashes of mud. *Why* had no one come for her? She had carefully chosen a horse reared in Wyndham Priory stables and did not doubt that it would return there, since she had positioned herself so close to the house. She had assumed that rescue would follow swiftly on the heels of her unattended mare, and that she would be conducted into the Priory and introduced to its elusive master. And then he would give her a hot drink, and tuck a blanket around her, and she would look up at him with a charming smile of gratitude, and he . . .

She was in the midst of these quite pleasant romantic imaginings, when Mr. Lacey, with her mare in tow, came peltering down the lane. His game bag was still attached to his saddle, and his face wore a worried look. Julia had leapt to her feet when she heard the horses, but now she cried involuntarily, "Oh, Bertie, do go away!"

"Well thank you very much," he said, dismounting.

"Oh, Bertie, I—" she began, coloring up. "But you've ruined *everything*."

"Good," he said shortly. "Cut line, Julia, what's the game? How did you come to fall off your horse? And what are you doing *here*?"

"I didn't!" protested Julia. "That is, I—oh, it is all such a mull! It's wet, and I've turned my ankle. And the horse was supposed to go to the Priory!"

"Well, it didn't, you ninnyhammer!" said Mr. Lacey, inferring from this tangled speech that Miss Wentworth had parted company with her horse voluntarily. "And a deuce of a pucker there would have been if I hadn't intercepted it before it came back without you. Were you trying to set the place about its ears?"

"Why of course not! I took *such* pains that no one at Ilcombe Hall should know anything of it," she said indignantly. "Oh Bertie, it is the most capital scheme! I shall stay here until Mr. Neville rescues me!"

"You'll do nothing like, I promise you. Lord, if I ever knew such a cork-brained wag-feather as you. What a dust up there would be if the Nonpareil found you in his front yard without a maid or groom. Bound to think you're a lightskirt. Shame your mama," he added succinctly. "Mine too."

Julia, to whom this possible construction on her behavior hand not previously occurred, said uncertainly, "Nonsense!"

Mr. Lacey decided to press his advantage while he might. "Ought to take you home now. Can you stand on the ankle?"

She did so, wincing slightly, and when he was satisfied, he said, "Serve you right if you had to sit out every dance of the Season."

She turned to him a face stricken with horror. "What a *dreadful* thing to say. I have a mind to stay here after all. You can't make me come with you. You've no authority over me!"

"No, but her ladyship does, and very likely she'll pack you off to Bath at once if she gets wind of your tricks," replied Mr. Lacey mendaciously.

"Bertie, you are an odious blackmailer!"

Mr. Lacey was spared further enumeration of his character defects by the sudden appearance of a large, and (to their guilty eyes) rather frightening-looking person with an equally intimidating firearm, who pronounced himself Mr. Neville's gamekeeper and inquired, in no very civil tones, as to the nature of their business. "For we don't hold with trespassers here, nor," he said, eyeing Mr. Lacey's full game bag, "with poachers neither. Hear tell things got werry lax in his late lordship's time, but the new master's a high stickler."

To be addressed in such a fashion on land that had been in her family since the Conquest by some villainous rogue who clearly had no notion of the proper deference owed to persons of consequence was too much for Julia. She drew herself up and said majestically, "It may be of interest to you to learn that *I* am Miss W—ow!"

"Miss W-Wilson," injected Mr. Lacey hastily, releasing Julia's arm from the pinch he had given it. "My—my sister. Thing is, lost our way. Visiting the Hall. Don't know the country."

"Name of?" prompted the gamekeeper.

"Smith," replied Mr. Lacey, whose wits had quite failed him.

"Thought you said this was your sister."

"I did," said Mr. Lacey, startled.

"Trying to humbug me, are you? You'll catch cold on that, you will. You said it was Miss Wilson."

"Eh?"

"Different last names," explained the gamekeeper patiently, but with a touch of malice.

"Oh," said Mr. Lacey, inspiration coming to his aid at last. "Different fathers!"

Julia decided things had gone far enough. "I am sure our parentage can be of no conceivable interest to this person. I am tired, and I have had a fall. I should be pleased to go home now."

"That's werry nice, Miss, but the whole story's a bit smoky, if you get my drift. If the gentleman will just open his game bag we can see if aught's amiss."

"Now see here," fulminated Mr. Lacey, complying nonetheless.

"Werry fine birds, they are, sir, and no mistake," said the gamekeeper. "Only I'll warrant they belong to Mr. Neville's table and not yours."

"They do not," protested Mr. Lacey hotly.

"Then perhaps you'll come round to the Priory, Mr. *Smith*, and take it up with the master. Begging your pardon, sir, but I have my orders."

"No! That is, take the blasted things. I don't want 'em."

"Knew you'd see reason, sir. You two be off now, and if you want to go hunting in the Priory park, you ask the master next time."

"Do you know," said Mr. Lacey through gritted teeth, when they had been released at last, "that it took me all morning to get those birds."

Julia, whose sole object all day had been to secure an introduction to Mr. Neville, found herself unaccountably relieved that it had not taken place under such inauspicious circumstances, and she could scarcely sympathize with Bertie's making such a fuss over such a paltry thing as a few birds. Still, her ever dimming recollections of her dear papa suggested to her that gentlemen had very peculiar notions about the importance of such objects, and she strove to give the subject her attention. "I'm very sorry you should have lost them, when you were so kind as to come and fetch me," she said meditatively. "Only think of Mr. Neville's being so top-lofty as to keep everyone out of the park! And to employ such an *odious* gamekeeper. I wonder if I should mention it to him when we meet."

Mr. Lacey's reply to this lay somewhere between a choke and a snort.

"I'll contrive something, Bertie, never fear," said Julia, interpreting his response correctly. "But just now I must think of something to tell Mama, because I have quite ruined my best riding habit."

Lady Wentworth, however, was much distracted by her own worries, and the sad state of Julia's apparel did not, for once, excite her comment.

"It is most dreadfully provoking," said her ladyship peevishly, when she caught sight of her daughter. "I have spent the entire morning looking for my best ivory fan, and now Roberts tells me she is sure we left it behind at the Priory, though I cannot think how we could have done so. Only Roberts has come down with a chill, and no one else besides myself would recognize it or know where to look for it, so I am very much afraid I will have to call at the Priory and meet that wretched man who took our home away from us. And how my nerves are to bear it I'm sure I don't know!"

4

THE DAYS BETWEEN Caroline's uncomfortable encounter with Lady Buxton and the promised delights of Lady Bassett's party passed in a flurry of activity only someone who had spent a year in attendance on the sickroom, and another in deep mourning, could appreciate. Lady Withering took her to the theater and Bond Street, though she would not accompany her to the museums, for, "if it got out that you have a taste for that sort of thing, people might think you were a bluestocking, and then where would you be?" Undeterred, Caroline went accompanied by a footman, and reveled in the anonymity and stimulation of city life. She could not be prevailed upon, however, to indulge in shopping, no matter how her ladyship cajoled and tempted her with descriptions of the latest French modiste, or painted in the most heart-wrenching detail the certain evils of appearing a dowd. Caroline replied that she had a trunk full of clothes from her first Season, scarcely touched or never worn at all because of her mourning, and that she could not afford to trick herself out in the latest styles. Nor would she allow Lady Withering to do so. She did not, however, disdain the suggestions of her ladyship's dresser, Miss Clara Barnes, as to how to adapt these creations with a tuck here or a cluster of artificial cherries there, a compromise by which her inspired godmother at last broke the stalemate. The result of this happy collusion was that even Lady Withering could find no fault with her goddaughter's wardrobe. In celebration, she bought her an expensive shawl of the finest Norwich silk, and pressed it on her so firmly that Caroline could not in all politeness refuse.

Despite her brave words to Lady Withering, Caroline dressed for her first London party in two years with some misgivings, and a flutter in her stomach. At least her appearance gave her no cause for anxiety; her godmother had sent Barnes to put the finishing touches on her toilet, but she could find little to do but comment on how beautifully the jonquil robe, open down the front over a slip of ivory satin, became Miss Wentworth's slender figure. A spray of tiny yellow roses arranged amid her dark ringlets set off her coloring to perfection, and a string of fine pearls, a gift from Caroline's grandmother, was her only jewelry. She looked both elegant and unpretentious, and Lady Withering, when she set eyes on her when she came down to dinner, was moved to compliment her exquisite taste.

Lady Bassett's drawing rooms were overflowing by ten-thirty, and she was still greeting latecomers at the head of the stairs. Caroline had to admit that she was enjoying herself immensely; it was a pleasure to be able to talk and laugh and meet old acquaintances again, and she had to own that the stimulus of so many new faces—after the confinement of the Priory—acted as a tonic to her spirits. After Lady Buxton's odious comments at the Frant dinner, she was reasonably certain that the nature of her family's circumstances was known to the ton, and while she did not expect to be snubbed, precisely, she had every expectation of being made to feel the diminishment of their estimation. She had told herself that if she suffered another such evening at Lady Bassett's she would withdraw completely from society, whatever the consequences. But so far, she was agreeably surprised to discover that a number of people sought her out, and she met with no more than a modicum of condescension, and very few knowing looks. She was chatting quite happily on the sofa with Lord Wynchwood, a charming sprig of fashion whom she dimly remembered meeting at her come-out, and who was entertaining her with all sorts of *on-dits* about the people present, when she happened to catch Lady Withering's eye, and to see her godmother turn on her a stricken look. She started up at once, thinking the good lady ill, but she was waved back to her seat.

Had she known it, the emotion swelling her ladyship's bosom of puce satin was most akin to remorse and a guilty conscience. She had failed of her duty, she had not dropped a hint in Caroline's ear when she had meant to, and now the latecomer greeting Lady Bassett at the head of the stairs was none other than Lord Ridley.

Caroline, following the direction of her godmother's gaze, saw him too, and was able to keep her countenance by exerting a stern measure of self-control. Lady Withering, watching her covertly, was relieved to see that she did not betray herself by so much as a blush or any display of self-consciousness, and she began to breathe easier. Caroline listened to Lord Wynchwood's agreeable prattle with half an ear, the other part of her attention focused across the room. She knew he would come to her; at some time a first meeting was inevitable, and after they had got over this hurdle, they could both relax and meet in future, if not as friends, at least as the most civil of acquaintances.

She felt rather than saw his presence beside her. "Ridley," said Lord Wynchwood suddenly, "I hadn't heard you were back in town! May I present Viscount Ridley, Miss Wentworth? He seems to be most eager to make your acquaintance!"

"You are out there, Geoffrey," said Lord Ridley, smiling and raising her hand to his lips. "Miss Wentworth and I are old friends."

As she looked into his laughing blue eyes, her first thought was that he was as handsome as ever, and the second, less charitable, that he did not look like a man just out of mourning for a beloved young wife. She said coolly, "How do you do, sir? It is a long time since we last met, and I trust you are well."

"Oh, quite well, thank you," he said, smiling down at her. "Geoffrey, I perceive your aunt is trying to get your attention. There—by Lady Jersey."

Lord Wynchwood excused himself regretfully and yielded his place on the sofa to Lord Ridley. "I had not heard you were in London again," he said in a low voice.

"Seeing you here, looking just the same—it made me feel for just an instant that nothing had changed!"

"A great deal has changed," she said calmly, in a normal tone. "We were so sorry to hear of your bereavement. I know you had our letter of condolence, but my mother was sorry not to have been able to wait upon you and her ladyship's mother, because we were in mourning too."

He bowed slightly. "Thank you," he said in a less intimate voice. "But you haven't told me why you've come up to town. Is your family here?"

"They will be shortly. Julia is making come-out this season, and then we will join my Aunt Needham in Bath."

"Bath?" he cried in horrified accents. "My dear girl, you won't like it at all. There won't be a soul there a day under fifty years old, and all the balls end at eleven."

She laughed. "So I understand. But Mama thinks the waters will do her good, and we mean to live a quiet life, you know. I daresay it will suit us very well."

"I hope it may suit your mama." He rose to his feet. "I see my cousin over there, and must pay her my respects. I am most grateful that chance has thrown us together again, Ca—Miss Wentworth. I hope to have the pleasure of seeing you before too many days. I will be spending the whole of the Season in London."

"Then I daresay we shall run into each other from time to time, though I doubt whether the circle of our common acquaintance is very wide," she said with unruffled equanimity, holding out her hand.

"My dear girl! I mean to call on you, you know."

Caroline murmured that she was sure her mother and Julia would be glad to see him when they came up to town.

"And what about you, dear Miss Wentworth?" he said, holding her hand in his and fixing her with a searching look. "Will not you be happy to see me?"

"Oh, most certainly," Caroline said in what she hoped was a quelling manner. "We are always happy to see old friends!"

*   *   *

Caroline's immediate wish, upon Lord Ridley's quitting her, was for peace and solitude, but even if she could have prevailed upon Lady Withering to depart immediately, she was sensible that such an action would give rise to the sort of tattle and speculation she most wanted to avoid. Accordingly, she told her godmother that she was feeling the heat a little and wanted to revive herself with a cool drink and some fresh air before she rejoined the company. Lady Withering patted her shoulder sympathetically, but charged her not to be too long. Having procured a glass of lemonade, she made her way to a small room off one of the drawing rooms and threw open the window, pulling a chair up to face it so that she might have the restorative benefits of the night air.

This was very cold, and she shivered a little, but she did not move to close the casement. The room was dim and suited her need for privacy perfectly. In a moment or two she would have to return to her godmother, but first she must still her rioting emotions. She found herself quite unreasonably out of sorts, and really did begin to have a headache. She would not deny that Ridley was still very attractive—certainly that!—and for just a moment—just one—she too might have pretended that things were as they were two years ago, with nothing changed between them. But then to have spoken so intimately, to have presumed so confidently her delight in receiving him, when he had treated her so unfeelingly, seemed to her the behavior of a coxcomb. As if she had been nursing an unrequited passion for two years, while he had married someone else! She could admit that her own behavior might also have been at fault, since he clearly believed that his marriage and the withdrawal of his attentions notwithstanding, she might now be gratified by an attempt to attach her. This knowledge did little to lessen her vexation, and prevented her, along with the unwillingness to let him know how much he had formerly wounded her feelings, from permitting herself the satisfaction of giving him a sharp set-down.

She discovered that, other than feeling cross as a cat after the encounter, she had suffered no real ill effects from it,

and was inclined to hope she had kept her countenance
rather well. She was on the point of rising to rejoin the
party when she heard voices in the doorway. She hesitated
just a moment before making her presence known, aware
that she could not be seen from the door and not wanting
her flight from the drawing room to become common
knowledge, and then the nature of the conversation made
her suck in her breath and sit very still indeed.

"Coming it much too strong, Robert!" cried a voice Caroline at once recognized as belonging to Lord Wynchwood.
"If you didn't come up to town to indulge a flirt with Arabella Grantham, why are you here? I've never known you
to set foot in Grovesnor Square so much as a day before the
Season begins! Don't tell me it's still on with that high-fly-
ing Incognita of yours!"

"La Perdita?" answered another voice, much deeper than
his lordship's. "Certainly not. She left my protection some
time ago, and—"

"But what a prime article!"

"An expensive virago, I assure you." Caroline could hear
the sardonic note in his voice, and conceived a degree of
antipathy toward the unknown speaker. "As for Miss
Grantham, you know I don't go in for that sort of thing: all
simpering titters, and that detestable archness that girls just
out of schoolroom seem to think marks the manner of a
fashionable woman."

"Humdudgeon! She's a diamond of the first water."

"Without the least amount of wit or conversation. And
with very coming manners besides."

"I'll tell you what it is, Robert," said Lord Wynchwood
judiciously, "it's that you scared the poor girl half to death.
I've seen you do it before, so don't say you haven't.
There's the poor thing like a rabbit in a snare, knowing you
have the power to blight or launch her social aspirations
with the raising of an eyebrow, all atremble with the fear of
displeasing you. No doubt it amuses you, but—"

"You are wrong, Geoffrey. It does not amuse me."

"Does it not? Beg pardon, then! I thought you looked
amused when the unfortunate girl was so flustered she

tripped and almost swooned into your arms, and all you could do was hand her over to her mama, with the recommendation that she take her out of the crush. And you know the room *was* very hot," added his lordship a trifle indignantly.

"My dear Geoffrey," said the other with a little laugh, "it was very likely her mama who tripped her, and if you could have seen how *meltingly* she looked as she fell into my arms, you would have laughed too. The girl should have been an actress. I—or rather my fortune—have been hunted by every stratagem known to the female mind, and I hope I'm not such a gentleman as to fall victim to blandishments like that."

"Robert," said Geoffrey, thunderstruck, "you ain't *complaining*?"

"I own it probably doesn't become me to do so," said his friend in a voice that sounded singularly unrepentant to Caroline, "but since the day I discovered my first true love would as soon have married a baboon possessed of my fortune and consequence, I have been, shall we say, a trifle on my guard. The devil of it is, one can never get away from matchmaking mamas, and now I've even been pursued into the country. Not two days ago I had the most uncomfortable interview with the former owner of an estate I've purchased—well, with his widow, that is—and all the good lady could do was thrust her daughter at me with the baldest of hints, and invent excuses for calling to collect some forgotten item three different times, just in case I hadn't noticed the girl was a beauty the first time out. I should have thought that delicacy of feeling . . . but no, nothing would do but that I should feel free to call on them in town, with her ladyship also venturing to wish that I might make the acquaintance of her other, *older* daughter, who, I gather, is an antidote already on the shelf. No doubt I am to have *her* pitched at me as well. I tell you, Geoffrey, it's the outside of enough!"

Caroline's fists were clenched in tight balls in her lap. "I heard you bought Wyndham Priory," she heard Lord Wynchwood say, "but I say, you can't mean, that is, was it

Miss Wentworth you heard was an antidote? I assure you it's no such thing," he added, assuring himself of Caroline's undying gratitude. "Tolerably handsome girl. Charming."

"I'll have to take your word for it," said—for it must be he—Mr. Neville, "as I have no intention of pursuing the acquaintance."

"Pity," said Lord Wynchwood ambiguously. "But tell me, Robert, why did you buy the place? Not that I haven't heard that it's devilishly fine, but won't you have to lay out a lot of blunt to bring it up to scratch?"

"That's precisely what I intend to do. The workmen have already started on the house, and all the banging and sawing drove me up to town early, in reckless disregard for my social reputation," said Mr. Neville with a laugh. "Would you believe me, Geoffrey, if I told you I bought it because I was bored?"

"No," said Lord Wynchwood, "I would not."

Miss Wentworth, in the silence that followed, was scarcely able to master the impulse to start up and slap Mr. Neville's face, regardless of the consequences. She was saved by Lord Wynchwood, who interjected, "Stop cutting a wheedle, Robert. *You* bored? Half the ton wants to *be* you. Why, just the other day I heard some young cawker say he was wearing his neckcloth in the *Neville Knot,* and wondering if you would let an audience in to watch you dress, like Brummell."

"My dear friend, I stand rebuked. Here is proof indeed of the worthiness of my existence," said Mr. Neville in a light voice, but with a self-mocking note of bitterness beneath his languid tone. "Now I think I shall quit my refuge, and take leave of my hostess before Mrs. Grantham and the divine Arabella run me to earth. Coming?"

Caroline felt as if she were inhabiting some particularly ghastly nightmare. Were all men such odious cockalorums? First Ridley and now this! Not all of his aunt's ill-natured cataloging of his sins began to encompass such pride, such insufferable conceit! She was filled with the overwhelming desire to tip him a settler, as Bertie would say, or at the very least ring a peal over him for harboring notions that must, if they were known, disgust every person of proper feeling. That she had no idea what her adversary looked like was a small difficulty, but not an insurmountable one. She entertained herself for some moments by imagining various rejoinders, each more clever than the last, by which she might depress Mr. Neville's insufferable pretensions.

Further reflection brought her the unwelcome thought that chasing down Mr. Neville, even in order to snub him, was more likely to confirm his illusion of being pursued than otherwise, and that, not knowing the true cause of her rancor, he would probably attribute her behavior to general incivility and want of conduct, or worse, to resentment of his purchase of Wyndham Priory. Thus stymied, she was forced to confront the lowering idea that there might be just a pinch of justice in his remarks about her mother and sister. She knew her mother too well to believe that she behaved with true impropriety, but she suspected that Julia had enlisted her in her schemes, and that she had been cajoled into overcoming her initial loathing of the very idea of Mr. Neville by the dazzling prospect that her favorite daughter might have a chance to make a brilliant match. Caroline had to own that Mr. Neville's reaction to these enticements, while revoltingly top-lofty, was just what she had warned Julia against when she had first set her cap for him. Never had she more wished that she had greater influence over her sister, or her mother more firmness in censuring her behavior.

Feeling really wretched now, Caroline decided that the only way to escape further mortification would be to avoid Mr. Neville's acquaintance altogether, and to convince Julia and her mother to do so as well when they came up to town. If necessary she would disclose enough of the dreadful conversation to discourage her sister's forward behavior, but she suspected that Mr. Neville might well have accomplished that on his own. Odious man! At least he would be her ally in averting the acquaintance, for nothing could be clearer from his remarks to Wynchwood than that he wished all the Wentworths at Jericho.

Upon that melancholy reflection, she closed the window and returned to the drawing rooms, concocting as she went a story about a shocking tear in her hem which had needed repair, and the very real headache which had necessitated her lengthy absence from the company and which would make it desirable for her to return home at her ladyship's earliest convenience.

Lady Withering having had the foresight to engage a very deaf coachman, the two ladies were free to enjoy what her ladyship termed a "comfortable cose" on the way home. Caroline's throbbing temples and mental exhaustion made it difficult to resist the clop-clopping of the horses and the gentle sway of the carriage, but she made an effort to answer her godmother's inquiries in an animated tone. Lady Withering meant to do well by her, and it was not her fault that an evening which had begun on a note of promise had yielded two distinctly distressing interviews. So she praised the refreshments, the musicians, and the company, and was rewarded by her ladyship's complimenting her on maintaining her countenance so well with Lord Ridley, and remarking that she had always known that her goddaughter was a girl of great good sense. "Though I did wonder," she added with a low tone, "when you were gone so long, whether you were quite as cool as you looked. Well, it's all over now, and you need not let it trouble you any further. But it's a pity Mr. Neville left before you returned, and I particularly wanted to present you!"

"Oh no, ma'am," cried Caroline in horrified accents, sitting up straight against the squabs, "I beg you will not!"

"Not present you to the most fashionable man in London? My dear, all he has to do is talk with you for ten minutes altogether, and your career will be made. He's a regular Croesus, and related to half the houses in England. His great-grandmother was a duchess!"

"I know he's full of juice," muttered Caroline mutinously. "But it's Julia who wants a social career, not I."

"My love, where *can* you have learned such a vulgar expression?" cried Lady Withering, startled. "Now listen to me, my dear," she said, patting Caroline's hand, "I hope you will not be prejudiced because of the way that *dreadful* woman acted the other night, and the remarks she let fall about her nephew. I have told you no one can place the least reliance on what she says. Now I know very well that it may be painful for you to meet Mr. Neville, because he has bought the Priory. But you must be sensible and master your feelings, as I have good cause to know you can do, in a much more difficult case."

"But he is so excessively proud and unpleasant," said Caroline feelingly.

"I thought you were not acquainted with him?" gasped Lady Withering.

"I am not, exactly," admitted Caroline, unwilling to divulge that she had been eavesdropping on his conversation. "But I cannot help believing that I should dislike him particularly, and I daresay he would feel quite the same about me."

"Nonsense, Caroline! You must be mad to talk so. And I *beg* you will not be so foolish as to be uncivil to Mr. Neville, or to repeat to anyone else what you have just said to me. If you want to throw your own chances down the wind, at least think of your sister. I've told you Robert Neville can make your career, but he could just as easily ruin you, *and* Julia, and me as well, if the truth must be told. And he will certainly do so if you carry on in this dreadful way," exclaimed her ladyship piteously.

"Of course, I should not be uncivil to *anyone*, ma'am," said Caroline with a laugh, "only please believe me when I say that it would be much better if you do not make the introduction at all. That way the great Mr. Neville will have no chance to ruin either of us, and I daresay we shall rub along quite happily."

"Well, perhaps you are right," said Lady Withering dubiously, "but promise me that if you should meet him you will not do anything to make him take you in dislike."

"I promise," said Caroline cheerfully, "but ten to one it will never happen."

5

HAD MISS WENTWORTH been able to place her bet in any of London's more famous gaming houses, where such issues as which of two venerable old dowagers would be the first to die or whether or not a member would succeed in killing a bluebottle before he went to bed were considered the proper subjects of speculation, she might have had some hopes of increasing her purse, for she did not encounter Mr. Neville at any of the entertainments she attended. Once or twice a hopeful hostess would indicate that he might be expected, but as he never materialized to gratify these hopes, Caroline began to relax. She amused herself for a time by imagining his appearance, and in her mind's eye endowed him with the fobs, seals, scented handkerchiefs, and other attributes of the dandy set, as well as that group's notorious incivility. If general report did not lie, his face she must concede as handsome, even allowing for the undeniable partiality inspired by a handsome fortune. For his expression she got no further than a Byronic scowl, but that was enough. Caroline was of the opinion that Byron was vastly overrated.

The days passed happily enough, and Caroline even discovered that she had acquired a little circle of admirers, and not a few female friends. As she had been burned once, she was on her guard to distinguish the gentlemen enjoying a mild flirtation from those in earnest, and, as she had foreseen, the latter group was comprised mainly of men of independent fortune seeking either a companion to their old age or a mother to their luckless children. She held them all at a distance, which did her standing no harm at all. Just let

anyone suggest she was hanging out for a rich husband
or—what had that dreadful woman said?—on the "scramble for a match!" Meanwhile she enjoyed the rout parties
and driving in Hyde Park or taking a turn in Green Park
with some ladies of her acquaintance. She was even introduced to Arabella Grantham, and was prepared to like her
excessively and champion her cause. To her considerable
disappointment, she found Miss Grantham rather too vain
and a dead bore besides, though she did have to admit that
she was quite as beautiful as Lord Wynchwood had described her.

Lord Ridley had cut up her peace a bit by sending up a
bouquet the day after Lady Bassett's party with the inscrip-
tion "As ever, Ridley," and by calling one morning while
she was out walking in the park. She expected that, having
discharged this obligation, he would not trouble her again,
and so she was surprised a few mornings later when the
butler opened the door to the ground floor saloon and announced him. She exchanged one speaking glance with
Lady Withering and smoothed the skirts of her rose-colored
jaconet muslin dress with rather nerveless fingers.

"How do you do?" he asked cheerfully, bowing over
Lady Withering's hand with an air of self-possession Caroline could only admire. "I trust I don't disturb you, but I
was hoping to persuade Miss Wentworth to drive with me
in Hyde Park this afternoon. It's such a perfectly splendid
day!"

"That's very kind of you," Caroline said coolly, "but I'm
afraid I'm engaged."

"My love, are you perfectly sure?" asked her godmother,
surprisingly. "I recollect your telling me that you were engaged tomorrow, and that you would hold yourself free to
run some little errands for me this afternoon. If that is the
case I'm sure I could excuse you."

"If Miss Wentworth has undertaken some commissions
for you, I should not dream of enticing her away, ma'am,"
said his lordship with unruffled amiability.

"Oh no, ma'am, I do assure you you're mistaken!" cried
Caroline, a trifle desperately. "I am engaged for this after-

noon, and it is tomorrow I will undertake the errands. I beg
your pardon! I hope you weren't depending on me."

"Certainly not, my dear. I seem to have mistaken the
dates, that's all. Tell me, Lord Ridley, how is your dear
mama? It is quite an age since we've met, and you must
convey my compliments when you see her next."

The next few minutes were spent in such pleasantries,
and Lord Ridley rose promptly at the end of half an hour to
take his leave. No sooner had the butler closed the door on
him when Caroline said, "Godmama, you encouraged
him!"

"Yes, so I did."

"But why, ma'am? A week ago you congratulated me on
putting him behind me, and in fact I mean to do so."

"Well, my love, we musn't be too hasty," said Lady
Withering with a little shrug. "I own that he did not behave
just as I'd like when you had your Season, but nothing
could be more proper than his behavior to you now, and
perhaps he is trying to make amends."

"Or perhaps he is just seeing if he can make me fall in
love with him again," said Caroline bitterly.

"Oh, I know you will be cautious, my child! But if you
should be fortunate enough to engage *his* affections, there
is no reason he should not marry you this time! His wife
left him quite plump in the pockets, you know."

"I see!" cried Caroline, flaring up. "And we should settle
quite happily on *her* money, is that it?"

"There is no need to fly into a miff, Caroline. You must
not do anything you do not choose. But if it does not bother
Lord Ridley to live on his late wife's bounty, surely you
need not scruple to let it trouble *you*. I merely ask you to
entertain the possibility that his lordship may be in earnest,
and treat him accordingly. Suitable husbands do not grow
on every bush, you know, so take care you don't turn missish and spoil your chances!"

Caroline had by now learned better than to argue with
her godmother's, and, it seemed, the whole of London's,
implacable determination on this subject, so she bit her lip
and was silent. Fortunately, her ladyship's mind was rarely

so attached to a topic that she could not be diverted from it with relative ease, so that a remark from her goddaughter about the appearance of the Duke of Clarence at Sunday services in the Chapel Royal caused her to forget her lectures on Caroline's matrimonial prospects, and pursue instead a much more agreeable gossip. The good lady spent a pleasant half hour regaling her charge with a history of this illustrious personage, including his longtime link with his actress-mistress, his many bastards, and the possibility of his entering into lawful wedlock at long last, so that she was quite in charity with Caroline again by the time the footman brought in the mail with a letter to Caroline from her mother and sister.

This consisted of a brief note from Lady Wentworth, indicating that she and Julia would arrive in London on the following Tuesday, and charging Caroline to make sure that Fenwick and the other servants had removed the Holland covers and brought the house into a suitable state of readiness by that day. Her sister had added some impassioned lines at the bottom of the sheet, crossed and recrossed, describing the awe-inspiring Court dress Mrs. Lacey was having made for her, her excitement at the prospect of her come-out, and the impatience with which she endured each day's delay in quitting the dull society of the country.

The Lacey's have been everything that is kind, wrote Julia in a childish scrawl, *although I am sorry to report that Bertie has behaved in quite an odious fashion. I would not have believed him to be so stuffy.* Here another sentence of apparent vehemence was appended, but Caroline could not make it out. *You will also be interested to learn,* her sister continued, *that we have made the acquaintance of Mr. Neville, who bought the Priory. He is very handsome, but his manners are a little stiff. Mama says he was much taken by my beauty, though I can't say whether that will signify, as I had not expected him to be quite so old. I fear he will not be well-liked in the neighborhood, as he is said to be a "high stickler" and turns people off of his property at the slightest excuse.*

Caroline could only wince at Julia's description of Mr.

Neville's manner to her and their mother, but she was encouraged to hope that her sister's eagerness to set her cap for the Nonpareil was dampened by the discovery that he was a man of two-and-thirty years. As she could do nothing more until they came up to town, she resolved to put the matter out of her mind and to enjoy the first ball she had been invited to attend, at the mansion of the Marquess and Marchioness of Milton. The marquess was a crony of the Prince Regent, and Lady Withering had suggested that it was not impossible that Prinny himself would grace the gathering with his presence.

Though Lady Withering was a very good ton, she and Caroline owed their inclusion in this grand affair as much to Caroline as to her ladyship's social connections. Lord Wentworth had run in the prince's set, drinking and playing deep many evenings at Carlton House, and his subsequent ruin was viewed with pity rather than censure by its members. The marquess remembered Caroline as a taking child in leading strings and convinced his wife to send round a card for her ball to the house in Park Street.

As the first major party of the Season, the ball was almost certain to be a success. Nevertheless, Lady Milton left nothing to chance, and when Lady Withering's carriage drew up before the mansion, a number of policemen, link boys, and extra servants were thronging the street in anticipation of what her ladyship delightedly termed a shocking squeeze. Caroline's gown of figured lace over a robe of soft white satin became her dark coloring very well, and the length of silver net draped round her shoulders brought out the sparkle in her gray eyes. The banks of flowers and the brilliance of the chandeliers set off the young ladies' ball dresses to perfection, and the warm light of hundreds of candles cast a flattering glow over the ballroom. Caroline knew a moment of uncomplicated happiness. She was young, she was in London, and she was looking her best. For this evening at least, she would ask no more of life than that.

Since she had been out two years, she did not have to wait for permission to waltz in public, and her hand was quickly engaged for the first dance. Countess Lieven passed her on the floor, in the company of an extremely handsome man who seemed to be enjoying her conversation. Caroline dropped her a curtsy, and the countess returned a civil nod and moved on. Caroline was not taken with the haughty countess—who was reported to have claimed "It is not fashionable where I am not"—but she knew better than to risk offending her. In social circles, even the unknown Mr. Neville did not wield as much power as the countess, and she was second to none in her zeal for exacting deference from those of less exalted ton.

Caroline was engaged for the quadrille by Lord Wynchwood, and when he came up to claim her hand she greeted him with relief and a degree of warmth she had not bestowed on her other partners. His lordship had easy manners and a self-deprecating charm which made her feel relaxed in his company, and she found herself speaking to him confidingly, as if they were old acquaintances. She particularly enjoyed the fact that even though he flirted with her outrageously, he seemed to *like* her as well, and on the whole he reminded her more of Bertie in his manner toward her than the sprig of fashion he aspired to be.

The ballroom and saloons were filling up with latecomers, and Caroline was diverted by Lord Wynchwood's seemingly endless fund of harmless gossip about anyone she inquired about. He was never spiteful or cruel, but she was surprised to discover that no one, including her godmother, knew more about ancestry and family connections, or could judge more accurately where a match would be likely to be made, or what a gentleman had paid for his stable at Tattersall's. She guessed he knew a great deal more than he was telling, and liked him for his reticence.

Suddenly the musicians, responding to an unseen signal, broke off playing, and a hubbub at the door indicated that His Royal Highness had arrived at last. "Oh botheration!" exclaimed Lord Wynchwood, as he escorted Caroline to the edge of the ballroom, where the other guests were pressed up against the gilt chairs lining the walls. "Now we won't finish our dance."

Caroline started to reply, but her eye was drawn to the prince, where he stood greeting the marchioness in a splendid field marshal's uniform, his chest gleaming with medals, and a curving ornamental saber fastened round his huge waist. Behind him stood a man in evening dress who Caroline was suddenly quite sure must be Mr. Neville.

His hair was pomaded and perfectly arranged à la Brutus, and a starched frill showed itself between the lapels of his extravagantly swallow-tailed, tight-fitting cutaway. His waist was hug with fobs and seals, and there were perfect rosettes on his dancing slippers. His face must be called handsome, but he looked down his long nose with a supercilious air, and dabbed at it now and then with his handkerchief, as if he smelled something bad.

Caroline yielded an irresistible impulse. "Lord Wynchwood," she said to her companion, "who is that man over there? A very Tulip of Fashion! Is he a member of the dandy set?"

"That man—you can't mean—the prince?" replied Lord Wynchwood in a thin voice. "That is to say, the uniform's a bit much and all that, but . . . military fever, you know! Wellington gathering his forces . . ."

"I know! I mean, I am acquainted with the prince, and of course that is not whom I meant. *That* man, with the air of an exquisite. I am persuaded from what I have heard that it must be Mr. Neville."

Lord Wynchwood made a strangled sound that made Caroline turn her gaze toward him in concern. He was quite red in the face. "My dear sir, are you quite all right? Shall I ask for a glass of champagne?" She looked round and noticed, for the first time, that the man Countess Lieven had been dancing with was standing quite close to her, and was regarding her rather steadily through his quizzing glass. She was by no means sure she cared for this scrutiny and raised her eyebrows at him, putting up her chin a little.

"No! That is . . . I assure you, ma'am, you are *quite* mistaken. That is Francis Ogilvy. *Here* is Mr. Neville," he said, giving Caroline a pitying look and presenting the man with the quizzing glass.

Caroline, blushing furiously, was surprised to see that he looked amused rather than wrathful. She also saw at once that she had mistaken what it meant to be a Nonpareil. His dark blue coat fitted admirably without padding across his shoulders, and his satin knee breeches showed no crease at all. His silk stockings and his waistcoat were of the plainest elegance, and every other man in the room looked either overdressed or in slight disarray. His dark hair was fashionably brushed and arranged, but it did not have the sculpted, lifeless look of the man who had caught her attention. Only his eyes, which were regarding her sardonically, and had a rather metallic gleam, were the way she had imagined them.

"I beg you pardon," she said, feeling she ought to say *something* because both Mr. Neville and Lord Wynchwood were staring at her, "I seem to have got it wrong."

"Robert, you are quite set-down!" cried Lord Wynchwood. "Francis Ogilvy! Why, ma'am, he carries a golden chest around with him wherever he goes, and takes snuff with a silver shovel. But let me present Mr. Robert Neville, quite the most important figure in Society outside of the great Brummell himself. The Nonpareil, the Arbiter—"

"Enough, Geoffrey," said Mr. Neville in a languid tone, not taking his eyes from Caroline's face.

Caroline felt a spurt of irritation at his manner, and experienced a strong desire to complete the snub that she had begun in such an innocent—but not entirely unsatisfactory—manner. "I am very sorry, Mr. Neville," she said in a colorless voice. "I have quite mistaken what it means to be a dandy, and I can see you must know best. I know it is of the greatest importance to men of your set, and I can only plead a lengthy absence from London as the cause of my ignorance."

Lord Wynchwood gasped. Mr. Neville's lips twisted slightly. "No doubt a *very* lengthy absence, Miss . . . ?"

"Miss Wentworth," said Caroline firmly.

The half-smile died. Mr. Neville gave a polite little bow. "You'll forgive me, ma'am. My condolence on the loss of your father."

"Thank you, sir. And in return may I thank you for your many kindnesses to our family, particularly to my mother and sister, during a very uncomfortable time for us all."

He had the grace to look embarrassed, though he could not know that Caroline was privy to any of his conversation with Lord Wynchwood. Caroline was conscious that she was probably throwing her social future out the window, but she was in the grip of an exhilarating recklessness and could not regret her thrusts. Lord Wynchwood, looking from one to the other without comprehension, remembered that some discomfort was bound to attend the first meeting of a Wentworth and the man who had bought the Priory, and endeavored to smooth it over.

"Miss Wentworth has just been telling me how much she is enjoying London, after the quiet of the country," he said.

"Indeed?" inquired Mr. Neville, raising an eyebrow.

"Oh, yes!" cried Caroline, determined that he would not think she was pining for Wyndham Priory. "I collect that it is highly unfashionable to appear too pleased, but I cannot help it—my father's illness was a lengthy one, and we could never go to the theater or to look at pictures or go to balls such as this! So I admit to enjoying myself, and if that makes me a rustic, then so be it!"

"You are hardly that, Miss Wentworth," he said with a glint in his eyes.

"Then do *you* own to enjoying such things, Mr. Neville?"

"On occasion. Much depends upon my company."

Caroline considered this. "If I should apply that to my own case, I should still find great cause for enjoyment, because it has been so diverting to meet new people and to renew the acquaintance of such notable and interesting gentlemen as Lord Wynchwood."

The object of this compliment flushed and bowed slightly, and Mr. Neville said with a smile, "Lord Wynchwood is a sad rattle, as he will be the first to tell you."

"I'm afraid it's true, ma'am," said his lordship with a grin. "I am no pattern card for the perfect gentleman."

"Nonsense," said Caroline sweetly, speaking more to Mr. Neville than to Lord Wynchwood, "you are most truly a gentleman, because you are never above your company, nor do you act bored, no matter what the provocation! You do not do justice to your disposition: your conduct is such that you do not need to play the coxcomb in order to be noticed."

The gentlemen were spared the necessity of replying to this rather unsettling comment by Prince George, whose stately progress down the line of guests halted in front of them. Whatever his private ailings, and they were many, the Prince Regent's public manner was invariably charming, and while his absurdities, his outlandish tastes, and his notorious love affairs often rendered him contemptible to the ton, few were immune to feeling pleasure at being singled out by their future sovereign. Caroline enjoyed such a sensation now.

"Miss Wentworth, is it not?" asked His Royal Highness, chucking her under the chin in a fatherly way, but managing, nonetheless, the briefest of glances at her bosom. "How very lovely you look this evening!"

Caroline curtsied and thanked him prettily. The prince had been her father's friend for years, so she was used to such encounters, and he always flattered her and Julia whether they were in good looks or not. Still, it was quite agreeable to her vanity to be the center of the room's attention for just a moment, quite as if she were a Renowned Beauty or a Famous Wit.

"I understand my mother will be receiving your sister at her drawing room this year," he said. "What a pity her illness has put off the presentations, but we have every hope she may soon be recovered. Such a taking little puss, your sister!" he said, apparently relishing the memory. "I look forward to seeing both of you there. My compliments to your mother," he added and then moved on.

"Well, Miss Wentworth," said Lord Wynchwood teasingly, "you appear to have made a conquest. The other ladies are quite put out with envy!"

Caroline laughed. "I'm afraid it's no such thing," she said, casting off her own vanity with unimpaired cheerfulness. "He sometimes distinguishes my sister and me because our father was a part of his set. I think he may feel a little guilty because he encouraged him to play so deep, but there is not the least need. In any case," she added with a mischievous sparkle, "I fear he can't quite forgive me my name, which my father gave me particularly to flatter him. I was born in the year of the Prince's marriage, you see."

"Wentworth?" asked Lord Wynchwood blankly, puzzling this out.

"Caroline."

"As a tribute, it would seem to have gone rather amiss," said Mr. Neville with a short laugh. The Prince Regent's disastrous marriage to Caroline of Brunswick, whose name he could not bear to hear uttered in public, was the subject of much private gossip but little public comment. "Miss Wentworth, the music seems to have started up again. May I ask if your hand is engaged for this dance?"

"This is bare-faced piracy, Robert!" exclaimed Lord Wynchwood. "Miss Wentworth was dancing with *me*."

"You'll perceive the music stopped, and now another dance had begun," said Mr. Neville coolly. "Miss Wentworth?"

Caroline was so surprised at his wanting to dance with her that she accepted him without thinking. They went through their paces in the set for some minutes without speaking, and Caroline was glad to concentrate on the steps so that she would not have to engage in polite conversation with him. She began to wonder if the silence was to last through the dance, when he said, "You dance very well, Miss Wentworth."

"Thank you, but I fear I am sadly out of practice. Of course we did not dance at the Priory."

"But you have had a Season in town, have you not?"

"Oh, less than a month, before Papa took ill. After that I'm afraid we did not go out at all."

"What did you do, then, if it does not make you sad to speak of it?"

She raised her eyes to his and put up her chin. "It does not make me sad in the least. I was in charge of the sickroom; my sister was too young, and Mama was . . . not well herself. And then after my father died we had books, and the horses, and trying to keep up with managing the estate." Her voice had softened, and she was unaware how much affection for her lost home had crept into it. "Mr. Neville . . . ," she began, rallying herself for one last effort to convince him that her dislike of him did *not* originate in the loss of the Priory, and that she was able to discourse on the subject in a perfectly rational manner.

"Miss Wentworth?"

"I know there must be some awkwardness between you and the members of my family on the subject of Wyndham Priory, and I daresay it is best to avoid the topic altogether. . . ."

"That would certainly be my inclination, ma'am."

"But . . . well, I mean no disrespect to my father, sir, but he did leave his estates in very bad loaf," she went on, ignoring the snub, "and even if we had been able to keep the Priory, which we were far from able to do, we could not have kept the land or the house in good heart." She lowered her eyes to his waistcoat. "Do you know what I'm trying to say?"

"Yes," he said, surprised, "I think I do."

"The thing is, some of the neighbors are bound to . . . well, there have been . . . there were . . . Wentworths at the Priory for a very long time, but when they see you mean to put money into the estate and stand on easy terms with them, then they will come around. That is all I wanted to say."

"Thank you, Miss Wentworth. I shall certainly follow your excellent advice," he said with a bantering tone, because he could see she was close to tears. Mr. Neville was an accomplished flirt, and no mean master of the art of small talk, but his attempts to draw her out further met with a steady resistance. He was somewhat puzzled by Miss Wentworth. He was used to being courted and flattered, and to casting females into exquisite confusion with the force of his compliments, but he was experienced enough to know that there was another kind of lure used to attract men of his sort—that of a strategic rebuff. However, he did not think Miss Wentworth's imperviousness to his charm—though in fairness to himself he had not tried very hard to charm her—was in any way artificial. Though he had no illusions about himself and the world he led, he was not used to being told—almost in so many words!—that he was a dandy and a coxcomb. He knew he could ruin Miss Wentworth with a few well-chosen comments in Society's ear, and he thought he knew she knew it too. She appeared not to care, but he had no wish to ruin her. As a matter of fact, he was rather intrigued.

"I wonder what it is that I've done to that chit to make her take against me?" he remarked to Lord Wynchwood, when he had escorted Miss Wentworth off the floor and her hand had been claimed for the next dance. "I never set eyes on her two years ago; that was when my mother took ill and I was scarcely up at town at all, so it can't be that."

Lord Wynchwood, who liked Caroline and had no desire to see her career blighted by a few ill-considered remarks, said hastily, "Don't refine too much upon it, Robert! The family's in a very bad way—under the hatches! Well, I don't have to tell *you* that. Shouldn't wonder if it's a strain for the girl losing the Priory like that, and then meeting up with the new owner. Dandy set! Ha! I never thought I'd live to see anyone plant you such a facer. Still, I'm sure she didn't mean it. Good enough girl, and very clever. I should think it shabby of you to try to ruin her chances, Robert," he said sincerely. "She'll be in a deuce of a pucker if she doesn't land a husband with some juice."

"What a flattering portrait you and Miss Wentworth paint of my character, Geoffrey," said Mr. Neville. "I'm quite undone. No, I don't think it can be the Priory, though I own I thought that at first. But she said—well, never mind. I wonder what it can be? I wonder if it would amuse me to try to find out?"

6

CAROLINE HAD ALWAYS meant to retire, effectively if not completely, from the social lists as soon as Julia had made her come-out, and after her interview with Mr. Neville she decided there was little point in pursuing any other plan. In normal circumstances, Lady Wentworth would probably have waited to bring Julia out until Caroline had settled, or, failing that, had retired after an unsuccessful season or two to make way for her more marriageable sister. However, as it had always seemed to both Caroline and Julia that it would be very unfair to the younger sister not to have her share of society simply because the elder did not marry early, and because they could not afford to keep the London town house for more than one Season, it was agreed that the sisters would go out in company together. Still, Caroline had thought she might decline attendance at some of the more glittering events of the Season, and let Julia shine on her own. Caroline had had such a chance herself, and knew the value of it.

She now had to acknowledge ruefully that it is one thing to contemplate making a sacrifice, and quite another to be faced with little choice. She fully expected that Mr. Neville would speak ill of her to his acquaintances, and she looked to see some considerable diminution in her friendships and court once his unfavorable opinion got about. She braced herself to bear this humiliation, but thought it might be preferable to avert it by staying home. It was little comfort to her that she had brought it on herself, after she had promised her godmother that she would not. She had behaved badly, and she knew it, forgetting what the barest civility rendered obligatory. Still, she could not help laughing when she remembered the expression on Mr. Neville's face when she suggested he was a member of the dandy set. If only she had stopped there and had not succeeded in letting him know she thought him top-lofty as well, and had not instructed him in how to better his relations with his neighbors! Her consolation was that she strongly suspected that Mr. Neville cared not a pin what she or anyone else thought of him, and so might not make the exertion to revenge himself on her for her rudeness.

Lady Withering was naturally curious about what had passed between her goddaughter and Mr. Neville, and had not failed to note, along with everyone else in the room, that they had danced together. The rapturous effect this had on her, as well as the pleasing speculations about Caroline's meteoric rise in Society once it was known that the Nonpareil approved of her, was only slightly dampened by Caroline's inarticulate protests and obvious embarrassment. Caroline found herself quite incapable of making her godmother acquainted with the true nature of her conversation with Mr. Neville, but she revealed enough to hint that Lady Withering should not expect him to call, or to distinguish Caroline with any favorable attentions.

Lady Withering was undaunted. "Very likely not, I should say! It would be beyond anything wonderful if Mr. Neville were to single you out when he has his pick of all the beauties in England. However, he has only to seem pleased with you, or drop a favorable comment, and you will be *besieged* with attention. Everyone will be guided by him, you know!"

Caroline hung her head guiltily and decided that this was not the time to tell her godmother that she would not be attending the Duchess of Middleborough's card party after all.

The day of her mother and sister's arrival in London, and of Caroline's removal from Lady Withering's house, came at last, and Caroline was glad to see that the orders she had given Fenwick about the opening of their house in Mount Street had been followed down to the last vase of flowers.

The house was expensively furnished, and, when Lady Wentworth had last had a free hand, in the first stare of fashion, but now the Egyptian motif—with the lotus bowl chandeliers, the hieroglyph paper with matching ibis border, and the painted columns—was a bit démodé, and had even begun to appear in hotels. Her ladyship's taste was fortunately not so romantical as to run to couches in the shape of crocodiles, and when the sphinx-topped pyramids and miniature obelisks were stored out of sight, the rooms were really quite charming. It might be wondered at that the London house had been furnished at the expense of Wyndham Priory, but Lady Wentworth was of the opinion that shabbiness in *historical* furniture was not only to be expected, but might even be deemed a virtue, whereas the interior of one's London house should reflect one's position in the ton down to the last gilded lighting sconce. As the Prince Regent endorsed this view heartily in his own opulent decor in Carlton House, Lord Wentworth had been persuaded without too much difficulty to concur.

Julia was in such a mood of exaltation at being in London at last that not even the dust of the road and the wearying carriage ride had depressed her spirits, and she went about directing the disposition of her trunks and bandboxes with manic glee. Lady Wentworth, a notoriously poor traveler, had retired almost at once to her room to submit to the soothing ministrations of her harassed maid. The two sisters and Mr. Lacey were presently installed in the blue saloon, enjoying their reunion.

"Only wait till you see my Court dress, Caro!" cried Julia rapturously. "Bertie's *dear* Mama was so kind. And she has given me ball gowns and walking dresses too! Oh, I don't think I can bear to wait another day to make my come-out!"

"And *I* don't think I can bear another day of hearing about it," said Mr. Lacey frankly. "Nothing but talk of female fripperies, balls, and such mummeries the whole time! Not much in my line," he told Caroline unnecessarily. "Got to be a dead bore."

"Not as much of a bore as *your* going on and on about the Nonpareil," retorted Julia hotly. "You should have heard him, Caro: 'bang-up team,' and 'slap up to the mark,' and 'prime cattle,' until I thought I would *scream*. And that was just the *horses*."

"Thing is," said Mr. Lacey, who had been treated a number of times to the edifying sight of Mr. Neville's four highly bred lively ones proceeding down the road at a spanking pace, "he's a notable whip."

"That was no reason to make a cake of yourself! Gaping at him with your mouth open like some moonling."

"I did *not*. Besides, *I* didn't visit the Priory three times on some flimsy excuse, and set the whole neighborhood to gabbing."

Caroline, intercepting a speaking glance from Julia to Bertie, correctly divined that there was more to be said on the subject, and remembered that she was not supposed to be privy to this information. "Oh, Julia, you didn't!"

"Told you," said Mr. Lacey, with satisfaction.

Julia looked a little guilty. "Well, there was nothing improper about it, as I merely accompanied Mama, and we did *not* go to call on Mr. Neville, but to recover some articles we had left behind. We had to remove in such haste, you know! I shouldn't wonder at it if we haven't left a great many things at the Priory, and I'm sure Mr. Neville can't be so top-lofty as to object to our collecting them. In fact, he was quite civil. Well, not *excessively,* but I daresay that's because he felt the awkwardness as much as we." She looked thoughtful. "He did not say he meant to call on us in town, but Mama is quite certain that he will. Besides, she means to send him a card for my come-out."

"Oh no!"

Caroline's vehemence startled her sister and Mr. Lacey. "Why, whyever not, Caro? Mama is persuaded that it would be positively insulting if we did not. And besides that, he is quite rich, and extremely handsome, if one does not mind that he is so old."

"Can't seem to rid herself of the notion that the Nonpareil is going to go top over tail for her," said Mr. Lacey, by way of explanation.

"He is much more likely to blight your career altogether," said Caroline. shuddering a little, "and I'm afraid it is partly my fault. I . . . I met him, you see, and I fear we have taken each other in dislike. Such a proud, cynical man, with a conceited notion of his own worth. We must *not* invite him here. He is sure to think we are chasing him!"

"Oh pooh," cried Julia, with a touch of petulance. "I am sure you have mistaken the matter. I know you too well to believe that you would ever be uncivil to anyone. In any case, even if he has taken you in dislike, Caro, which I feel sure he could not, it need not signify. It is my come-out, and I hope I will not make any man think I am *chasing* him."

Mr. Lacey made an inarticulate noise in his throat and rose to his feet. "Must be off. Promised my uncle I'd be in time for dinner, and he's a dev—a high stickler. Won't do to set his back up."

"Oh Bertie!" said Julia, forgetting her pique, "shall you have any fun in London?"

"I mean to!" he said with a grin. "My uncle's well enough, but he dislikes trouble. Told my father I could do as I like in London, but not to expect him to rescue me from any bumblebaths. Sets a great store by appearances. Shouldn't want to disappoint him."

"And you *will* come to my come-out, won't you? That is to say, it's not that I'm in a *quake*, or anything of that nature, but I should very much like you to be there."

"Of course," replied Mr. Lacey, understanding perfectly, "and I shall hope to have the honor of standing up with you," he added punctiliously.

"Oh, *Bertie!*"

7

CAROLINE WOULD HAVE been dismayed to learn that, in addition to sending Mr. Neville a card to her ball, her mother had, a few days later, formed the intention of sending one to Viscount Ridley as well. A brief interview with her bosom-bow Amelia Withering sufficed to acquaint her with the particulars of his renewed attentions to Caroline and with her friend's hope that this time his intentions might be in earnest. Shortly thereafter Ridley presented himself at Mount Street, and as the young ladies were out shopping (Julia not sharing Caroline's scruples in this regard), Lady Wentworth received him alone. He was perfectly affable, and more than capable of charming his way into the good graces of matronly females such as she, and his extreme good looks and address made her think he might do very well for Caroline, if only he could, as Wentworth might have said in a vulgar moment, be brought up to scratch. Lady Withering had informed her of Caroline's reluctance, but Lady Wentworth could not but feel that she could overturn any such objections by the force of her own will, if the chance should present itself to dispose of her elder daughter so easily. Nevertheless, though she took care to inform Lord Ridley of the date of Julia's ball, and promised to send him a card, she did not disclose the invitation to Caroline.

Lady Wentworth would have received with injured incredulity any suggestion that she was lacking in affection for her elder daughter, but she was not of a naturally maternal disposition, and Caroline was such a very uncomfortable child. She was never quite sure what Caroline was thinking, except when Caroline was exhorting her to do something quite against her inclination—generally in order to fulfill some nicety of her daughter's conscience—and in fact her ladyship harbored the lurking suspicion, never fully expressed, that Caroline did not always quite *approve* of her. Julia, on the other hand, though inclined to be a bit too much in alt to be a perfectly restful companion, always entered into her feelings in every particular and was the mirror reflection of her young ladyship besides. It would be nice to suppose that, while Julia was her mother's favorite child, Caroline had been her father's, but Lord Wentworth had preferred the prince's company to any of his family's, and had lost interest in them altogether when his wife failed to supply him with an heir.

Preparations for Julia's come-out occupied the household for days before the event took place: a band must be engaged, furniture moved, the chandelier polished, and the hundreds of spare glasses and plates removed from storage and washed. The bills for champagne and candles alone threatened to be staggering, and there must be ladies' beverages as well, and a fine dinner to serve to select guests beforehand, with an elegant supper to follow. Julia wanted to decorate the ballroom in pink silk canopies, to set off her coloring, but more practical heads prevailed, and she settled on floral sprays instead.

Her taste for pink, however, was satisfied in the choice of her ball gown, which was of white satin, with a Russian bodice and inlets of pink satin down the front. It fastened with exquisite pearl rosettes, and like Caroline's dress, was ornamented only with her very good strand of pearls. When she descended the stairs to dinner on the evening of her party, both Caroline and Lady Wentworth were rapt in their admiration. A small wreath of white-and-pink roses adorned her shining gold hair, and excitement tinted her cheeks with a delicate blush. Her blue eyes were startlingly bright, and if the expression in them was rather too willful to convey the impression that she was an innocent bud just unfurling her petals, she still looked, as her mother put it, like the veriest angel.

Caroline had arrayed herself quietly, in orange blossom sarcenet, set off with a shawl of the lightest gauze. She did not want to look as if she were competing with Julia, and she was reasonably satisfied when she completed her toilette. She gave one brief, wistful thought to the diamonds, not the Wentworth diamonds but her own more delicate necklace, that would have become the neckline of her dress so well, and then fastened on her pearls. Her mother had said she need not contribute them to the sale because their value was not substantial, but Julia's dejection over the other jewelry compelled her to make a sacrifice of her own. She was glad now that she had done so, because her sister had ceased to lament the loss of the jewels, and had even begun to discuss her diamondless Court presentation in a cheerful tone.

Lady Wentworth had feared, in her heart of hearts, that good ton and old connections would not be enough to completely overcome the family's lamentable change in circumstances when it came to filling her drawing rooms, and in this she was not entirely mistaken. Lady Sefton and Lady Jersey had declined, and though the latter had written a very civil note of regret, there was no mention of vouchers for Almack's. The party was a trifle thin of members of the very first circles, but Julia's loveliness, and the loyalty of old acquaintances, contrived to make it a success nonetheless. Long before the Wentworths had received the last of their guests, Julia's hand had been solicited for almost every dance, and Caroline found herself with almost as many partners as her sister.

Lord Ridley arrived in good time to stand up with Caroline for the first two dances. She was vexed, but not surprised, to discover that her mother had invited him; she feared that it would be very difficult to convince her mother to discourage any kind of eligible *parti*, and determined that the only way to greet him was without embarrassment and with a certain willful obtuseness.

Caroline would have been hard put to explain why she resisted Ridley's particularity of attention to her, or why she trusted him so little. Of course his past behavior to her had been unfeeling and perhaps unkind, but she might have forgiven him if she believed him sincere in his regard for her *now,* or at least truly resolved to make amends. But there was something about his assumption of intimacy that grated on her nerves, and so far from being penitent, he seemed to conduct himself as if his marriage and her wounded heart had never occurred, and they might go on just as before. Caroline had to wonder at the perversity of circumstance, which appeared to be offering her what she had most thought to desire, and of her own character, with its vague and unsettled suspicions.

Ridley, perceiving none of this, saw only that she was elusive, and set out to attach her once more. He was used to thinking of her as his uncritical admirer, warmed by the flames of first love, and the flattering recollection of her obvious regard for him had occasionally surfaced during his brief, but not entirely felicitous, marriage. He knew he had not used her well when he had never had any intention of offering her matrimony, but an agreeable flirtation had blossomed into affection, and he had let his attentions grow too pronounced. He had liked to think of her, not broken-hearted, but repining tenderly under the cruel necessity that had separated them. When he went out into Society once more after his wife's death and discovered Caroline at Lady Bassett's, his initial object in seeking her out had only been to gratify his vanity by discovering whether she still nursed a *tendre* for him, but after some time in her company he began to think that, now that his wife's fortune made him independent, it really might be very comfortable to marry again. He had no doubt that Caroline's poverty, if not her earlier partiality, would make her receive his addresses with pleasure, and he attributed her present reticence to maidenly caution, and a not-unnatural desire to pay him back a little. He was certain enough of the outcome to indulge her, and to wait till she had played her little game out.

"My dear girl," he told her as they took their places on the floor, "how can your mother have contrived to bring off such a splendid ball as this? It is quite the most magnificent of the Season!"

"Oh we are not so far under the hatches as that," responded Caroline wickedly. "Besides, it's early days yet."

"You know perfectly well I meant no such thing," he said calmly. "Her ladyship has been in town less than two weeks, and that is very short notice for such an affair."

"Well, Lady Withering was of the greatest help to us, and before my father died we used to give a great many parties, you know!"

He lowered his voice. "Permit me to say how very sorry I am about the loss of your home," he said, anxious to assure her that he knew all about it, and did not mind. "It must be very distressing to you and your mother and sister, and I am glad to see that you are all in good spirits. If I can be of service to you in any way, I beg you will let me know."

Caroline inclined her head, not trusting herself to speak.

They danced on in silence for a while, and presently Lord Ridley said, "They tell me Neville is making great changes at Wyndham Priory. I must say that on my one visit I was enchanted, and thought everything there the vision of perfection. *I* certainly would find nothing to change, but then Mr. Neville has not had the privilege of seeing it when the Wentworths were in residence."

Caroline wondered at his putting this construction on what was one of the most unhappy episodes of her life, and did not reply.

"You do not speak. Forgive me, the topic must pain you. I only wish you to understand how perfectly I enter into your feelings on this matter. I can only think how fortunate it is that you will not have to meet Mr. Neville very frequently in Society."

Caroline considered telling him that her mother had sent Mr. Neville a card for the ball just to see what his reaction would be, but as she was quite sure that this was one function the Nonpareil would be most unlikely to attend she thought better of it. Instead she said, "As to that, we are a little acquainted with him, and while we are not, as you say, likely to see much of him, I see no reason why we should not meet with tolerable ease. It is hardly his fault that my father squandered his fortune, or that the Priory is in such a ramshackle state that it is in desperate need of repair. And if he should restore it to what it was in my grandfather's day, I assure you the tenants will have no cause to regret the change of ownership, nor perhaps the neighbors either," she added with a touch of bitterness. Caroline had to wonder at herself for defending Mr. Neville, whom she despised, to Lord Ridley, whom she had once loved. She decided that even the former's contemptuous civility was easier to bear than Ridley's crushing solicitude.

Lord Ridley smiled down into her eyes. "You do not do yourself justice," he said, "but I've no wish to cross swords with you. I can see you must be upset, and will say no more. May I venture to hope that you will do me the honor of letting me lead you into supper? I know you too well to think you would *outrage* propriety by standing up with me for more than two dances, and I'm engaged for the next set with your lovely sister. I hope I can compel her to talk about *you*."

Caroline put him off with some excuses about her duties as hostess, and her mother needing her, but had no real expectation of avoiding him. She wished Lord Wynchwood, or one of her reliable friends, might have asked her first. Caroline saw with surprise that her distant manner seemed rather to encourage Lord Ridley than not, and wondered why that idea should have so little attraction for her.

Last of all the guests to arrive when Lady Wentworth had already joined her party in the ballroom, was Mr. Neville, who climbed the stairs unhurriedly and surveyed his fellow guests coolly, as if unaware of the flutter he was causing in so many breasts. Her ladyship all but tripped over her skirts in her haste to greet him and tell him where to find her lucky daughter. Julia's triumph swelled her throat, and caused her to stammer in reply to his civilities. Lady Withering, more in possession of her faculties, asked him how he did, and suggested that while she was not quite sure that Miss Julia Wentworth had any dances free, he might find some other of his acquaintances already in the ballroom.

When he had taken himself off, sauntering across the room and stopping to exchange salutations with his friends, Lady Wentworth turned on her friend in wrath. "What do you mean by that, Amelia!" she hissed, the magenta feathers of her headdress quivering with indignation. "You know perfectly well he came to see Julia, and you positively discouraged him!"

"What I know *perfectly well,* Susan," replied Lady Withering, "is that if you pitch your daughter at him in that manner he is quite capable of giving you, and Julia, an embarrassing set-down. It will do her no harm if he knows she is surrounded by admirers, you know. It is more than enough that he came here this evening. You may take it from me that Julia is quite creditably launched!"

"I can see that quite well, Amelia. I've had dozens of compliments on her beauty, and the Countess of Wigmore was obliging enough to say that she could see where she came by her looks. But that is no reason to let her dance with Bertram Lacey, whom she's known since he was in short coats, if Mr. Neville should want to stand up with her. She'll be quite throwing away her chances, after I have been to such *trouble* to bring it off. You know I had to contrive opportunities to bring her to his notice at the Priory, just in hopes that this might happen."

"Susan, you aren't thinking seriously that Robert Neville will fall victim to Julia? Innocent buds aren't in his line."

"I don't see why not," replied her friend. "Wentworth was five-and-thirty when he offered for me, and I wasn't a day older than Julia."

And look where that got you, thought Lady Withering, and closed her lips.

Julia watched the approach of her most illustrious guest with a mixture of satisfaction and anxiety. She did not for a moment doubt that her own and her mother's lures had borne fruit, and that his appearance at her ball was a tribute to her grace and beauty, but she was also aware that Mr. Neville's eyes, when he regarded her, were far from warm with admiration, and seemed rather to be as cold as steel. She had had, at the Priory, the unpleasant sensation that he was laughing at her, as if she were an amusing child. Her admirers had all been much younger men, and she had to own that she was a little out of her depth. When she had flashed him her most dazzling smile and expressed the hope that they might meet up at town, he had even turned the subject by inquiring whether she was still at her lessons, for all the world as if she had just cast off her leading strings. The recollection threw her into confusion, and made her wonder what on earth she might say to him to convince him that she was no schoolroom miss, but a worthy candidate to become the Rage of the Ton.

Words failed her, however, when he bent over her hand and said in a light tone, "My congratulations, Miss Wentworth. London appears to like you very much."

Julia blushed and murmured that the party was a shocking squeeze and expressed the hope that he might enjoy himself nevertheless.

"Oh I mean to," said Mr. Neville, used to such wooden responses from debutantes. "Lady Withering tells me that it is quite useless to hope for the chance of standing up with you, however."

Julia looked up at this. "Oh no! That is to say, all the dances are taken except the waltzes, and Mama is old-fashioned enough to insist that I must not waltz in public without the approval of one of the patronesses of Almack's, but I daresay if *you* . . ."

"My dear child, I wouldn't dream of doing such a thing," said Mr. Neville, becoming bored with this game. "Countess Lieven would never forgive me, to say nothing of the others! My credit is not good enough to withstand such boldness, and neither is yours; even old Douro can't break the rules of Almack's with impunity."

Julia favored him with a radiant smile, sure now that he would dance with her if he could. "And who, pray, is old Douro?" she asked archly.

"Arthur Wellesley, ma'am."

She continued to look blank.

Mr. Neville smiled. "The Duke of Wellington, Miss Wentworth."

"Oh, of course," said Julia dismissively, thus disposing of the most famous military hero of his age, and the man who was preparing, even as they spoke, to check the advances of Napoleon on the Continent. "But military gentlemen can't expect to cut a figure in Society, after all."

"Just so," said Mr. Neville with a sardonic lift of his eyebrow, "I'm told they generally have far too much to do."

Julia was spared the necessity of replying to this by the arrival of Mr. Lacey to claim her hand for the next dance, and Mr. Neville, after exchanging a few words with Bertie on the stabling of his horses in London, and bowing deeply to Julia, withdrew.

"Oh, Bertie," said Julia mistily when he led her out onto the floor. "Isn't it wonderful? I'll be the envy of every girl in London when it gets out that Mr. Neville came to my come-out."

"I own I never expected to see *him* here," admitted Mr. Lacey, grudgingly. "Not his sort of affair at all."

"Perhaps he had a *particular* reason for wanting to come," suggested Julia sweetly.

"Gammon! He didn't look moonstruck to me."

"Pooh! How would you know?" pouted Julia.

"Got eyes, haven't I? Julia, you won't lose your heart to this fellow, will you? Ten to one he's just amusing himself. Can't say for sure, but it seems to me he's paying as much attention to your sister as he did to you."

"What? Oh well, I daresay he feels obliged to, because all *my* dances were taken," Julia said complacently, looking over to where Caroline and Mr. Neville stood talking. "Caro told me particularly that they had taken each other in dislike. And speaking of that, what do you think of her Lord Ridley? Such a handsome man, and such pleasing manners! Caro must be quite *aux anges!*"

"Hmmmph!" responded Mr. Lacey noncommittally. "I say, Julia, how came you to be to be out riding in Sir Barnaby Pilbeam's carriage without a groom? Saw you, you know. Daresay I'm not the only one. Fellow's forty if he's a day, besides being a shocking loose screw. Dresses like a man-milliner too!"

"Mama says he has sixty thousand pounds," Julia said primly.

"Well, what does *that* signify? You ain't saying you mean to *encourage* him?"

"Well, no," said Julia thoughtfully, "though Mama did say I must be careful whom I hint away. But I promise you I didn't give him the least encouragement."

"Except for riding with him in an open carriage, without a groom."

"Well, I own I was not sure if was quite the thing, but he said there would not be room for the groom."

"*That* I can well believe. Fellow's built like a pudding."

"Yes, and he wears a corset too, because when I dropped my reticule he tried to retrieve it for me, and he could not. He told me he had injured his back, but it *creaked*! And you should have heard him when he came to pay a morning visit. Mama was afraid he might expire on the stairs, and then what should we have done? We were on pins and needles till he came through the door."

"Might have been a good thing if he did," muttered Mr. Lacey.

"Well, perhaps, since he is so old, it would not have been so very surprising. Do you think he can be senile?"

"Never heard that he was. Why?"

"Because he *would* chuck my chin and put his arm around my waist, though I didn't like it, and you know the only person who used to do that was old Mr. Stanton, and you remember *he* was quite senile, and had to be led around."

Mr. Lacey, uttering a stifled oath, did a brother's duty and made Lady Wentworth's veiled warnings rather more explicit. "Lord, if you ain't the veriest baby," he concluded unwisely.

"I am *not*!" Julia retorted hotly. "I can take care of myself, I promise you."

Mr. Lacey's first response to this was inarticulate. "No need to fly into a pelter," he said bracingly after a moment. "But promise me if you do get in a scrape you'll let me help. Here, Julia," he said, turning the subject, "is your mother feeling quite the thing? Meant to ask and forgot!"

"I should say she's in a high gig," said Julia frankly. "Why do you ask?"

"Because when we took our places in the set she looked quite queer. Kept winking and jerking her head at Neville over there. Doesn't have a tic, does she?"

"Certainly not!"

"Well, I expect it's nothing to worry about," Mr. Lacey said judiciously. "Probably just the excitement."

Caroline had regarded the specter of Mr. Neville bearing down on her with quite as much trepidation as her sister, but for a different cause. She had been as amazed as Mr. Lacey to see him enter the ballroom and watched with alarm when he engaged Julia in conversation. When this passed off with apparent amity, she decided that he was not hellbent on depressing their pretensions to Society after all, and even that, his unpleasant boasts to Lord Wynchwood to the contrary, he must have found her sister more attractive than he would admit. Whatever the truth of the matter, the last thing she expected was that, out of a crowded roomful of people, Mr. Neville would make his way over to *her*.

Mr. Neville's approach, most irritatingly, had the effect of making the rest of the circle disappear. He raised his quizzing glass and looked at her. "Satisfied?" he asked, smiling slightly.

"I beg your pardon?"

"With the success of your sister's debut."

"Oh, most certainly," she responded, made reckless by his disregard for the niceties of conversation and by her overmastering desire to cross swords with him every time he came within her range, "especially now that you have been so obliging as to help bring her into Fashion."

"Yes it is excessively kind of me, is it not?" he said with a note of mockery. "Don't pay me Spanish coin, Miss Wentworth; it's apparent to me that you and your sister stand in no need of help from one of the dandy set."

Caroline's lively sense of the absurd came to her rescue,

and instead of blushing hotly and stammering a reply, she burst into sudden laughter. "That is most unhandsome of you, Mr. Neville, when you know I have already apologized for that *unfortunate* mistake. As for paying you Spanish coin, was it not Lord Wynchwood who called you the 'Arbiter of Fashion'? And much as it goes against the pluck with me to minister to your vanity," she said maliciously, "you must know that it does my sister a great deal of good socially for you to be seen at her come-out!"

Mr. Neville gave her one of his real smiles—not the one he kept for social occasions—a slight, contemptuous curl of the lips—but one that lit his eyes with amusement and softened his habitual aspect of cynical reserve. "Your sister's charms are quite manifest, Miss Wentworth. But have you no thought to spare for yourself?"

"Naturally, if there is any need."

"Then you don't wish me to—how did you phrase it?—be so obliging as to bring you into Fashion?"

"Certainly not! And if I were not sure that you are quizzing me I should tell you it would be quite useless for you to try!"

"Oh, I daresay the case is nowhere near as hopeless as that," he said languidly.

Caroline choked. "I *wish* you would stop making me laugh. I am perfectly serious. I have no wish to become the rage of the town, or any other figure you seem to believe it lies within your power to create. As if I didn't know I had sunk quite beneath reproach in your estimation after our last conversation," she added cheerfully.

"Oh no, ma'am, quite the contrary," he said, trying the effect of a compliment.

He received only an inclination of the head so eloquent of dubiety that he was at once pleased and taken aback. He was used to casting females so addressed into a state of fluttery confusion, but the most hardened flirt in London had grown bored with the expected. He had his own rather ruthless way of dealing with any girl who set her cap at him too obviously, but a female of marriageable age who had taken him in dislike was a novel experience. He rather expected it would prove to be a salutary one as well. He began to be interested in discovering what he could provoke her to say next.

"Tell me, Miss Wentworth, are you as averse to receiving compliments as you are to cutting a figure in Society?"

"Mr. Neville," said Caroline, meeting his eyes with a level gaze, "as you are apparently determined to undermine my composure with such remarks, do you not think it is expecting a great deal to see your 'compliments' received with anything but caution?"

"Bravo!" he said admiringly. "I am quite set down. But if it will not try your composure too far, tell me, pray, whether you always say precisely what you are thinking?"

Caroline laughed. "I'm sure it seems that way to you, when you've no idea what curbs I've been putting on my vexatious tongue! Mr. Neville," she said frankly, "I can only think that it is fortunate that we are not destined to see very much of each other, because every time we meet I come within ames-ace of giving you a trimming. I am sure it can't be very agreeable!"

Her laughter was reflected in his eyes. "If you don't wish me to pay you compliments, ma'am, you shouldn't leave me such an obvious opening," he said. "I collect you do not mean to go into seclusion?"

"Of course not."

"Then I fear I must disappoint you. It is quite likely that we will see each other after all, and I shall engage to prepare my poor ego for the shattering treatment it must endure at your hands. In fact, if you will permit me, Miss Wentworth—"

"Ca—Miss Wentworth, Mr. Neville, forgive me for intruding, but your mama has sent me to remind you that it is time for us to go down for supper," said Lord Ridley at her elbow, laying a proprietary hand on her arm. "And your friend Mr. Lacey is getting up a party to, as he calls it, 'snabble all the lobster patties,' so I suggest we've no time to lose. Neville, your servant."

Borne away on this irresistible tide, Caroline had little time to ponder her conversation with Mr. Neville. She was quite puzzled. His manner upon their meeting held all the height she was prepared for by his aunt's and his own remarks, and nothing in her brief acquaintance with him led her to suppose that he was not as spoiled and idle as his reputation suggested. Her first knowledge of him had been when he uttered such words to Lord Wynchwood as must make her forever hold him in contempt, and her remarks to him at the Marquess of Milton's ball were of a nature that could not lead him to mistake the intensity of her dislike. Yet so far from blighting her social career, as she had expected, he had signaled her out, and treated her sallies with good humor, and shown that he had a strong sense of the ridiculous himself. He had even, for what she did not doubt were malicious purposes of his own, begun a light flirtation with her. It was impossible to uncover the intricacies of his mind, but she was determined not to permit him to cut up her peace. She told herself that his civilities to her, if they could be called that, must spring from a desire to recommend himself to her sister, and then wondered why that was such a singularly unsatisfying reflection.

She would certainly have been incredulous if she knew that among the many celebrants of Julia's triumph there were several who found her the more attractive of the two sisters. One of these was Lord Wynchwood, who expressed the view to his friend Mr. Neville that while Miss Julia Wentworth was undoubtedly a diamond of the first water, Miss Caroline Wentworth had taste, and superior sense as well. "And what kind of rig are you running, Robert? I shouldn't have thought either one of them was in your style."

"You don't think I might have fallen victim to a lovely face? It's happened before, you know."

"I know it, Robert, but if you wanted to pay court to the Beauty, why did you spend as much time with her sister? You mark my words, they'll be laying odds at White's tomorrow on which one's your latest flirt."

"My dear Geoffrey, didn't you ask me not to ruin the elder Miss Wentworth's matrimonial prospects last time we met? Am I to be scolded for taking your advice? I merely wanted to set her feet firmly on the social ladder!"

"Humbug!"

"You don't believe I acted out of kindness?" inquired Mr. Neville in a disinterested tone.

"Out of *what*?"

. "My dear boy, it's not impossible."

"I know that, Robert," retorted Lord Wynchwood seriously. "When Bingham lost his inheritance to you at White's and was at point-non-plus of despair, I know very well that you forgave the whole debt. *On-dit* of the town, it was."

"Geoffrey, this conversation is beginning to bore me. I haven't the faintest notion what you're referring to."

"Have it your way, Robert. But it's too bad of you to amuse yourself with the Wentworths. Especially when you told me you thought the younger one had set her cap for you and had coming manners besides, and that you particularly did not wish to further the acquaintance. And while I'm sure you'll acknowledge now that Miss Caroline Wentworth is not a fubsy-faced ape-leader, or whatever it was you called her, it would be too cruel of you to take them up just to administer a snub in the end."

"Good God!" cried Mr. Neville, much struck. "Did I say that?"

"You know you did. Well, words to that effect."

Mr. Neville slapped his hand to his forehead. "Where was this?"

"At Lady Bassett's rout party. You really don't remember?"

"Was I foxed?"

"A trifle disguised at the most. What *is* it, Robert?"

"Bear with me. Was Miss Caroline Wentworth by chance in attendance at this party?"

Lord Wynchwood furrowed his brow. "Believe she was, yes!"

"Aha!" cried Mr. Neville.

8

MR. BERTRAM LACEY had lost no time in attempting to acquire what Caroline called "town bronze." He did not like to admit it to the Wentworths, for whom the subject might still be a sore one, but the finest model for any aspiring gentleman to copy was without doubt Mr. Robert Neville. Accordingly, though his father's allowance did not reach a level of munificence which would enable him to patronize Stultz or Weston, he was able, through the help of some new friends, to discover an up-and-coming tailor who initiated him into the mysteries of superfine or Bath suiting, and made for him, in addition to a greatcoat with a beaver collar and a modest six capes, a blue morning coat with brass buttons, a buff-colored waistcoat with just a hint of stripes, and pale buff stockinette pantaloons. A pair of tassels for his Hessians, a higher crowned hat, and yellow gloves (not, alas, in chickenskin) completed the outfit in which Mr. Lacey would make his debut in the fashionable spots of daytime London. His evening dress, while not slap up to the mark, was regretfully deemed adequate to the needs of a young man whose aspirations must necessarily exceed the depth of his pocketbook.

His uncle, though retired from Society, was nevertheless wise in the ways of young men, and wrote him a letter of introduction to Mr. John Jackson's Boxing School at Number 13 Bond Street. Gentleman Jackson's manners and dignity, in addition to his remarkable habit of treating his most aristocratic and least exalted pupils with exactly the same degree of civility, could not help but inspire adoration in the breast of one such as Mr. Lacey, and almost from the very moment he entered the premises his greatest aspiration was to be allowed to put on the gloves with this acknowledged master.

His uncle also personally conducted him to Manton's, bade him look around, and said, if he behaved himself, his nephew might expect a capital piece to take back with him to the country. As Mr. Lacey's handsome selection was a mahogany double gun with elevation, hammers, and gravitating stop holes, furnished with brown leather, and costing the heart-stopping sum of 67/2/0, he made very sure that he would in no way incur his relative's displeasure during his stay in town. His uncle, content that he had fulfilled his duty, now left his nephew to his own devices.

In addition to the wholesome pleasures of pugilism and firearms, however, London offered other distractions that Mr. Lacey, being only human, could not help being tempted by. His obliging new friends from Jackson's soon made him acquainted with such diverse attractions as the sparring matches at the Fives Court, the Cock-pit Royal, the bold Cyprians at Covent Garden Saloon, the Cocoa Club (where he saw Mr. Scrope Davies, the friend of Byron), the melodramas at the Surrey Theater, and the subscription rooms at Tattersall's, as well as a number of snug little gaming houses in Pall Mall.

Mr. Lacey knew very well that despite the air of respectability of these establishments, a green 'un from the country would be a likely prey, and he had no desire to be thought a flat, or to end up in Dun Territory. Still, it was very agreeable to be treated as an equal by Lord Shipley and Mr. Carleton, both great-goers, and after a few modest days he began to find himself more at home at Turf and Table than he had intended.

His first efforts met with considerable success, for he enjoyed a run of luck at the tables that left his pockets full of guineas, followed by a fortunate bet next day on the horses. He began to outfit himself with a bit more largesse, and to think his earlier caution unwarranted. It was all so easy and pleasant that it went to his head, and the example of his friends, who seemed to live from day to day on the brink of

ruin and still contrive to stave off insolvency, did nothing
to bolster his determination to remain out of debt.

In no time at all he found himself, if not quite all to
pieces, seriously embarrassed. His belief in his natural ability at cards had undergone severe reevaluation, and only his
countryman's shrewdness had saved him from losing a considerable sum on a showy bit of horseflesh much favored
by his companions in a match at Tattersall's. To make matters worse, the tradesmen among whom he had bestowed
his custom began to demand immediate payment, almost as
if they scented his difficulty. Mr. Lacey now began to discover that privileges accorded Mr. Carleton or Lord Shipley, with their trustees and their connections, were not
necessarily extended to Mr. Bertram Lacey of Ilcombe
Hall, and one of the mysteries of London life was now
made more clear to him.

Sick with apprehension about the effect the news that he
had swallowed a spider might have on his uncle, or worse,
upon his dear papa, he placed one last, desperate bet on a
sure thing disclosed by a jockey friend of Shipley's. If it
won it would go a long way toward meeting his obliga-
tions, and Mr. Lacey fervently promised the Fates that if his
supplication was favored he would make haste to mend the
error of his ways. The Arbiter of his Fortunes did not disappoint him; the horse came in first, and Mr. Lacey, much relieved, went home with a tidy sum in his pockets.

Mr. Lacey's friends, less chastened and a trifle pot-
valiant after their celebration of this extraordinary event,
urged him to reinvest his blunt at the tables, now that his
luck had manifestly turned, and to seize the opportunity to
get clear of his debts altogether. Mr. Lacey, however, was
made of sterner stuff. He settled his debts of honor and
those of the tradesmen he thought most urgent, and put
down something on account with the others. Then he
squared his shoulders, prepared to pack his bags, and, with
only one cowardly, regretful thought of Manton's finest,
laid the remainder before his uncle.

Expecting a thundering scold, Mr. Lacey was not disappointed. "Of all the cork-brained, bird-witted . . . !" His

uncle had not run out of expressions of displeasure even
after five minutes of very colorful vituperation. "Didn't I
warn you to stay out of gaming-hells? And horses! Humbug! And pray tell me, sir, what is it you propose that I
shall do with *that*?" he added, gesturing wrathfully at the
pile of unpaid bills his nephew had produced. "Well, sir? I
wish you will tell me!"

"Nothing!" replied Mr. Lacey penitently. "That is, I only
wish you would advance me the sum for just a little while,
so that I can settle my debts before I leave London. I am
aware," he added, hanging his head, "that you *can't* wish
me to remain with you under the circumstances, so I mean
to go home at once and lay the matter before my father.
You can be sure that he will repay the loan immediately,
and I will undertake to pay him back out of my allowance,
even if it takes me a *year*," he said gloomily. He was aware
that these arrangements were more appropriate to a miscre-
ant schoolboy than a young man of fashion, but he was too
relieved at having the matter out in the open to care.

"Hmmm, well, don't be too hasty, my boy," said his
uncle, in a more benevolent voice. "No need to turn tail because you can't pay your stick. It's a damned imposition, of
course, but I daresay I can lend you the money, and your
father need never know. Thing is, I know Augustus, he'll
cut up stiff if he gets the news. Bound to keep you under
lock and key for at least a year." Mr. Lacey shivered. "Not
that you don't deserve it, but you've only done what nine
out of ten young fools do when they hit the town. Did it
myself, once. Daresay you've learned your lesson?" he
asked, giving his nephew a shrewd look beneath his bushy
brows.

"Oh yes, sir!" cried Mr. Lacey joyfully.

"Good. Then we'll say no more about it. But, mind you,
this is the last time I tow you out of the River Tick. If I hear
you've so much as laid a farthing on a game of speculation
I'll pack you back to Ilcombe Hall on the stagecoach, and
think what a mortification *that* would be to your papa! So
no more betting, sir, while you are under my roof. I trust
we understand each other?"

Mr. Lacey agreed, consoling himself with the reflection that his uncle was a right 'un after all.

While their old friend was becoming sadder and wiser in the ways of the town, the Wentworth sisters were enjoying the fruits of what must be considered, under the circumstances, a remarkable social success. Within a fortnight Julia was in the happy position of finding herself with three engagements in the same evening, and had gained sufficient confidence to give Sir Barnaby a sharp set-down, and order Fenwick to deny her when he called. Fortune, in the form of Mr. Neville, had smiled upon her come-out, and no girl in such a felicitous position need fear for partners at a ball, or suitors in her train.

The Nonpareil's luster cast a similar glow over Caroline's second Season, and she found that she attracted a great deal more attention than she had in her first. The ton had discovered her to be a "quite pretty girl with excellent style," and her court now included men of fashion and consequence, of an appropriately marriageable age. The gazetted fortune hunters, afraid of being left out of the latest fad, paid their tribute, but in such a way as to raise no hopes that their intentions were serious. The house in Mount Street filled up with flowers and cards, and Lady Wentworth, when she was not exhausted by her unselfish ministrations to the needs of her children, was in transports of rapture.

Not everyone rejoiced equally in the Wentworths' good fortune. Lady Oversby, whose own daughter was making her come-out this year, told her friend Lady Bridle that while the Wentworth girls were pretty-behaved enough, especially the older, and the younger was undeniably a Beauty, it was a mystery to her why the Nonpareil should want to make up to the daughters of a ramshackle ne'er-do-well like Evelyn Wentworth, when just the *slightest* notice of a far more worthy candidate would have been enough to give her a start in the world. Lady Bridle, whose only daughter was safely married, was unable to console her friend for Mr. Neville's lack of attention to the somewhat bird-witted Maria, but pointed out that obviously he had no need to consider fortune in setting up his latest flirt. "And mind you, the family's an old one, and they are, or were, very good *ton*," added her ladyship, adding even further to her friend's discomfort.

"But which one is it?" asked Lady Oversby querulously. "My Horace says he was particular in his attentions to both."

"Oh, the Beauty, without doubt," replied Lady Bridle, with an air of superiority. "Can you imagine Robert Neville with anything else?"

Equally vexed were Lady Jersey and Lady Sefton, because, as Sally Jersey remarked to her friend at the next assembly at Almack's, "It was too bad of Robert not to let us know he meant to go to the Wentworth chit's come-out, when I had already sent my regrets. It is so irritating to be behindhand when Robert makes one of his discoveries! Evelyn Wentworth's daughter too! I sent vouchers right away, of course, though I'd meant not to. They're all to pieces, you know, and I never could abide Susan Wentworth! Sybil Frant vouches for the elder sister, and I must say she seemed a modest girl of excellent principles, with a great deal of countenance too, but the younger is little more than a schoolroom miss. Robert will find her a dead bore within a month."

"Ten to one he's hoaxing us somehow," Maria Sefton said thoughtfully. "I don't believe for a minute he's the least bit taken with the newest pretty face. He's hardened his heart to them these ten years, and from what I hear of this one there's nothing to make him lose it now. You know he bought Wyndham Priory from the Wentworths?"

"Certainly I know it," replied Lady Jersey in frosty accents.

"Depend on it, he's playing some deep game of his own. I don't see quite what it is, but I'll lay odds he means to amuse himself at our expense. You mark my words!"

Something of that nature had also occurred to Lady Withering, whose impeccable social connections had made her aware of the sort of speculation about Mr. Neville and the Wentworths within the confines of White's and other clubs. This confirmed her in her opinion that men were quite odious, but nevertheless she felt it incumbent upon her to drop a word in the ear of her goddaughter. A little more acute an observer than Lady Bridle, she had no fear that Mr. Neville was setting up Julia as his latest flirt, because it was clear that his attentions, at least on the evening of the ball, had been directed at Caroline. This, in combination with Caroline's avowed dislike of him, made her deeply suspicious, and she determined that her goddaughter should not be hurt again. "For there's no denying what an attractive man he is, my love, and I can't count how many diamonds of the first water he's made the object of his gallantry. But I shouldn't want *you* to wear the willow for him, my dear Caroline!"

Caroline replied that she had no such intention.

"No, of course you do not," said Lady Withering soothingly. "But he may be getting revenge on you, Caroline, or playing some game of his own, and I wish you will not be taken in by him. He is quite an accomplished flirt, and I fear it is unlikely that he will form a lasting attachment, and people will talk, you know."

"I hope, ma'am," said Caroline, blushing hotly, "that no one is saying I have set my cap for him, or some such thing?"

"They are far more likely to say it of Julia than of you," said her ladyship frankly. "There is not the least cause for alarm, my dear; just be a little on your guard. I beg you will not be offended at my saying so, especially since I know you do not quite like him."

Miss Wentworth, her pride wounded, had no trouble whatsoever in resolving that, the next time they met, she would treat Mr. Neville with a hauteur so chilling as to put all the idle tongues to rest, and to banish from the Nonpareil's mind any expectation that she would be in the least gratified by even the smallest of his attentions.

Viscount Ridley, much to his chagrin, also found that Mr. Neville had indirectly thrust a spoke into his wheel. His

courtship of Caroline, which had begun as a somewhat
half-hearted attempt to make amends for his earlier treatment of her, was threatened by the increased circle of eligible suitors who now paid court to her with varying degrees
of seriousness. Lord Ridley was not unaware of the advantages of his face and figure, and he was convinced that Caroline's somewhat distant manner masked the same decided
partiality she had shown him before, but he had expected to
be shown to exceptional advantage beside her aging and/or
desperate followers, and to win her with very little exertion
on his own behalf. He considered withdrawing altogether;
there were prettier girls (like the stunning Julia!) and certainly richer ones, but Lord Ridley, who could never bear to
be bested at games at Eton, found he had no taste for being
cut out on any playing field at all.

He determined to fix his interest as soon as possible, in
order to follow up the advantages of long acquaintance,
and, apparently, the present favor of Lady Wentworth. Accordingly, he began to send floral tributes with a regularity
that delighted the florist who enjoyed his patronage rather
more than their recipient. He also began to call in at Mount
Street with the air of one who stood on easy terms with the
family, thus arousing vengeful thoughts in the circle of
those less favored. He did not often find the Wentworth
ladies alone, but one lovely afternoon Julia was out driving
in Sir Waldo Eppingly's phaeton, and Caroline, recovering
from a slight cold, had refused a like offer from Mr. Stan-
hope. Lady Wentworth, hearing that it was Lord Ridley
who had called, overbore Caroline's objections that she
was feeling a bit out of sorts and did not wish to receive
anyone, and directed Fenwick to show his lordship into the
saloon.

Lord Ridley was pleased to discover that his assiduous
attentions to Lady Wentworth—the little compliments, the
sly references to past triumphs, and the solicitude with
which he inquired into the minutest change in the state of
her health—had at last borne fruit. After a few minutes' exchange of pleasantries her ladyship rose, pleading a
headache, and requested him, with a smile, to observe the

proprieties and not sit too long alone with her daughter. Then she exited in a graceful cloud of lavender silk, with an all-too evident look of satisfaction.

Caroline knew that her mother could not have concealed it from her if Lord Ridley had asked permission to pay his addresses to her, so she did not fear the embarrassment of a proposal. Had Ridley known it, she had received one or two already, and had declined them. It was not precisely something one wished to become accomplished at or inured to, but she had to own that it was relief to know that one need not react with a stammer or blushes, and that in time it might even be possible to remain tolerably in possession of one's composure.

She had underestimated Lord Ridley, however. Her mother's partiality was for the moment assured, and he thought he need not scruple to broach the subject of marriage to his intended bride before he made a formal declaration of his intention to do so. He began by quizzing her on the number of admirers she and her sister had acquired, and asked her what she had to say about London *now*.

"Why, just the same as I said before," replied Caroline with a smile. "That it is most delightful to be able to spend the Season here."

"And do you still mean to go live with your aunt in Bath? I daresay it will fret you dreadfully, after the gay life you lead here. Besides which, the town is full of cripples and eccentrics!"

"Well, of course we mean to go," said Caroline, surprised. "Mama could never accomplish such a move on her own, and in any case it would be a grievous trespass on Lady Withering's kindness if Julia and I were to foist ourselves on her when we've sold the town house. And besides," she added with a mischievous twinkle, "I've nothing whatsoever against cripples or eccentrics."

"Well," he said slyly, "it's certain that neither of you will be residing in Bath very long. No one who knows the lovely Misses Wentworth can doubt that we will soon be reading about the engagement of one or the other in the *Gazette*! And an exalted match at that, I shouldn't wonder."

She fixed him with her level gaze, a little less color in her cheeks. "Do you think my purpose—our purpose—in coming up to London was to find a rich husband?"

"Not your purpose, perhaps, my dear Caroline," he said softly, "but it is certainly your destiny and your duty to marry, and marry as well as you can. As for Julia, even your mother would not deny that she is on the catch for a fortune at the very least, and perhaps a title as well. She might even aspire to Robert Neville," he said with a little laugh.

"You make it sound so bloodless! So mercenary!" cried Caroline.

"You pea-goose, of course it's bloodless and mercenary both. You can hardly hope to ignore worldly considerations when they have such unpleasant ways of thrusting themselves upon your notice. You may take it from me that there are many worse things than selling yourself, if not to the highest bidder, at least to a degree of comfort and independence. You will not be very happy without either one, you know."

"Were *you* happy, then?" Caroline could not forbear asking.

"I was not so dreadfully unhappy as you might imagine," he said, smiling and taking her hand, "and I mean to be much happier next time."

"I'll allow you to have the better knowledge of your own character and prospects," Caroline replied, carefully withdrawing her hand, "and you must be the judge of what will make you happiest. But I have no intention of selling myself, as you put it, even for a fortune the size of Golden Ball's."

"And shall *you* be happy then," he asked with a small smile, "with your home gone, and your friends, submitting to your aunt's decrees, or your mother's? It is not a very rosy prospect, and I fear it will be quite impossible to endure."

Caroline would not give him the satisfaction of knowing that she shared this same fear. "You are mistaken if you think I'll be moped to tears, pining for company, or chafing under what you call my aunt's *decrees*. I assure you she is quite amiable," she said lightly, "and I hope to form at least a few agreeable friendships."

"And would it not be a great deal more agreeable, my dearest Caroline," he said, a smile lighting his handsome eyes, "to be married to a man who holds you in the greatest affection and esteem? A man who is, while not precisely rich, sufficiently affluent to provide you with enough of life's elegancies to make you comfortable? Surely your scruples could not make you regard such a prospect with horror?" he asked, laughing at her.

"Charles—" Caroline began, frowning.

"No, don't rebuke me! I know that I have not yet spoken to Lady Wentworth, and I will not pursue the matter until I have satisfied the proprieties. But only consider: there need be no consideration of compromise or mercenary concerns between *us*. You must be well aware that I have always cherished the tenderest feelings for you, almost from the moment we met."

Caroline forbore to remind him that his tenderest feelings had not prevented him from marrying someone else, and said only, "We were once very good friends, Lord Ridley. But that is all, I think."

"I see that I have pressed you too soon, and I shall give you time to find your feet in London," he said with just a touch of acid. "I can imagine how enjoyable it must be to be the object of so much attention, and I would not willingly interfere with any of your pleasures. But I mean to induce you to marry me in the end, you know."

"By pointing out to me my destiny and my duty, I suppose! And picturing in the blackest terms my probable fate if I do not accept," cried Caroline, stung by his implication. "Oh I beg pardon, that was uncivil! But you must understand that I will neither accept nor reject an offer of marriage on the basis of *missish* scruples or because I would prefer to conduct a lot of silly flirtations! I hope my character may be stronger than that."

Lord Ridley colored a little, but said calmly, "Perhaps I have erred in broaching the subject at all at this time. I should have dwelt more on the steadfastness of my regard for you, and less on the evils of your situation that might impel you to accept the protection and consequences of my name and fortune. Pray let us talk no more of this at this time, and find some other subject."

"Lord Ridley, I cannot help but feel that it would be best if we were never to return to the subject at all."

"My dear girl, I know you cannot mean it. I will speak to your mama—"

They were interrupted by a commotion below, followed by Fenwick's discreet tap on the door. "Beg pardon, miss," said the butler in stricken accents, "Mr. Lacey has called."

Lord Ridley said in an undertone, "Surely he can be denied, Miss Wentworth? I would not wish to leave you until we have resolved our little misunderstanding!"

Caroline looked uncertainly at the butler.

"It appears to be a matter of some urgency, miss. And not being wishful of disturbing her ladyship . . ."

"Of course, Fenwick. Show Mr. Lacey up at once."

Lord Ridley was not pleased. "I shall withdraw, then, and leave you to your tête-à-tête," he said stiffly. "Your servant, Miss Wentworth. Lacey, yours," he said as Mr. Lacey entered the room.

"Now Bertie," said Caroline, when the door had closed behind him, "what is this all about?"

Lord Ridley, hurrying out into the street in something of an ill temper, was further discomposed by colliding, in a rather rough fashion, with Lord Wynchwood and Mr. Neville almost on the Wentworths' doorstep. Ridley, like most other aspiring men of fashion, was jealous of Robert Neville, and was quite put out to see that he, along with another man of considerable address, was obviously about to call at the Wentworths'. He was not so annoyed, however, that he did not apologize profusely for his clumsiness and express the regret that he had not met Mr. Neville at any of his engagements during the past week.

Mr. Neville replied civilly but briefly that he had spent the week at Wyndham Priory, consulting with his foreman.

"Ah," replied Lord Ridley with a knowing look, "then I collect you are wanting to see the Wentworths on some matter of business. I can perhaps spare you some trouble. Miss Julia is not at home, and Lady Wentworth is resting with a headache."

Mr. Neville gave him the look he used to depress pretension, and Lord Ridley flushed.

"And Miss Caroline Wentworth?" prompted Lord Wynchwood, incorrigibly.

"She is at home, but engaged with a Mr. Lacey," he replied, with what he hoped was chilling dignity. "Some havey-cavey business of the boy's, and they made quite sure they were not to be disturbed. But I must say no more. Good day to you."

"Geoffrey, I collect I have made another enemy," said Mr. Neville to his friend.

"Well, if you *will* level your glass at a person in that way you can hardly expect him to like it. Besides, he seemed all in a pucker of his own making. Shouldn't be surprised if it has something to do with Miss Wentworth!"

"Ah," replied Mr. Neville, remembering Ridley's proprietary arm on Caroline's arm at the Wentworths' ball, "sits the wind in that quarter?"

"Shouldn't wonder at it," said Lord Wynchwood judiciously, drawing from his nearly inexhaustible fund of knowledge about the ton. "The *on-dit* is that two years ago he was most particular in his attentions, but then Wentworth looked about to cock up his toes, and the family withdrew to the Priory. Ridley got himself engaged to the Harrington chit—you remember, Dysart's daughter—within a fortnight. Got the earl to pay his gaming debts and come down handsome all round, so who's to blame him? But the thing is, there's just something about the fellow I don't like. Can't quite put my finger on it, but there it is."

"Well, his neckcloth *was* quite sadly out of frame," remarked Mr. Neville absently.

"Yes, poor fellow," laughed Lord Wynchwood. "What shall we do now?"

"My dear Geoffrey, your memory really is atrocious. We are about to call on the Wentworths."

"But Ridley said—"

"Just so," said Mr. Neville. "I own that we should probably tarry a few more minutes for, ah, developments to proceed. But I must admit I'm curious to know what 'havey-cavey' business Miss Caroline Wentworth is involved in, and I'm quite consumed with desire to learn what is making that—do you hear it?—infernal noise!"

9

UPSTAIRS AT Mount Street, Mr. Lacey was endeavoring to apologize to Caroline for the manner of his intrusion, and for routing her most persistent suitor. "Cross as a cat he looked too! Can't say that I blame him. You too, Caro," he said thoughtfully. "You look blue as megrim. And your nose is red."

"I can see that I chose the wrong day to wear lawn green," said Caroline, smoothing down her dress of jaconet muslin.

"You ain't pulled down?" persisted Mr. Lacey.

"I am attempting," said Caroline with some asperity, "to recover from a slight cold by spending a quiet and uneventful afternoon at home. Come on, Bertie, cut line! What can you have done to give Fenwick such a Friday face? It takes a great deal to put him out of countenance, you know!"

Mr. Lacey groaned and put his head in his hands.

"As bad as that? May I respectfully suggest that a handsome *douceur* will go a long way toward making amends, at least as far as Fenwick is concerned?"

Mr. Lacey raised his head. "Dash it all, Caro, I'm not caper-witted. Slipped him a note when I came in. Shouldn't wonder if I hadn't better double it," he said gloomily. "Ought to give you something too, for damages and food and the like."

"Damages? Food? Bertie, have you been carousing below stairs?"

"Worse," he replied, in the same melancholy voice. "It's Sal Atticus, you see."

"No, I don't see," said Caroline firmly. "Bertie, are you *foxed*?"

"No," he said earnestly, running his hand through his hair, "and I *wasn't* either. Well, just a trifle concerned, certainly not castaway. But I promised my uncle, and he'll never believe that I—oh, Caroline, what am I to *do*?"

"I suggest you begin by telling me who or what Sal Atticus is," said Caroline dryly.

"Oh," replied Mr. Lacey, disconcerted. "Sal Atticus. The Sapient Pig."

Some hitherto mystifying elements of Mr. Lacey's earlier remarks now began to make themselves uncomfortably clear. "Do you mean to say you've brought a *pig* to this house?"

"Had to," said Mr. Lacey, with a sad shake of his head. "Couldn't think of any place else."

"Good God! Where is it now? You haven't let it loose somewhere inside?"

'Certainly not," exclaimed Mr. Lacey scornfully. "It's in a crate, in the kitchen. Thing is, crate was a little big for the door."

"Well, never mind that now. You'd better tell me why you find Mount Street the only acceptable refuge for an animal of, shall we say, such inconvenient dimensions, instead of the butcher shop, for example! And be quick about it, before Mama comes downstairs, or Gaston returns from his afternoon off and turns Sal Atticus into Sapient Sausages!"

Mr. Lacey had endeavored to conform to his uncle's strictures in every respect, and had sensibly removed himself from the path of temptation by avoiding the company of his erstwhile gaming companions. A chance meeting in St. James's Street, however, had elicited an invitation to join Lord Shipley and Mr. Carleton on what the former described as a capital lark, a visit to the Female Satyr in Haymarket, and as Mr. Lacey did not see any possible way to get into financial difficulties in the course of this unexceptionable adventure (the admission price being only one shilling), he entered into the project with enthusiasm.

"What is a Female Satyr?" asked Caroline with unbecoming curiosity.

Mr. Lacey was glad to be able to display his superior knowledge of the world. "Woman with a horn growing on her head, like a ram."

"Was she born with it?"

"Shouldn't think so. Shipley says it grew after she—dash it all, Caroline! Not a proper subject for ladies! Don't ask me any more; never saw her myself."

When the trio of friends arrived in Coventry Street, the premises of Mr. Weeks, where this attraction was on exhibit, was unaccountably closed, and the only solace offered after such an undeniable disappointment was a rather seedy inn, which plainly did not count members of the Quality among its usual customers. They were nonetheless respectably entertained with a tolerable burgundy, however, and in good time were, as Mr. Lacey put it, slightly shamefacedly, ripe for a spree.

The opportunity obligingly presented itself in the form of a loud and rather boisterous argument between a gentleman of somewhat raffish appearance and his equally dubious companion, who were so far into their cups as to make appeal to a wider audience in an attempt to settle their bet. The raffish gentleman was presently discovered to be the owner of the heretofore unknown Sal Atticus, and was so bold as to declare that the fame of this surprising creature would shortly rival that of General Tom Thumb himself. The abilities of the Sapient Pig were too numerous to detail, but included spelling, reading, playing cards, and casting accounts. The animal could even—and this was the subject of his vigorous dispute with his companion—tell any person what o'clock it was to the minute, and that by his own watch. The company was much inclined to skepticism, and added their wagers to the pot on the side of Doubting Thomas, but Mr. Lacey, previously a stranger to porcine accomplishment, unaccountably threw in his lot with Sal and the raffish gentleman. Nothing would do but that the interested parties must remove to Spring Gardens, where the curiosity was being housed, preparatory to going on display at the Royal Promenade Rooms.

Roused from a heavy slumber, Sal Atticus was at first reluctant to display his remarkable skills and had to be coaxed with a number of those edible treats a pig might be expected to prefer to telling time. Rising at length to the occasion, he did not disappoint. It was, according to Mr. Lacey's pocket watch, precisely eight o'clock at that point, and Sal, with the briefest of squints at the position of the hands, counted out eight beats with one ponderous trotter.

"You're bamming me!" interjected Caroline.

"I am *not*. And I was never so glad of anything in my life, because I'd begun to think the whole thing was a hoax. But it *wasn't*."

"What next? Did this remarkable animal challenge you to a game of hazard?"

"No! That is, it wasn't the *pig*. Though Scunthorpe—the raffish gentleman—got it into his head that Sal could read minds too, but I wouldn't lay my blunt on that. Devilish hard to prove, I should think!"

Mr. Lacey, with ill-gotten gambling gains once more lining his pocket, found himself solicited to join his affable hosts in a card game, and felt it would be uncivil to refuse. By the time he had recalled, somewhat belatedly, his promise to his uncle (aided in this respect by the waning effects of the burgundy), he was too far ahead to withdraw from the table. "Thing is," he said wonderingly, "couldn't lose! Had to accept Scunthorpe's vowels, and didn't want 'em. Said he'd come round with a bank draft next morning, but the fellow never showed up. Shabby, but I was just as glad to be quit of him, I can tell you. Forgot all about it. Then today some chap pulls up in a wagon, with the pig in a crate. Tried to send him back, but he said the exhibition closed down the first night; some trouble with the law! Said a gentleman gave him a guinea to deliver Sal Atticus to my uncle's house. Had to give him another guinea to bring it round here, before my uncle saw him and nabbed the rust. But now what am I going to do?"

"But Bertie, I don't understand why it's so important that

your uncle and Sal Atticus be kept apart! Had he a particular aversion to pigs?"

Mr. Lacey had forgotten that Caroline was not in possession of what must be considered a vital element in his story
and went on to relate, in a somewhat less animated fashion,
an edited version of his adventures upon the town.

Caroline was sympathetic. "Oh Bertie, you are in a
scrape! I must say your uncle was a brick, and I quite see
why you don't want to disappoint him."

"He'll send me packing if it gets to his ears," he said
glumly.

"Very likely. We must see that it doesn't. I don't suppose
you could contrive to send, uh, Sal down to Ilcombe Hall
without his hearing about it?"

Mr. Lacey shook his head. "Get to my father's ears.
Worse," he added darkly.

Caroline got to her feet. "I can see that resolution is
called for. Take me down to Sal Atticus at once, and then
we will decide what must be done!"

Caroline had a moment to regret her bravery when she
descended into the nether regions of the house on Mr.
Lacey's arm, to be met by an astonishing crescendo of
snorts more reminiscent of a steam engine than of one of
God's creatures. She mentally revised her estimation
of Sal's size upward. She also had cause to regret that her
trifling indisposition had not rendered her sense of smell
less acute.

"Good heavens!" she cried when the animal was at last
revealed in all his porcine splendor. "I'm quite at a loss for
words. I can only hope that Gaston will find himself in the
same case, but I fear that is too much to hope for. Bertie,
your watch if you please!"

"Caro, you ain't thinking of making it do *tricks*?"

"Certainly I am. How else are we to know that this is the
real Sal Atticus? They might have bamboozled you and
substituted some quite ordinary pig. There is only one way
to find out!"

Mr. Lacey, grinning, handed over his timepiece. Caroline

crouched beside the crate. "Now, sir, if you please, tell us the hour," she said, addressing the pig.

Sal Atticus peered up at the proffered article hopefully, as if wondering whether it might consist in some form of the afternoon snack which would be so welcome. The snorts increased.

At that moment, Fenwick was opening the Wentworths' front door to Mr. Neville and Lord Wynchwood, who had completed their walk around the neighboring streets and returned to satisfy their curiosity. The butler's face was impassive, despite the extremely disconcerting noises issued from below stairs.

Mr. Neville's lips twitched. "Entertaining Prussians, Fenwick?"

"I believe it is an animal of the swine race, sir," said the butler with majestic restraint.

"Indeed?" said Mr. Neville, raising an eyebrow. "Are the ladies at home?"

"I shall endeavor to inquire," said Fenwick, "if you—"

A piercing shriek interrupted this ceremonious discourse, and the two gentlemen hurriedly followed the butler down into the kitchen without further ado.

A remarkable scene met Mr. Neville's startled gaze. Unthinking, he raised his quizzing glass to bring it into focus, but magnification did not serve to further illuminate or explain. Miss Wentworth, in a clearly disheveled state, was kneeling beside the crate of the largest porker he had ever seen, pulling, with the assistance of Mr. Bertram Lacey, what appeared to be a watch chain out of the animal's mouth. For one brief moment, the power of speech unaccountably left him.

Lord Wynchwood sprang to the rescue. "Miss Wentworth! Are you all right? Did the brute bite you?"

Silence fell on all the human inhabitants of the kitchen. Caroline knew an instant of pure horror as her eyes traveled upward from Mr. Neville's gleaming hessians, his well-molded buff-colored pantaloons, his exquisitely cut blue coat, his snowy neckcloth. It was the expression on his face which overset her gravity and made her turn away her head and seek refuge in her handkerchief. She was destined, apparently, never to make a very favorable impression on the Nonpareil, and her hopes of greeting him with quelling hauteur were quite undermined. "Oh, it's no such thing," she said, a trifle unsteadily. "But I'm afraid he has eaten Mr. Lacey's watch."

"Grandfather gave it to me," said Mr. Lacey, whose awe of the present company appeared to have rendered him insensible.

Lord Wynchwood, blinking, showed himself every inch the gentleman. "Miss Wentworth, I fear we are intruding. We heard a cry and feared someone had taken hurt. We will return another time. Neville?"

Mr. Neville, whose besetting vice was thought by many of his friends to be a disconcerting enjoyment of the ridiculous, stood his ground. "You wouldn't care to tell us, I suppose," he said in a languid tone, "how you came to feed Mr. Lacey's grandfather's watch to a pig?"

Caroline was forced to withdraw into the shelter of her handkerchief again. "I expect you will find this rather hard to believe," she said judiciously, "but as a matter of fact we did not offer him the watch as a treat. He was merely supposed to look at it, and tell us the time." She was spared the necessity of seeing how her listeners absorbed this information by Sal himself, who, abandoning optimism, decided the timepiece was inedible after all, and disgorged it from his mouth. "Oh look, Bertie, he's dropped it. I'm sure it will be good as new when it's been round to the jeweler's."

"Ah well, then, all's well that ends well," said Lord Wynchwood in a tone that indicated that the pig's powerful presence was not having a tonic effect on his constitution.

Mr. Lacey, meanwhile, in response to an attempt to draw him out on the subject, was regaling Mr. Neville with a brief and somewhat broken history of his association with Sal Atticus. Mr. Neville listened with an air of polite interest, broken only by the occasional necessity of wiping his eyes. Caroline, watching him, abandoned her handkerchief altogether and succumbed to her most urgent inclination. Fenwick, returning a few moments later from the upper portion of the house, descended to a scene of almost unbridled mirth. "Begging your pardon, miss," he said, with an injured air, "but her ladyship will no doubt be wanting refreshments soon, and making inquiries. What *am* I to tell her about the animal?"

"Oh nothing!" cried Caroline. "I mean, at least not yet. I know this is a dreadful nuisance for you, Fenwick, but Mr. Lacey and I will think of something, I promise you!"

"Very good, miss, but may I venture to hope it will be *soon*," he muttered darkly.

"Impudent fellow," suggested Lord Wynchwood when he had retired.

"Not at all. Only he is quite the model of rectitude, you know, and he had a great deal to suffer with trying to preserve his sangfroid in the face of some of my father's gamier escapades. I daresay he thought those days were behind him," said Caroline, thoughtfully.

Mr. Neville, giving a little choke, said; "On one point at least I may be able to enlighten you. There was a small article in yesterday's news, to which, I must admit, I did not attend with the degree of interest I might *now* lend to such a subject, describing the closing of an exhibition of a performing pig on grounds of fraud!"

"Well it can't be Sal Atticus then," declared Caroline, "because Bertie *saw* him tell the time."

"Shall we put it to the test?" asked Mr. Neville wickedly.

"Robert!" cried Lord Wynchwood in stricken accents.

"Coward," said Mr. Neville scornfully. "I perceive that where Miss Wentworth was in error was in standing, perhaps, a little too close to the crate." He pulled out his elegant timepiece and dangled it peremptorily in front, but out of reach, of the pig's snout. "The o'clock, sirrah! At once!"

Sal's reply to the undoubted voice of Authority, though voluble, left something in doubt as to his meaning. His general attitude, however, was becoming intransigent. An animal of his dimensions required a great deal of sustenance at frequent intervals, and no such nourishment was apparently forthcoming. He began to squeal and butt his head against the crate.

"Good God, don't let him out!" cried Lord Wynchwood, turning pale.

"It gives new meaning to the term 'bacon-brained,'" said Caroline with feeling.

"Not at all," replied Mr. Neville with a smile. "I believe pigs are considered to be quite intelligent. He may not tell time or play cards perhaps, but you may be sure his master clued him somehow, so he knew how many beats to count out."

"I don't suppose he can read minds after all?" asked Caroline, her eyes brimming with laughter. "How very disappointing!"

Mr. Neville raised an eyebrow. "My dear Miss Wentworth, I assure you that it is a great deal more comfortable for him that he cannot."

"Westphalian ham," murmured Lord Wynchwood.

"Rillettes de porc," suggested Mr. Neville meditatively.

"Sausages!" cried Mr. Lacey.

"Oh that is too bad of you all!" exclaimed Caroline. "You are not suggesting that we just *eat* him! When he has been a performer! And you *said* that he was quite intelligent," she said, rounding on Mr. Neville.

Mr. Neville folded his arms and looked at her curiously. "And pray what do you suggest is to be done with him, ma'am?"

"Can he not be sent to the country somewhere to—to reproduce? I am sure he would be happier on some farm than he is in London!"

"And London would be a dashed sight happier too," said Lord Wynchwood faintly.

"In short, an honorable retirement!" cried Mr. Neville. "Now why did I not think of that?"

"Lord Wynchwood," asked Caroline with a gleam of mischief in her eye, "you have a country estate! Will you not give Sal Atticus a home?"

His lordship turned quite ashen. "Well, I don't—the fact of the matter is—my sister! Doesn't much care for pigs. Butcher shop! That's the thing!"

Mr. Neville shook his head sadly. "That's quite beneath you, Geoffrey."

"Then why don't *you* take the wretched brute, Robert? I daresay you have farms enough at the Priory!" retorted the exasperated Lord Wynchwood.

"*Would* you?" asked Caroline maliciously, expecting to see him thrown into confusion.

"Dash it all, Caro," interjected Mr. Lacey. "We've no right—"

"Yes," said Mr. Neville, cutting across this protest, "I will."

All his subsequent difficulties were made worth it by the effect these simple words had on his listeners.

"*You*?" cried Miss Wentworth and Lord Wynchwood in unison. Mr. Lacey's jaw dropped.

"Yes, certainly," he said with a small smile.

"You wouldn't just take him down to Wyndham and—and eat him there, would you?" asked Caroline.

"You have my pledge that he will be safe from any appetite but his own."

"Oh famous!" cried Mr. Lacey, unable to believe his good fortune. "Thank you very much, sir!"

Caroline said in a softened voice, "And you have my thanks too. We didn't mean to involve you in this, and I fear we have used you most shamelessly. But I think it will answer very well. The Gryders, you know, have a breeding sow, and I'm sure they would be happy to take him in." She stopped and colored up. "Oh, I beg your pardon! Of course I did not mean to tell you what to do, that is—"

"On the contrary, I am happy to be guided by you," he said kindly. "You know the tenants better than I. However, I feel I should just mention that all I have up at town at the moment are my carriage and my sporting curricle, and I doubt whether either one is the appropriate conveyance for a passenger of such, ah, prodigious girth."

"Good God, no!" cried Lord Wynchwood, shuddering. "Even your credit isn't good enough to carry that off!"

"Very well, then. I shall have to arrange for a cart to

carry it down to the Priory. I had better go at once—I'll send someone round as soon as possible."

"You shall do so at my expense, of course," said Mr. Lacey grandly.

"I'll do no such thing, halfling! I take it you are *giving* me the pig?"

"Oh yes, sir!" said Mr. Lacey, torn between the demands of his conscience and his wish to be guided by Mr. Neville in all things.

"Then we are quits. It's quite a valuable animal, I'm sure, so the advantage is all mine."

Mr. Lacey had not considered the matter in this light and pronounced himself satisfied.

"We'll be off, then," said Mr. Neville, earning a warm look of gratitude from Lord Wynchwood. "But if I may venture to suggest—some foodstuffs, and quickly too!"

The urgency of this matter was seconded by Sal Atticus, and Caroline and Bertie were left to forage in the kitchen, and to concoct some Banbury tale that would satisfy Lady Wentworth and the servants. Mr. Lacey's relief at being saved had dimmed a little in the wake of a very lowering idea. "We'll be the laughingstock of London by this time tomorrow," he said grimly, thrusting a handful of turnips into the crate.

"Very likely," replied Caroline, lost in thought.

10

LADY WENTWORTH was insensibly mollified to learn that she had been rescued from the consequences of a vicious practical joke through the good offices of Mr. Robert Neville. The Berners Street Hoax, in which Mr. Theodore Hook had laid a bet that he could make a modest house on a quiet street the most famous in London within a week (and then wrote hundreds of letters to tradesmen and such estimable personages as the Lord Mayor and the Duke of Gloucester asking all of them to appear at Number 54 Berners Street at the same time), was but six years' distant, and the resulting mêlée still an *on-dit* of London life. Lady Wentworth had the lowest opinion of those persons in Society who amused themselves by discomfiting the innocent, but she did not doubt that the perpetrator of the Pig in the Kitchen was some misguided admirer of Julia's, or failing that, the agent of some jealous mama, and she felt sure that the happy chance of Mr. Neville's appearance on the scene, and his willingness to involve himself in the successful resolution of such a distasteful problem, would serve to squelch any further attempts of that nature. The animal, before it was removed from the premises, had overset the entire kitchen staff, and driven her ladyship, newly emerged from her boudoir, to return almost at once to that restful sanctuary. Only the full force of the compliment to her Julia, once she perceived it, saved her from suffering one of her most intense spasms.

Julia, hearing that Mr. Neville had called with Lord Wynchwood while she was away, was in a flutter of excitement. Despite her early bet with Mr. Lacey, she had had no real hope of attaching the Nonpareil once she had met him; he was too hardened a flirt, and though he undoubtedly found her beautiful, she could not believe his attentions were in earnest. In fact, other than some pretty speeches at her come-out, he had scarcely distinguished her at all, and since she was made rather more uncomfortable by his presence than she would admit, she found herself more relieved than offended. The news that he had called, however, and rescued the household from an embarrassing and somewhat inexplicable incident, tickled her vanity and set off some not unpleasing speculations. She had no real liking for Mr. Neville, but to captivate such a man would be a triumph indeed! Even St. Paul's would be scarcely large enough to accommodate the wedding guests. . . .

Lord Wynchwood, however, put quite a different and less gratifying construction on the incident in which he had played a minor and most unwilling role. "Damn it, Robert, I believe you've gone short of a sheet," he said to his friend. "What on earth came over you? When this leaks out you'll have all of London laughing! Even Queen Charlotte couldn't emerge from this one in credit."

"Calm yourself, Geoffrey," said Mr. Neville cordially. "It is only a pig, albeit a somewhat remarkable one. Do you know, London can go to the devil, for all I care. I haven't enjoyed myself so much in years!"

"*Enjoyed*?" sputtered Lord Wynchwood.

"Yes. I find Miss Wentworth's conduct in the matter outside my usual experience of delicately nurtured females, and therefore delightful." He looked thoughtfully at his friend. "If you must talk about this despicable incident, my dear rattle, you would oblige me by keeping her name out of it, and the boy's. It can all be some dreadful mix-up, or a hoax, and the removal of the beast put down to one of my distempered freaks. But the boy was quite concerned, you know, that the truth not get back to his family."

Lord Wynchwood studied his friend with interest. "Robert, you *haven't* done all this just to impress Miss Wentworth? It's not in the least like you!"

"Oh, I shouldn't think it would do me any good. It's

quite obvious that she thinks me the most useless fribble in nature."

"I thought you were tired of fawning females and their toad-eating mamas," said Lord Wynchwood with a smile.

"Just so."

"I know what you're about," said his lordship, after puzzling this out for a few moments. "You're trying to make her fall in love with you, just to teach her a lesson. It's too bad of you, Robert! I never knew you to make guileless innocents the object of your gallantry!"

"You have a very strange notion of gallantry, my dear Geoffrey!" replied Mr. Neville amiably. "What sort of dalliance takes place in the kitchen, in the presence of a pig?"

"All the same," persisted Lord Wynchwood, "I've no wish to see you make a cake of yourself. Take care you don't end up falling into the parson's mousetrap!"

"You astonish me! I thought you were convinced I was a merciless heartbreaker," said Mr. Neville with a wry smile.

"Humdudgeon!" cried Lord Wynchwood. "I just hope you know what you're about!" He said no more on the matter, and ventured to ask his friend's advice on Lord Iversley's breakdowns, and whether the chestnuts or the grays would make the more suitable addition to the Wynchwood stable.

Mr. Neville was by no means certain that he could have articulated the precise nature of his interest in Miss Wentworth, had Lord Wynchwood persisted. His attention was fairly caught, and his hunter's instinct aroused, by her indifference to him, and so far from despising her because she deprecated his position in life, he was inclined to give her a great deal of credit. He suspected that his ill-chosen remarks at Lady Bassett's had somehow come to her ears, and in that case could not blame her for choosing to dislike him.

He was more at a loss to understand his own desire to convince her that he was not such a worthless creature as she might suppose. He wasn't even sure why he liked her enough to make any exertions on her behalf—she had more countenance than beauty, and she was certainly somewhat heedless of convention. He supposed some of it might be pity for her straitened circumstances, and the part he bore in her change of fortune, but he felt no such obligation to Lady Wentworth or the divine Miss Julia. Previously the only ladies he had found interesting for any period of time were women of rather less virtue than Miss Wentworth, and he had never found himself with the slightest desire to become leg-shackled to anyone. But the episode with the pig had acted on him in a curious way—the discovery that a young lady of Quality could possess such a lively sense of fun, and show so little embarrassment at being discovered in a situation highly inappropriate to any aspirant to social heights, threatened to upset all his calculations. He admired too her affectionate loyalty to Mr. Lacey. It was quite a lowering reflection that the only girl of birth and breeding he had met in years whom he did not regard as a dead bore thought he was a coxcomb and little better than one of the damned bow-window pieces at White's.

The novelty of feeling something stir in his heart that was not mere diversion was not an entirely agreeable sensation, as Mr. Neville had no intention of getting into dangerous waters with Miss Wentworth, or of placing his unfettered future in jeopardy. He really thought that, were it not for the strength of his own character, as well as an inherent distaste for allying himself with a family which had encompassed such a ramshackle care-for-nothing as Lord Wentworth, he might well stand in some danger. He perceived that, despite his inclination to the contrary, it might be just as well to avoid becoming too particular in his attentions.

He did not hesitate, however, when, driving down Bond Street a few days later, he encountered Caroline, accompanied by her maid, coming out of Hookham's Library. He pulled the curricle to a stop, and entreated her to allow him to drive her to her own door. To his surprise, she accepted at once, taking his hand and climbing up, saying, "Mr. Neville will see me home, Betty."

"Thank you," she said calmly when she had taken her seat. "I'm so glad to have the opportunity to speak with you again! I most particularly wish to thank you once more for rescuing us from—from the appalling bumblebath in which we found ourselves the other day."

Mr. Neville noted that her manner toward him was once more distant and correct, with none of her earlier laughing recklessness, and wondered whether someone had warned her against him. "You mean, in which Mr. Lacey found himself, don't you? He confessed nearly the whole of his adventure to me, you know."

She gave him a warmer look. "I did not know how much he had told you. He was very afraid the news of his scrape would get round, but it has not. I imagine we have you to thank for that as well."

"You imagine far too much, Miss Wentworth," he said diffidently.

"As you will, sir. But I must assure you nevertheless that we are very grateful."

Mr. Neville narrowed his eyes and looked at her. "I do not want your gratitude, Miss Wentworth."

"Then you must take care not to excite it," replied Caroline with an unruffled countenance. "Now tell me, how does Sal Atticus get on in his new home?"

"Oh, he is quite blissfully installed at the Gryders' farm, I believe. I suspect it takes very little to content a pig."

"I wonder if he will miss his old life," Caroline remarked quizzically. "It's all very well to be retired, but he is used to something a bit more *stimulating*, even if he didn't really read or play cards or any of those things. It is sad to think of him falling into ordinary sloth."

"Very true," agreed Mr. Neville. "I cannot but think that idleness may lead him into a woeful deficiency of purpose which may quite undermine his character."

Caroline choked and bit her lip.

"However, it may relieve your mind to know that Gryder believes there is every reason to hope that, er, Sal will become the father of a large family of hopeful piglets before long. I trust," he said with suspicious meekness, "that the prohibition against turning him into bacon or ham does not extend to his descendants as well?"

"Certainly not! Unless," she added with a gleam in her eye, "one of them should show an interest in reading minds!"

Mr. Neville remarked that he had not envisaged this possibility but was prepared to meet it. He then said, in a more serious voice, "Miss Wentworth, I wonder if I might presume on your superior knowledge of the Priory to ask your advice about a matter there. If it distresses you to speak on such a subject, please let me know at once and I will say no more."

"How can you say so, when you know perfectly well I have given you unsolicited advice on at least two occasions?" asked Caroline with a smile. "Mama is convinced that I am quite lacking in proper feeling, and I'm afraid she may be right."

Mr. Neville could not think of any response to this that was not highly uncomplimentary to Lady Wentworth, and so was silent.

"What is it you wished to ask me?" said Caroline with a searching look.

"It's about Mrs. Murdoch," he began ominously.

Caroline stiffened, remembering Julia's comment that Mr. Neville was said to be a "high stickler" at Wyndham Priory. Mrs. Murdoch had been the Priory's housekeeper since before Julia and Caroline were in leading strings, and she was afraid that Murdy's ready tongue, long tolerated by themselves, might have excited his disapprobation.

"There is no need to poker up, you know," he said, watching her clouded expression. "It's nowhere near as bad as all that."

"Oh dear!" cried Caroline. "Has she given you one of her thundering scolds? She doesn't mean anything by it, you know. I fear—" She stopped, seeing the amused expression on his face. "Well, perhaps she wouldn't exactly dare to give *you* a set-down, but she does take liberties, I'm afraid. I do hope she hasn't set your back up by flying into a miff?"

"I have no fault to find with her character or her housekeeping," said Mr. Neville, smiling faintly. "Though I feel quite sure she does not approve of *me*. That, however, is hardly to the purpose. She informs me that she plans to leave the Priory and my service at the end of the year."

"Oh no! When she has been there her whole life!" exclaimed Caroline involuntarily.

"Exactly. What I should like to know is whether your mother has offered her a position, or is it merely pique at, forgive me, the change of ownership? You must know that she is extremely attached to your family."

Caroline shook her head. "We would have liked to offer her a position, but we were—are—not in a position to do so. Poor Murdy! She offered to take reduced wages, but I never thought she could be happy away from Wyndham. It was her home as much as ours."

"I beg your pardon, Miss Wentworth," said Mr. Neville, affected by this disclosure; "I should not have brought the matter up."

"No, you were very right to," said Caroline firmly, "but I wonder what maggots she has taken into her head? Oh! Perhaps it is Fenwick!"

"Fenwick?"

"Why yes! Our butler. He is planning to retire when we sell the London house and move to Bath, and if I'm not mistaken, he had always nursed a *tendre* for Jane Murdoch. I never knew it was mutual," she said wonderingly. "Perhaps they plan on marrying and settling in a cottage somewhere, or on running an inn."

"If that should prove to be the case, I might be able to assist them," said Mr. Neville.

Caroline's eyes flew to his face. "That is very kind of you."

"Not at all," he said smoothly. "I undertook to provide for the servants of Wyndham in the purchase agreement. Don't concern yourself; I will find out the truth of the matter from Mrs. Murdoch and make what arrangements are necessary. I am obliged to you for your assistance."

Caroline longed to ask him why he had purchased the Priory in the first place, but his manner seemed to indicate that the subject was closed, and she could not answer for her temper if the answer was, in fact, the one he had given Lord Wynchwood. Presently the curricle drew up in front of the house in Mount Street, and Caroline, alighting, was handed down her parcel of books.

"Are you a great reader, Miss Wentworth?" he asked, surprised at the weight of the bundle.

"I don't know how to answer that, Mr. Neville," replied Caroline with a smile. "Certainly it is one of my greatest pleasures."

"Do you mean to read all these, then?"

"Oh no! Some are for Julia, and one is even for Mama. Hookham's were able to supply me with Miss Austen's latest novel, *Mansfield Park*."

"Miss Austen? The author of *Pride and Prejudice*?"

"Why yes. Have *you* read *Pride and Prejudice*?" she asked with considerable surprise.

His mouth twitched. "Miss Wentworth, the *prince* has read *Pride and Prejudice*!"

"Ah. I collect it was the fashion, then, when it came out."

"Something like," he said with a smile. "But that is *not* why I read it, my dear Miss Wentworth. My aunt most particularly recommended it, and I have always placed the greatest dependence upon her judgment in such matters, for though she is not quite *blue,* she is very well read."

"Your aunt? L-Lady Buxton?" asked Caroline incredulously.

"Good God, no! My Aunt Buxton is not a great reader, having, I fear, a great deal else to occupy her mind," he said grimly. "May I presume, then, that you have met Lady Buxton? You have not mentioned it, you know!"

Caroline thought that his aunt's abominable behavior could not be too little spoken of, and that there was so little to relate that could be told with propriety to her nephew that the subject must always be a matter of the greatest constraint. She murmured that her acquaintance had been a very brief one, at the Frants' dinner, and that she had not seen her ladyship since.

Mr. Neville, watching her carefully, said bluntly, "Nor would you wish to, I imagine. You need not tell me she was shockingly rude. I can see it by the way you are struggling to school your countenance into tact. It is quite unnecessary, you know!"

"Thank you, but I had much liefer not cross swords with you over your aunt, as well as everything else," Caroline said with a smile. "And you still have not told me what you thought of Miss Austen's book."

"I found it very amusing," he said, in perfect truth, accepting her efforts to turn the subject. "But you don't think, perhaps, a trifle hard on the masculine sex?"

"It seemed to me perfectly accurate in every respect," Caroline replied decisively.

He laughed. "Did it? Am I to believe you found Mr. Darcy an agreeable hero, then?"

Her lip quivered. "Mr. Neville, you must know that Mr. Darcy, besides being quite high in the instep, suffers from rather abominable pride. But he is certainly an *agreeable* character, as you put it, bec—"

"Am I to take it that this is the sort of man women prefer?" he interrupted.

"I did not say he was the sort of man women prefer," Caroline replied coolly, enjoying herself. "I said I found him accurate in every respect."

"Well done, Miss Wentworth. An expert thrust!"

"And I began to say," continued Caroline, trying not to laugh, "that while Mr. Darcy behaves in quite an odious manner at the beginning, by the end his conduct is everything that must be pleasing."

"And *that* is your notion of accuracy?" asked Mr. Neville, raising an eyebrow. "How like a female to believe that a woman's influence can render a proud man compliant and good-natured!"

"You mistake me," she said as he handed her up to her front door. "That is a notion on which I place no dependence whatsoever! Good-bye, and thank you for escorting me home!"

11

CAROLINE WAS OBLIGED to exercise considerable self-discipline in order to prevent Mr. Neville from intruding on her meditations. His imperfections—his indolence, his selfishness, his heartless disdain for his fellow creatures—were manifest, but Caroline was forced to acknowledge that they were combined with good humor and considerable charm as well. He had displayed a tactful concern for his housekeeper, and his conversation gave every indication of a well-informed mind. He had rescued Mr. Lacey (and herself) from embarrassment with the good-natured aplomb of an older brother, and (she was quite sure) had prevented the story from getting about. Yet there was something in his manner to her that was mischievous and threw her into confusion. She was determined to despise him, and yet she could not. If only he did not make her laugh! He certainly had the knack of penetrating her reserve and goading her into saying the most abominable things to him. For reasons best known to himself he had adopted a friendly manner toward her, but she felt he was quite capable of withering her sensibility with a ruthless set-down should she take him at his word.

Her godmother's warning had not fallen on deaf ears. She thought it not at all unlikely that his ultimate goal was, if not to snub her, to fix his interest with her out of pique at her treatment of him. And the likely outcome of *that* could only be a broken heart, and she would die before she gave him that satisfaction. She could not trust him; therefore she must be on her guard. She must banish him from her thoughts, and banish him she would.

Lady Wentworth, whose speculations about Mr. Neville and Julia had nourished quite unjustified hopes in her capacious bosom, was inclined to believe that the Nonpareil would lead her daughter onto the floor for her first waltz at Almack's or gratify her maternal solicitude with some other gesture of marked preference. Accordingly, she escorted Julia and Caroline there in excellent spirits, with every expectation of a happy outcome. She was destined to disappointment. Mr. Neville did come, but with the sole apparent purpose of flirting with Countess Lieven, and while Julia's hand was solicited for the country dances, she was forced to sit fanning herself on the sidelines when the fiddles struck up the first waltz. The unwritten rule of Almack's, like its insipid refreshments and rigid entrance requirements, was inviolable: no young lady could waltz without the express approval of one of its patronesses. Julia sat watching her sister dance with Lord Wynchwood while Mr. Neville was absorbed in the witticisms of the countess, and felt herself grow flushed and irritable. One or two of the other belles of the Season, already admitted to membership in the magic circle, cast her condescending glances from the floor. Julia ground her teeth, and considered a strategic retreat from the field of combat.

She was startled to find herself suddenly confronted with the formidable personage of Lady Sefton, on the arm of Lord Ridley. She rose to her feet, blushing, and dropped a curtsy.

Her ladyship gave her a thin smile with the air of one bestowing a coin on a beggar. "I see you are not dancing, Miss Wentworth. Allow me to present Lord Ridley to you as a desirable partner."

Julia, rescued from obscurity by a handsome Man of Fashion and address, albeit an all-but-acknowledged suitor of Caroline's, favored Viscount Ridley with her most radiant smile. "Thank you," she said fervently when he had led her onto the floor and encircled her waist with his arm, "did you ask her to present you?"

"Most particularly," he replied, nothing loath to excite

gratitude in such a lovely girl. He had, in fact, thought of asking Caroline, but she was dancing with Wynchwood, and her manner to himself, though perfectly correct, could not be in any sense be interpreted as warmly appreciative. Lord Ridley was growing a bit tired of the game Caroline was playing with him, and thought it might better serve his purpose with her if he were seen to flirt with someone else. When he saw Julia forced by convention to retire to the sidelines, he had hit on the nacky notion of using Caroline's own sister to awaken her to the dangers of continuing in her posture of feigned indifference. It was no trouble at all to convince Lady Sefton, with whom he had maintained a long-term but respectful mock flirtation, to present him as an eligible partner to Julia.

Julia was naturally a graceful dancer, but her previous experience of the waltz was with the dancing master her mother had engaged for her before her come-out, whose compliments might be considered paid for, and therefore not entirely reliable. Subsequent attempts with Mr. Lacey were also unsatisfactory, because he would not take it at all seriously, and talked when he should have been minding the steps, and laughed when she stepped on his slippers. She was grateful to Lord Ridley, who did not seem to know that this was the first time she had waltzed in public, and complimented her on the delightfulness of her dancing.

"And," he said, favoring her with one of his most charming smiles, "you will certainly not lack for partners now that everyone can see that you have the patronesses' approval."

"Thank you," she said again, a trifle breathlessly. "I shall not forget that you were the first to lead me onto the floor."

Really, the chit was quite charming, Ridley decided. It would certainly do Caroline good to see that her beautiful sister was demonstrably enjoying herself in his company. He would be happy to gratify Julia's vanity with a few compliments of his own. "The honor is mine, Miss Wentworth. You and your sister are quite the rage of the town, and those of us who are old friends must be grateful for any attentions you bestow on us."

Julia felt her confidence reviving in his company. "How can you be so absurd?" she said playfully. "Of course we will always make time for our special friends. At least I hope I always may!"

Lord Ridley looked over to where Caroline was chatting animatedly with Geoffrey Wynchwood. "Your sister does not partake of your sentiments, I believe," he said with a small shrug.

"Oh no! You must not think so!" cried Julia earnestly, her blue eyes filled with concern. "Caroline is very good, but she is very guarded. But I'm sure that she—how could she not—well, I must say no more!" She broke off with a little stammer, and blushed.

"Your sister may be guarded, but I perceive you are not," said Lord Ridley quizzically.

Julia studied her gloves with interest. "Mama and Caroline say I am too much in alt, and that I should learn to hold my tongue," she admitted. "But I think it most unfair of them, when everyone knows I am just like Mama, and she has always suffered from an excess of sensibility!"

"Well, I hope you will not curb your tongue when you are with me," he said with a chuckle. "I would prefer to say that you have a confiding disposition, and I think it is quite delightful!"

Julia raised her lovely eyes to his face. "Do you really?"

"Of course I do," replied Lord Ridley truthfully. "Why else do you think I asked you to dance?"

So far from conversing with Lord Wynchwood in a manner which would excite the jealously of her erstwhile lover, Caroline had discovered that something was troubling him, and attempted to draw him out.

"Beg you won't regard it, ma'am; I'm just a trifle blue-deviled," said his lordship with a touch of embarrassment.

Caroline was so surprised at this uncharacteristic mood that she hastened to hope that all was well with his family and friends.

"Oh, it's nothing of that nature, I promise you. At least not yet." He sighed. "The thing is, my brother is with Wellington in Brussels, and the chaps at Brooks are laying odds on how soon Boney's going to attack. You can't get better than ten to one on anything later than the end of June. They say Wellington will be lucky to raise a hundred thousand troops, while everyone knows Bonaparte will have half a million at his disposal! I know Stacy can take care of himself but . . ."

"But naturally you are worried," said Caroline, a little at a loss as to what to say to him. "Though surely there is every reason to have confidence in the duke, after his victories on the Peninsula. I've heard that in India they called him Wellesley Bahadur!"

"Wellesley the Invincible! Oh, I've no doubt that *he'll* come through all right. But Stacy's a hothead, a neck o'nothing rider, and a born soldier," he said proudly. "That's what worries me." He shook his head ruefully. "What bothers me is that we used to argue about Bonaparte, and I *defended* him. I wouldn't want Stacy to remember that."

"Lord Wynchwood," she said placing her hand on his arm with concern, "there is certainly no need to reproach yourself for that. I feel quite sure the duke himself has a sneaking admiration for Bonaparte, and I know for a fact that the Prince Regent does. He told my father that he hoped to do for London what the emperor has done for Paris!"

Lord Wynchwood laughed. "Well, he ain't going to do it, not if he holds to his taste for Chinese deformities! Beg pardon, Miss Wentworth; the patronesses would strike my name from the lists if they knew I was prosing on in such a dreary fashion! Here, Neville!" he cried, spying the imposing form of his friend approaching, "do you keep Miss Wentworth company while I secure a cup of claret! Miss Wentworth, would you care for some lemonade?"

Caroline declined this refreshment and gave Mr. Neville

a dry smile. "Abducted!" she exclaimed when Lord Wynchwood had gone.

"Miss Wentworth, I assure you I had every intention of joining your conversation," said Mr. Neville, amused.

"It is very civil of you to say so," commented Caroline, "but now I daresay I shall never know the truth."

"The truth is vastly overrated, ma'am," replied Mr. Neville languidly. "Wynchwood looked a trifle down pin this evening, didn't you think? I hope nothing's amiss."

"His brother is with Wellington at Brussels," Caroline said succinctly.

"Stacy? I thought he'd been with the duke a year or more," said Mr. Neville in surprise.

"I rather think it's been brought home to him that the French attack will almost certainly come soon."

"Lord yes! Bonaparte can hardly afford to wait till the duke unites our allies against him. Poor Geoffrey! Captain Wynchwood is just the sort of skitterbrain to find himself in the thick of things."

"Is it true that the emperor has five hundred thousand troops to our hundred?" asked Caroline thoughtfully.

Mr. Neville started to raise his quizzing glass, thought better of it, and dropped his hand. "Does the subject interest you?" he asked, surprised.

"Are you going to tell me, like Lord Wynchwood, that serious topics are off-limits at Almack's?" asked Caroline with a tremor of irritation in her voice.

"I have not the smallest inclination to do so, and I doubt it would do any good if I had."

"Then I will say that of course it interests me! I don't want to sound like an evangelical tractist, but how can we ignore the fact that men like Lord Wynchwood's poor brother might soon be *dying* or wounded, while we stand here—"

"Fiddling while Rome burns?" suggested Mr. Neville, gesturing at the orchestra, which had struck up the waltz again.

"Do you *never* find yourself at a loss?" asked Caroline in a stifled voice.

"Quite frequently," he said without conviction. "For example, I am not in possession of the information you require, though I think it very likely that rumor exaggerates the extent of Bonaparte's forces. I would not think it possible that he can have above two hundred thousand, but that is scarcely an informed military opinion."

"Then the outcome is not hopeless," reflected Caroline.

"Under Wellington? Most certainly not!"

"You sound as if you admire him," Caroline said, somewhat amused by his partisanship of a man who might be said to be the opposite of everything a Pink of the Ton would presumably extol.

"Does that surprise you?" he asked, raising an eyebrow.

"Well, he is not—that is, he—" She broke off, embarrassed, aware of what he might infer from her impulsive comments.

"No, he is not," agreed Mr. Neville, with a wry smile which showed her that he knew very well what she had almost said. "His utter lack of self-importance is nothing short of remarkable, and I believe it would be charitable to call his appearance plain. Nevertheless, Miss Wentworth, I do indeed admire him."

Caroline blushed hotly.

"You seem a trifle warm, ma'am," he said with a glint of malice in his eyes. "Are you quite sure you would not care for some lemonade?"

"No, thank you," she said ruefully. "I shall come about again, never fear."

"Oh, I have not the slightest doubt of that," he said with a small bow. "Points about even, I should say." He bestowed a thoroughly irritating smile on her. "Your pardon. I did want to solicit your hand for this dance, but I am persuaded you would come to cuffs with me were I to attempt to distract you from the contemplation of more *serious* matters."

Caroline, who had meant to refuse him if he asked her, found this curiously unsatisfactory. "What a completely *un-*

derhanded and detestable thing to say!" she said with feeling.

"I rather hoped you would think so."

That surprised a laugh out of her. "And the worst of it is, you make me quite detestable too, when I particularly vowed that I would curb my tongue."

A queer, twisted smile touched his lips. "Oh, I don't think it is in my power to do that. *Shall* you dance with me, then?"

"Certainly not!"

"Then I must make a strategic retreat. Until our next encounter, Miss Wentworth!"

The ride home from Almack's to Mount Street in their job-carriage afforded the Wentworth ladies none of the pleasures and satisfactions which usually attended the opportunity to digest and elucidate, in relative comfort and privacy, the evening's events. Indeed, it might be said that at least two of the carriage's occupants were in a decidedly ill humor, while the third was engaged in a powerful inner struggle which rendered her silent and unresponsive to both her mother's disapproval and Julia's attempts to provoke her.

Lady Wentworth found herself in the unwelcome position of entertaining the notion that her friend Amelia Withering might have been right; she had allowed herself to become quite giddy with Julia's success and, perhaps, a trifle premature in celebrating her daughter's conquest of the Nonpareil. He had certainly not distinguished her with his attentions this evening, and had even, insofar as he noticed anyone other than Countess Lieven, preferred Caroline's company to Julia's. She could not in justice fault Caroline for conversing civilly with Mr. Neville, but her inability to do so did not keep her from feeling out-of-reason cross with her oldest child. She could not help noticing, moreover, that so far from encouraging Ridley, Caroline had behaved with a frustrating absence of enticements and allure, which would, if she were not careful, overset all her ladyship's best-laid plans. Lady Wentworth had been the reigning belle of her Season, and could not but feel that her formidable expertise, although a trifle rusty from disuse, might now be of service in instructing her daughter, if only Caroline were not so mulish as to refuse to take the hint. Really, it was too bad of Caroline to disturb her peace in this fashion, and if it were not for her ladyship's unstinting selflessness in all matters concerning her children, she scarcely knew whether she would find the strength to make such an exertion.

"Caroline, my love," she began, fetching up a deep sigh and settling herself more comfortably against the squabs, "I must own that I do not *perfectly* understand your behavior toward Viscount Ridley."

"Nor do I!" cried Julia, nothing loath to enter into a diatribe on the subject. "You were quite horrid to the poor man."

Caroline, who had been staring pensively out at the passing street scenes, looked up in surprise. "Why, what do you mean, ma'am?" she asked, ignoring her sister's remark. "I danced with him once, and we had a pleasant conversation. I cannot imagine who might have been carrying tales, but I assure you, Mama, that I have done nothing whatsoever to invoke censure."

"Oh on, it's no such thing!" admitted her ladyship with some reluctance. "I have no fault to find with the propriety of your behavior. But you know, my love, if I may just venture a little hint, perhaps you are a bit too complacent and serene in your air and manner. A gentleman, I believe, likes to see some symptom of peculiar regard when he distinguishes you with his attentions. Otherwise he may suspect you don't participate in his sentiments. I very much fear that may be the case with Lord Ridley."

"Do you mean, Mama," said Caroline with a small smile, "that I should encourage him more?"

"Oh you really must, Caro!" said Julia feelingly. "Lord Ridley is *suffering*, and he is almost convinced that you do not care for him as you used to."

"I hope, Julia," said her mother with a frown, "that he was not so improper as to say such a thing to *you*."

"Well, no," admitted Julia, "but I could *tell*. He looked at Caro so *soulfully*. And when I told him we should always have time for our old friends, he did say that he feared that Caroline did not share my sentiment!" she added triumphantly.

"I note that he was not suffering too much to waltz with you," said Caroline dryly.

"No, and it was excessively kind of him! I thought I should sink when I had to sit there and watch that odious Lavinia Black and Helen Lovelace—who is really quite horse-faced in spite of her fortune—twirling around the floor in such a *superior* manner, and giving me *smirking* glances only because I had not yet secured the patronesses' approval. And then Lord Ridley asked Lady Sefton to present him as a desirable partner, and I could see that they were quite green with envy. And he dances divinely too, and says such pretty things! You don't know how lucky you are, Caro!"

"I must agree with Julia, Caroline," said Lady Wentworth warmly. "Lord Ridley's attentions to Julia only reinforce my belief that he is sincere in his wish to be of service to our family and to establish himself in our esteem. We need not look very far for his motive, I think. But you must take care, my love, or you will lose him! Your cool manner will convince him that you are indifferent to him, and then he will turn to someone else!"

"I am not . . . indifferent, ma'am, but I am not at all sure that I hold him in particular regard," said Caroline faintly. "A great deal has changed in two years, you know."

"Missish!" cried her ladyship scornfully. "You liked him well enough to pine for him, and to cherish a broken heart when he married another! Next you will be saying that you would not like to marry him at all!"

"I am not sure that I should, Mama," Caroline replied in a quiet voice. "I will admit that I was disappointed and—

and hurt, but I fear I might have been mistaken about Lord Ridley's character."

"Caro, how can you say so!" cried Julia. "When he is so handsome and so charming, and so good. I am persuaded you do not value him as you ought!"

"I should like to know," inquired Lady Wentworth in accents which unmistakably signaled the onset of an attack of nerves, "whether Lord Ridley has said or done anything in your presence that might be considered unworthy of a gentleman?"

"No, he has not."

"Well," said her ladyship, fumbling in her reticule for her vinaigrette, "I should never like it to be said that I wished for either of my daughters to marry against her inclination or her heart. My sensibilities would not have supported . . . such an arrangement in my own case, and I should never wish that either of my dear ones should marry merely to oblige me, or out of a sense of duty, however much such a sacrifice might add to my comfort and my peace of mind. I would have thought, Caro, that you were not in the same case as Julia and myself, but never mind. The viscount is a man of fortune and address, and should he offer for you I hope you will think very hard before you reject him, as it is by no means certain that you will receive another offer. It need not weigh with you," she said, sniffing a little, "but if he does ask permission to pay his addresses to you he will have the express approval of your poor mama. And I would certainly hope that in the meantime you set yourself to be agreeable to him, instead of casting out lures to your sister's beaux!"

Julia, who had been quite as annoyed as her mother over Mr. Neville's conversation with Caroline, was nonetheless moved to say, "Oh, no, Mama, you are unjust. Mr. Neville is not a beau of mine, at least not yet. And as for casting out lures, you know that Caro particularly dislikes him, and it was you who reminded her that she must be civil to him whatever her feelings!"

Caroline, hearing her case described without any roundaboutation, experienced a startling moment of self-enlightenment rather confounding in its intensity. It was an uncomfortable discovery, and one that did not in the least encourage her to confide in her mother or Julia. Since Lady Wentworth had quite exhausted her supply of selflessness for the evening and could only husband her reserves by reclining insensibly, eyes closed, against the comfortable carriage seat, the three ladies resumed their silence, and the ride home to Mount Street was accomplished in an atmosphere of general dissatisfaction.

12

JULIA'S COURT DRESS had been made by the most skillful costumier Mrs. Lacey's resources could command, and prior to coming up to London, Lady Wentworth, Julia, and Bertie's mama had all pronounced themselves more than satisfied with the result. Lady Withering, however, upon being applied to for her admiration, was unable to gratify her old friend by lavishly praising this magnificent creation, and even went so far as to suggest that without a few judicious modifications on the part of a truly up-to-the-minute French modiste, it would be quite apparent to all and sundry that the Wentworths, in addition to having lost their fortune and family seat, no longer moved in the first circle of Fashion.

Lady Wentworth, who had not come so far down the path of launching her child with brilliant éclat upon the ton without a substantial investment of her own time and self-esteem, could not tolerate the idea of Julia's appearing a dowd at her presentation. She was nevertheless irritated by the implicit criticism of her standards and taste. "My dear Amelia," she said in a marzipan voice, "it is so *excessively* kind of you to take an interest in our dear Julia."

Lady Withering was not deceived. "Now don't fly up into the boughs, Susan. The dress is quite beautifully made, and the material is exquisite. It needs just the *slightest* touch here and there, and then Julia will be in the first stare of Fashion. And you know, it is quite unreasonable to expect a country dressmaker to be perfectly à la mode; even a month or more is often enough to render an ensemble démodé in town!"

"I am well aware of that, Amelia," replied Lady Wentworth with a languid air, "but you know *dear* Clementina Lacey *would* make a present of her Court dress to Julia, and she was quite determined to patronize her own modiste. And then I have not been myself since the loss of my dear Wentworth, and Clementina insisted on lifting what burdens she could from my shoulders." She heaved a weary sigh. "Naturally, when she has been so kind, it would ill become me to complain, and like you, I realized it would be a trifling matter to alter the gown to the present mode when we came up to London. Only Julia has been so popular, and I have been so busy, that there has scarce been an hour to attend to it, and now I fear there will not be time to find a suitable costumier and commission the work."

"Nonsense," said Lady Withering, falling into the trap. "Would you like me to see to it for you? I could give it to the woman who is altering Caroline's dress, and I promise you no one will know that *that* is two years old! It should be quite a simple matter to update Julia's."

"Is Caroline having her dress altered?" asked Lady Wentworth blankly. "I hadn't supposed she would care enough to make the effort. She doesn't want to attend at all, you know. I've had to forcibly remind her of her duty to the family. What *would* Her Majesty think? Sometimes I don't know what gets into that girl!"

"I must own she does entertain some rather odd notions," admitted Lady Withering. "I offered to lend her my tiara for the occasion, and she refused, because Julia will not be wearing the Wentworth diamonds. My dear, did you *really* have to sell them before Julia's come-out?"

"I don't know," replied Lady Wentworth with an air of injury. "That horrid Mr. Lambert said we did, and went on and on about debts and mortgages until my head ached most dreadfully. And Caroline was almost as bad. I was quite powerless to resist, I can tell you. But now my poor Julia has to suffer. I know!" she added, brightening perceptibly. "You had much better lend your tiara to Julia. It is prettier than mine, and will set off her beauty to perfection."

"What a splendid notion," commented Lady Withering dryly. "Perhaps she could be persuaded to accept my diamond necklace as well."

"I have already tried to convince her to do so," said Lady Wentworth ingenuously, "but without success. It is extremely vexing," she added in a puzzled voice. "She says that if she cannot wear the Wentworth diamonds she will wear none at all. No doubt it is Caroline's influence! There is no end to the distempered freaks *she* has been getting into!"

Lady Withering closed her lips upon the thought that so far from emulating her sister's superior behavior, Julia was acting like a spoiled brat, and said merely that she hoped there was nothing amiss with her goddaughter.

"Not amiss, no! But she is a foolish, headstrong girl who does not seem to know her own interest!"

"Ridley?" guessed Lady Withering shrewdly.

Lady Wentworth nodded. "I have given her to understand," she stated in a wounded tone, "that the prospect of her marriage to him would be exceedingly agreeable to *me*, but she will not take the hint. She refuses to distinguish him with any particularity of attention, and I have warned her that she will drive him away with her coldness! And now he has asked permission to pay his addresses! Naturally I gave him every encouragement to expect a favorable outcome, but I can't be sure *what* she will do. I must *make* her know her own interest, because if I don't, he might change his mind and not want to marry *her*."

"Cramming the fences," murmured Lady Withering, whose husband had been a bruising rider.

"Don't be vulgar, dear," said Lady Wentworth sweetly.

"As you like, Susan," replied her friend with perfect condescension. "I must admit that I also encouraged Caroline to look with favor upon Ridley's suit if she were convinced of his sincerity. It appears, since he intends to make his declaration, that there can be no doubt on that score. But her heart has been bruised, and if it has not yet healed, I don't see how it can contribute to her felicity to force her into accepting him. If he can be persuaded to wait a bit, I feel sure he will meet with more success."

"But what," asked Lady Wentworth in stricken accents, "if she doesn't receive any other offers?"

In the face of this awful prospect, Lady Withering could only bow to her friend's superior judgment. "I don't suppose Julia . . . ?" she suggested hopefully.

Lady Wentworth shook her head mournfully. "She *would* send Sir Barnaby Pilbeam away, though I warned her she would be foolish to whistle away sixty thousand pounds merely because he is a trifle . . . large."

Lady Withering was betrayed into an undignified giggle. "My dear Susan, even if the ground didn't quite *tremble* beneath him, he cares for nothing but his dinner, and besides he is far too old for Julia."

"Well, I did wonder if she wouldn't be happier with an older man," said her friend reflectively. "Someone who would take care of her and not be always flying into a temper. Like me, she suffers from an excess of sensibility, and young husbands tend to be jealous and fly up into the boughs at the *slightest* provocation."

"Well, old ones get gouty stomachs," said Lady Withering.

"Yes," agreed Lady Wentworth with a sigh. "I had hoped that Mr. Neville might . . . That is, he did come to Julia's come-out, and everyone said . . ." She cast her friend a look of entreaty. "You don't think perhaps . . ."

"No," said Lady Withering, quite firmly. "I do not."

Lord Ridley, having received the impression from Lady Wentworth that his suit was not only welcome but sure to be attended by success, resolved to make his declaration in form without loss of time. He was persuaded, by his own partiality and her ladyship's optimistic wishes, that his attentions to Julia had roused Caroline to a sense of her own folly, and that his interests would best be served by pressing the matter without delay. He was, moreover, a considerably more acute observer than his beloved's mama, and he had not failed to notice Mr. Neville's growing interest in the Wentworths, and he attributed it to its proper cause.

He had no real fear that the Nonpareil would make a serious attempt to fix his interest—his efforts hitherto at avoiding the parson's mousetrap having bordered on the legendary—but his self-confidence was not so great that he could view a determined assault on Caroline by the most accomplished flirt in London with complete complacency. Far better then to enter into a betrothal now, before Neville could become a serious rival, instead of waiting until the end of the Season as he had planned. He could even imagine a certain discreet pleasure in having it known, when the engagement was announced, that it was he who had cut out the top-lofty Nonpareil.

Lady Wentworth had conferred the honor upon him of inviting him to the private family dinner to be held before Julia's presentation, and it was then that he intended to make his declaration to Caroline. He would not, of course, accompany them to the drawing rooms; that would have to wait until he and Caroline were married. But he relied on the intimacy and excitement of the occasion to further his suit, and looked forward to the event with the greatest anticipation of satisfaction.

Unhappily for the viscount, he could not have chosen an occasion less auspicious for furthering his romantic aspirations. The two girls found themselves somewhat unequal to the task of moving about gracefully in the wide hooped petticoats that were de rigueur for Court dress, and the magnificence of the pearls, lace, and delicate embroidery that decorated the outside of the stunning white gowns did not entirely mask the fact that they were exceedingly impractical outside the dressmaker's studio. In fact, Caroline began to find herself a bit out of sorts. "However did people get on in the last century?" she asked Julia with asperity. "It's quite as if one were walking around inside a barrel."

"I must admit I haven't figured out how we are to sit down," replied Julia, on whom the excitement of her presentation had not yet begun to pall. "Though *that* won't signify at Court, as we won't be seated."

"I daresay it will signify a great deal at dinner," suggested Caroline.

Julia giggled. "Perhaps we shall have to be served standing up, and then poor Bertie and Lord Ridley will have to stand up too. Oh, I wish we weren't having a dinner at all! I'm sure I won't be able to eat a bite."

On this point, Caroline was in perfect accord with her sister's feelings. Despite a certain willful obtuseness, she could not remain totally deaf to her mother's hints, and she knew that Lord Ridley had been granted permission to pay her his addresses. His inclusion in the family party, on an equal footing with Bertram Lacey, spoke volumes about her ladyship's expectations, even if her far-from-subtle declarations and animadversions had not. Caroline could only deplore the effective encouragement her mother was giving Lord Ridley, but her protests fell on deaf ears. Even Julia seemed to assume that her sister's reluctance stemmed from missish prudery and a rather unattractive desire to revenge herself on her suitor before she ultimately accepted him.

Caroline knew her own heart better. Even if his rather mercenary view of matrimony and his ready assumption of her willingness to receive his renewed attentions had been acceptable to her, she still would not have accepted him. It had been some time since she realized she no longer loved Lord Ridley, though she had entertained the notion of accepting him if he offered for her a bit longer out of a mistaken sense of duty and misplaced nostalgia. But for several days now she had known beyond doubt that she could not marry Ridley, or anyone. You could not marry one man when you were in love with someone else, and Caroline was painfully, hopelessly in love with Mr. Neville.

The discovery did not afford her any emotion but despair. The catalog of his acknowledged vices, which she had recited to herself many times before, was not sufficient to check the disastrous inclination of her feelings. She felt that her character must be shockingly deficient in some hitherto unsuspected way. Most lowering of all was the reflection that she *knew* he was amusing himself with her, and still she could not help yielding to his attractions. She had become one of his string of broken hearts, an object of pity and scorn like someone with a dreadful disease! Well, she would *not* go into a decline or act in such a way as to give rise to gossip, but it did seem manifestly unfair that both her London Seasons should end in such misery.

Fenwick, with the sharpened instincts of one for whom any change in domestic weather might have personal significance, noted that Miss Wentworth was unusually subdued during the course of the sumptuous meal he laid out in the dining room. Neither of the girls appeared to have much appetite, and the grilled oysters and loin of veal, removed with a beef soup, suckling pig, and assorted pâtés, went largely untouched by Miss Caroline, and only delicately sampled by Miss Julia. The two young men, he noted with approval, ate robustly. Perhaps the ladies' position, a sort of awkward perching on the very edge of their chairs, exercised a necessary control over their intake of food. Fenwick, who was very fond of Caroline, hoped it was no more than that.

Caroline was, in fact, finding her appetite quite destroyed by the meaningful glances Lord Ridley was bestowing on her over the platters, in addition to her mother's beaming smiles and almost flirtatious good humor. Moreover, he seemed, for reasons not entirely comprehensible, to have taken exception to Mr. Lacey's easy standing within the family circle, and behaved toward him with a mixture of condescension and hints that his own relationship with the Wentworths would soon undergo a material change. When the second course was brought in, his malevolent angel prompted him to bring up the subject of Sal Atticus.

"I understand," he said with a sly smile, helping himself to larded guinea fowls and green goose, "that the household was recently the victim of a most unfortunate practical joke, and that you owe your deliverance to the good offices of Mr. Neville."

Lady Wentworth, who did not like to be reminded of such an uncomfortable event, nodded regally. Caroline exchanged the briefest of looks with Mr. Lacey, whose fork was poised over the dressed crab.

"I believe, if I am not mistaken, that I called the very day the joke was played, indeed, almost at the very hour," he said, adding some asparagus and a spoonful of jellies to his plate. "It is most unfortunate that Miss Wentworth did not apply to *me* for help, as I cannot help feeling she would *now* do." He favored Caroline with an indulgent smile. "It must be excessively uncomfortable for you to be indebted to someone as, shall we say, high in the instep as Mr. Neville, particularly in your delicate circumstances."

Caroline had opened her mouth to offer a retort when Mr. Lacey said with a little choke, "Must protest. Not at all high in the instep."

Lord Ridley leaned back in his chair, examining his fingernails. "It is altogether natural that you would say so," he said meaningfully.

The import was not lost on Julia or Lady Wentworth. "Why, Bertie, what had you to do with it?" asked Julia.

"He was simply here when the joke was played," said Caroline, attempting a rescue. "He and I were trying to get rid of S—the pig when Mr. Neville called and was kind enough to take it off our hands."

"Coming it a bit too strong, Caro," said Mr. Lacey, who had read the challenge in Lord Ridley's eyes. He turned toward Lady Wentworth. "Fact is, ma'am, I owe you an apology. Got in the most dreadful scrape and was landed with the pig. Couldn't think what to do, so I brought it here."

"Oh, Bertie, how revolting!" cried Julia.

"Bertram Lacey, you can't mean to say that *you* are responsible for bringing that appalling beast into this house!" said her ladyship in a strangled voice. "Whatever will your parents say?"

"Nothing at all, for they won't find out!" cried Caroline, her eyes blazing. "The animal has been sent away, and I'm sure Bertie's involvement need go no further than this room. We have already seen that we can rely upon Mr. *Neville*'s discretion!"

"And upon mine, I hope," said Lord Ridley. "Mr. Lacey, my apologies. I had no idea, when you so earnestly begged admittance to Miss Wentworth's presence, that you were involved in any way in the affair. I trust I have not embarrassed you. I only wish you might have turned to *me* for assistance, when you must know that I would be only too happy to be of service to any friend of the Wentworths."

"Can't think why I didn't," said Mr. Lacey succinctly, between gritted teeth.

"That is very handsome of you, Lord Ridley," said Julia, fixing him with an approving smile. "I think Caroline is quite right; the story must never go beyond this room. Oh please, Mama; it would be so dreadful of us to get Bertie into trouble!"

"I am inclined to think," said Lady Wentworth, fanning herself with the air of one whose upright posture was in a decidedly perilous state, "that far too much has already been said on a topic that cannot but offend persons of refinement and delicacy. Moreover, while Clementina Lacey does not suffer from *my* exquisite sensibility, I fear such news might prove the undoing of the strongest constitution. I will, therefore, be silent." She rose, mothlike, from her chair. "Caroline, Julia, shall we leave the gentlemen to their port?"

Lord Ridley, who had discovered Caroline studying him with an air of grave attention, was suddenly reminded that the evening's main task was still undone. "May I hope, Lady Wentworth, that if Mr. Lacey will excuse me, I might solicit the honor of a private audience with your daughter Caroline instead?"

Her ladyship said instantly, "Yes—certainly! I am sure Caroline can have no objections, and Mr. Lacey will not mind sitting alone. You must take the yellow saloon. Come, Julia!"

Mr. Lacey not proving at all unwilling to sit alone with the port, Caroline was ushered out of the dining room with a rapt, somewhat envious look from Julia, and an apprehensive smile from her mother. When the door closed behind them in the yellow saloon, Caroline said, "That was not well done of you, Lord Ridley."

"My dear girl," said the viscount with a smile, "what I

have to say is for your ears alone. I had no choice but to ask
for a private audience."

"I refer to your treatment of Mr. Lacey," Caroline said
seriously. "You forced him to make an embarrassing revelation, and he was humiliated in front of you and my
mother and sister. And you—you practically accused him
of *toad-eating* Mr. Neville! He did not deserve that, Lord
Ridley. He has been a very particular friend of ours since
Julia and I were in leading strings!"

"And I have every hope he will be as particular a friend
to me," avowed his lordship, seizing her hands. "Miss
Wentworth, Caroline, I promise you I had no idea the silly
fool was involved in what I took to be a stupid practical
joke. I merely lamented your indebtedness to Neville, and
the awkward situation it put you in, so don't rip up at me,
fair tyrant."

"I assure you that Mr. Lacey and I did not find our 'indebtedness,' as you put it, awkward in the least," replied
Caroline, unmollified, and quite untruthfully. "And if Mr.
Neville found it so, he has not said so. There was no reason
at all for you to make it your affair."

"There was every reason," said Lord Ridley with somewhat forced amiability. The interview was not off to a
promising start, and he had gone too far now not to bring
matters to a close. "Any event which causes you distress is
an affair of moment to me, and I hope you will give me the
right as well as the reason to make you my concern." He
took even tighter possession of her hands and drew her as
near as her wide skirts would permit. "Come, my dear, let
us not play games. You know for what purpose I have
asked to speak to you this evening."

"Lord Ridley," said Caroline, carefully disengaging her
hands, "I am sensible of the honor you wish to pay me, but
I had much rather you did not."

His brows went up. "No?" he said softly. "I perceive that
you have not yet forgiven me for two years ago. Very well,
you must punish me a little. But while you do so, permit me
to tell you that I love you, have always loved you, and that
any unfortunate event which might have occurred to sepa-

rate us did not in the least alter my regard for you in any particular."

"Sir, the 'unfortunate event' you speak of was your marriage! How can you say so, in all respect to your wife?"

"I have already told you that I married my wife for her money," he said with barely suppressed irritation. "It was a bargain between us, with no love on either side. Whatever we were to one another, it never did, nor need it now, affect the way I feel about you." He laughed shortly. "You must at least be convinced of my sincerity in that regard, because no one could tax me with wishing to marry *you* for your fortune."

"Oh!" gasped Caroline. "Please, don't—"

"I do not hold it against you, nor the loss of the estate which gave the Wentworth name its chiefest esteem. I will never reproach you with it. Is not *that* sufficient proof of my steadfast affection?"

"Lord Ridley," said Caroline, recovering her composure a little, "there is no need to continue in this manner, which will almost certainly prove to be an embarrassment to us both should it be permitted to continue. Let me say without further loss of time that while I am grateful for your proposal, I am unable to do otherwise than decline."

Lord Ridley's smile faded. "What do you mean?"

"I mean," said Caroline as gently as she could, "that I am unable to return your regard."

Lord Ridley, whose countenance had darkened slightly as she pronounced these words, leaned against the mantelpiece with his eyes fixed on her face. "If I did not think that you mean to accept me in the end, I should really be quite angry, you know."

He had spoken mildly, but the expression in his eyes was not one to give her comfort. Trying to control her own growing temper, Caroline said, "Forgive me! I have no wish to occasion pain to you or anyone. But I wonder, if you have such regard for me as you suggest, that you think I would stoop to tormenting you or otherwise behave in what seems to me a particularly shabby manner. If you wish to pay me a compliment, you would do better to believe in my sincerity."

"One moment!" cried his lordship, his face now quite pale with wrath. "I think you had best explain yourself, Miss Wentworth. What kind of game are you playing with me? You say you don't wish to be my wife, yet you have received my attentions with enthusiasm, and your mother has given me every encouragement to believe my suit would be welcome."

Caroline was conscious of some embarrassment. "For my mother I cannot speak, though I must apologize if you feel you were misled. But for myself I must protest that I have been very careful not to treat you with any singularity, and indeed on at least one occasion you felt it necessary to complain to my sister that I did not encourage you enough!"

Lord Ridley appeared deaf to reason. "You have made me the laughingstock of London," he said between clenched teeth. "You have deliberately attempted to humiliate and embarrass me. Your actions are unworthy of a lady of Quality!"

Goaded beyond endurance by the injustice of this accusation, Caroline cried, "You are quite mistaken, Lord Ridley. One is not humiliated and embarrassed merely by an unsuccessful suit. One must first be courted and pursued in a very public fashion, only to be unceremoniously dropped when one's suitor marries someone else, after an interval so short as to occasion the most odious sort of gossip. *That* is humiliation, I do assure you!"

Lord Ridley strode forward and gripped her wrist, bending his head so that he could look into her face. "I was right, then," he said with an ugly smile. "You have done all this to spite me."

"No, you are wrong," said Caroline quietly, struggling to regain her composure. "But I do not know how to convince you. I am sorry for your estimation of my character, but I hope when we meet in future it might be as friends, or at least with the appearance of civility." She paused. "Lord Ridley, you are hurting my arm."

He said, in a voice unlike any he had ever used, "I shall make you very sorry for this."

Caroline tried without success to free her wrist. "Sir, you are not behaving like a gentleman."

He released her at once, sketched a mocking bow, and hastily left the room. A moment later Caroline heard him open the front door and quit the house.

13

CAROLINE'S AGITATION after this interview was so great that she felt physically weak, and uncomfortably close to tears. Sinking down into the sofa, she reviewed what had passed, which only served to increase the tumult of her thoughts. She had expected no little awkwardness to attach itself to her refusal, as Lord Ridley had, since they met at Lady Bassett's, steadfastly resisted all her hints that her feelings had undergone a substantial change. She knew that her mother had encouraged his suit, which did lend some justice to his feeling himself ill-used. But to put such a construction on her rejection of his proposal, to imagine himself the victim of an outrageous plot to humiliate and ridicule him, was, she feared, indication of a character that was seriously flawed. She thought her eyes were opened to it at last: the selfish disdain for her feelings two years before was all of a piece with his mockery of a marriage and his disproportionate reaction to her refusal. She was very much afraid that her instinctive but unwelcome conviction over dinner—that his unhandsome treatment of Mr. Lacey must be deliberate—was correct as well. Such malicious behavior toward one who was not his rival in anything but intimacy with the family did more to convince her of the good fortune of her escape than the viscount's rather ugly parting threat. She only hoped she could win her mother to a complacent view of the circumstances without disclosing any more of the unhappy details of the evening's events than was strictly necessary.

At the thought of her mother, Caroline's consciousness returned to the present, and she discovered almost with surprise that she was still in her Court dress, and would very soon be expected to depart for the drawing rooms. She felt quite unequal to encountering her mother and Julia's observation, and was sure that the news that she had rejected Ridley, when it was revealed, would inevitably give rise to a painful scene. It would be unpardonable to ruin her sister's presentation, but short of telling her mother that she had accepted the viscount, she did not see how a confrontation was to be avoided if they were to meet. The only recourse was to avoid such a meeting. She rang for Fenwick, who came with such alacrity she might almost have suspected him of lurking outside the door.

"Fenwick, I find that I am feeling unwell," she told him, reflecting that this was no more than the truth. "I am going to go up to my room at once."

"Oh, miss, I am very sorry to hear it. I do hope it wasn't the oysters," said the butler with concern. "Shall I send Betty up to you?"

"Yes, please. And could you tell my mother I will be unable to accompany her and my sister this evening, but that there is no need for her to come up. In case it is anything contagious, I should hate for my sister to be exposed on the night of her presentation. I will be quite well enough with Betty to look after me."

"Very good, miss," replied Fenwick with the tactful understanding which was the hallmark of the most successful of his kind, "and may I suggest a pot of hot tea as well?"

"You may indeed," she said with a grim smile. "Oh, and Fenwick?" she asked, turning back as he held the door for her.

"Yes, miss?"

"If this should somehow come to Gaston's ears, would you please be so kind as to tell him that dinner was excellent, and that I am *quite* sure it was nothing that I ate."

Caroline could imagine what her mother's feelings would be when she heard this news, but she had shrewdly guessed that, given a pretext for postponing an interview almost certain to undermine her emotional well-being, Lady Wentworth would weigh the desirability of Caroline's presence at the drawing rooms against the opportunity to maintain the unruffled tranquility of her spirits throughout the evening and decide in favor of the latter. At length she heard her mother and sister's carriage drive off, and she was able, with relief, to give herself over to the ministrations of her maid, and the comfort to be derived from a bracing cup of tea.

Caroline passed a rather restless night, awakening to the same troubled thoughts on which she had at length closed her eyes. The sun was streaming into the room, and she discovered that she had slept beyond her usual hour. She did not feel refreshed, or up to the day's exertions, but she could no longer postpone the interview with her mother. She sighed, and rang for her chocolate.

A few minutes later a soft knock fell on the door, and a slightly flustered and considerably relieved housemaid entered the room with a tray. "Oh, miss, I'm so glad to see you are up!" cried the girl. "Mr. Fenwick said you were taken ill last night, and were not to be disturbed till you rang for your tray."

"Thank you," replied Caroline, somewhat surprised at this solicitude; "I am feeling much better this morning."

"I'm sure Monsieur Gaston will be *that* relieved. Mr. Fenwick told him it wasn't the oysters, but when Miss Julia took sick in the night he would go on and on about typhus, and losing his place. In quite a taking he was!"

"My sister is ill?" asked Caroline, cutting across this recitation.

"Yes, miss. Her ladyship is with her now. I'm to ask you please to come to your sister's room as soon as you are dressed."

"Good God! Is it serious?"

"I couldn't say, miss. The doctor's not been sent for, I can tell you that. I think—" The girl gulped and stammered.

"Yes?"

"Well, she *might* have took sick at the Queen's drawing rooms, because Mr. Fenwick did say that her ladyship was in *such* a state when she came home last night, and Miss Julia looked all red-eyed like, from crying. He said—"

"That will do, Maria," interposed Caroline swiftly. "Is Betty with my sister?"

"Yes, miss, and Miss Jenkins is with her ladyship."

"Very well then, I will dress myself immediately. You need not stay!"

Caroline, who had flung on her clothes at random and done up her hair in a careless knot, entered her sister's room with the greatest apprehension. Julia lay propped up on her pillows, her face pale, her eyes glittering with unshed tears. There were dark circles under her eyes. Lady Wentworth gripped the edge of her armchair with clawlike fingers, her eyes closed, while Betty and Jenkins hovered over her with hartshorn and water, and burning pastilles. Her ladyship opened one eye at her elder daughter's entrance, but exhibited no further signs of revival.

Caroline hurried to her sister's bedside. "Dearest, are you ill? What is it?"

Julia gave her a wan smile. "I'm afraid it must be influenza. It came on me during the night—I feel like someone beat me all over with a cudgel, and I have such a headache!"

"And a fever too," said Caroline, laying a hand on her sister's forehead. "Oh dear, I fear you must be right. Did it come over you at your presentation?"

At this Lady Wentworth emitted a low moan of such a piteous nature that Betty and Jenkins redoubled their frantic ministrations. "Mama?" asked Caroline wonderingly. "Have you contracted influenza as well?"

Her ladyship opened her eyes with a visible effort. "There are things far worse than influenza," she intoned in apocalyptic accents.

"Should we not send for Dr. Dingle?" asked Caroline calmly. "I think he should examine you both. Perhaps you would be good enough to see to it, Betty. I cannot but feel that it would be better for my sister to lie quiet, and you may like to rest as well, ma'am."

"Yes, summon the doctor if you must," agreed her ladyship majestically. "Though there is little he can do for *me*, and I can't help thinking that a week or two of suffering in bed might be just the thing for Julia."

"Mama!" cried Caroline, horrified. "Jenkins, Betty, do you go at once and send for the doctor. I'll see to my mother and sister. I'll send for you when you're needed again."

"She's right, Caro," said Julia weakly when the maids had left the room, "I've done something very wicked." The tears started afresh down her cheeks.

"Well, whatever it is, you still need your rest, and you can tell me all about it later. I'm sure it can't be anything so very dreadful," said Caroline soothingly, handing her sister a handkerchief.

"You don't understand," said Julia in a smothered voice.

"Ruined," muttered her ladyship darkly. "We shall be quite ruined, and all my exertions will have been for nothing. We shall have to leave town at once."

"Mama, Julia is ill! There can be no question of leaving London. Whatever can have happened? Did you do something to offend the Queen?" she asked her sister.

Julia turned her face into the pillow so that Caroline had to strain to hear her. "I stole the Wentworth diamonds," she said.

Julia had sorely vexed her mother, whose patience was already tried by Caroline's absence and the suspected reason for it, by persisting in her refusal to wear any jewelry except Lady Withering's stunning tiara. The ball gown looked quite austere with a bare neck, but all Lady Wentworth's remonstrations could not avail against her daughter's resolve. At length she abandoned the struggle and decided to let Julia have her own way, for the gown really was improved by its most recent alterations, and Julia was looking truly breathtaking. Lady Wentworth never noticed that Julia clutched her reticule with rather more than the necessary care throughout the evening, or that this object appeared to bulge suspiciously. At the hour of the presentation, Lady Wentworth and Julia had already made their obeisance to the Princess Mary, and were just about to curtsy to the queen, when Lady Wentworth noticed that her daughter's neck was no longer bare. "And I can tell you, I don't know how I kept my feet," cried her ladyship with feeling. "Her Majesty had to ask me if I was quite well, and I don't to this moment know *how* I answered her." She fanned herself exhaustedly. "Fortunately, the Prince Regent was not in attendance, for he would have recognized the Wentworth diamonds at once. But someone else is bound to have done so, and everyone knows we have sold them!" she wailed. "Of course it will get out, and then what will we tell people? We will be ruined!"

Caroline had been listening to this recitation with growing wonder. "Oh, if someone asks you must say you had them copied before you sold them, and that these were only paste," she said distractedly. "But—"

"*Paste?*" sniffed Lady Wentworth in horror.

"Well surely, Mama, that is better than the truth," said Caroline with some amusement. "But—"

"That might answer," mused her ladyship, reviving a little. "It would be dreadfully mortifying, of course, but at least no one ever need know that Julia—oh, I can't bear to even think of it!"

"There is one person, at least, who will know the truth," suggested Caroline.

Julia emitted a low groan from the bed.

"You mean Amelia Withering, I suppose," said Lady Wentworth thoughtfully. "*She* is far too well acquainted with my views on paste jewelry not to suspect that the gems were real, and the matter is bound to come to her ears. But I'm quite sure we may rely on her discretion, my love, once we have acquainted her with the details. Though I own I cannot like to do so, when I know she will scold me most dreadfully, though I cannot see how any of this is *my* fault!"

"I was not referring to Lady Withering, Mama," said Caroline gravely. "I meant that the owner of the Wentworth diamonds, whoever he or she may be, might well have noticed they are missing, and suspect the truth. Julia, however did you come by them?"

"I didn't *steal* them," said Julia petulantly. "Well, not

precisely. They were just lying there, and I took them. I only meant to borrow them, for my presentation. It's not as if I'm some wretched housebreaker. I was going to send them back."

"Lying where?" prompted Caroline.

"In the cupboard, at Wyndham Priory. Where I used to keep my velvet pelisse, and some of my best shawls. You remember that Mama and I had to return to the Priory after it was sold to fetch one or two little things," Julia said with a touch of embarrassment. "When I opened the cupboard to look for my shawl—it was Norwich silk, you know, so I couldn't leave it behind—I saw the box. I recognized it at once, of course. And I . . . and I . . . I just took it!" she said, exploding into sobs. "Oh why did Papa have to gamble away all our fortune! It was quite m-monstrous of him, and it is so *odious* to be poor!"

"Julia!" cried her mother in a horrified tone. "I forbid you to speak so of your dear papa. What would people say if they were to hear you abuse him so shamefully?"

Julia's reply to this was a further display of the excess of that sensibility which her mother had hitherto regarded in a more favorable light.

"Don't, dearest; you'll only make yourself more ill," said Caroline, leaning over to bathe her sister's face with lavender water. She looked over at her mother. "But how is it that the diamonds were still at the Priory, ma'am? I am quite certain we made arrangements to turn all the jewelry over to Mr. Lambert before we left."

Lady Wentworth shrugged feebly. "I am quite at a loss to tell you. I too believed we had given everything to that wretched little man."

"You don't think one of the servants . . . ?" ventured Caroline.

"Certainly not," replied her mother icily. "How can you even suggest such a thing?"

Julia blew her nose. "I thought that somehow the diamonds must have been left behind by accident. Don't you see, it seemed like a sign that I was *meant* to wear them, because the new owner didn't even have them yet, and couldn't possibly miss them. It didn't seem like stealing, when they had always been *ours*. Wentworths have always worn those diamonds to their presentations! Only last night Mama looked so shocked, and I hadn't considered—oh, Caro," she wailed, "what are we going to *do*?'

"What surprises me," said Caroline in the calmest tone of voice she could muster, for it appeared that Julia was becoming dangerously overwrought, "is that the new owner must have expected to take possession weeks ago, yet we've heard nothing. Perhaps Mr. Lambert thinks *he* has lost the diamonds, and is quite frantic. In any case we must contact him immediately to discover the owner's identity."

"Oh, *must* we acquaint him with this dreadful news?" cried Lady Wentworth. "He is forever lecturing and censuring, and I cannot *bear* to think what he will have to say about *this*!"

"Perhaps we need not put him in possession of all the facts," suggested Caroline, "but I think we must send for him at once."

"Then you will have to receive him, Caroline, because I shall become quite ill myself if I must make any further exertion today," said Lady Wentworth in a nerveless voice.

"Perhaps I should receive him," said Julia faintly. "It should fall to me to make the explanations. It is all my fault."

"I'm sure he will absolve you from that responsibility when he knows you have influenza," said Caroline lightly.

"I am being punished," said Julia melodramatically. "I felt tired and a little hot yesterday, but it was not till after— till afterward that I was struck down. Perhaps I may not survive the illness. I'm sure I had much rather not if I am to be sent away in disgrace, with the whole town talking."

"Hush," said Caroline soothingly. "You are blue-deviled because of the fever. Let us try and see what we can do. Get some sleep now, and I will bring the doctor up to you when he arrives, and perhaps a glass of lemonade as well. Would you like that?"

"Oh, Caro," cried Julia, her tears starting up again. "You are so kind. But you had much better stay away, you and

Mama both. You don't want to catch influenza when you are going to marry—oh!" Her brain, confused by illness, had just recollected what the events of the last night had driven out of her mind. "*Are* you going to marry Lord Ridley? Mama said she feared you were not."

"No, Julia, I am not," said Caroline quietly, ignoring ominous signs that her mother was about to be rendered insensible by this intelligence.

"But he is so handsome and so good," muttered Julia sleepily, sinking deep into her pillows.

"Yes, dear," replied Caroline, gently tucking the bed linen around her sister's shoulders, "but we have decided we should not suit."

Lady Wentworth would have remonstrated, but Caroline laid a finger to her lips. "Forgive me, ma'am; for I know such news affords you no pleasure. But I think we had much better discuss it elsewhere and let Julia sleep. Let me take you to your room at once so that you may rest. Julia's quite right, you know; you must take great care not to catch influenza as well."

Lady Wentworth suffered Caroline to lead her from the room in silence, but when they had passed into the hall, she said tragically, "I know that it is quite useless to try to persuade you to accept Lord Ridley when you have made up your mind against him, because *my* wishes in that regard are of trifling consequence. You must have your own way. It does not matter what fate befalls the family."

Caroline said imploringly, "You know I would not willingly do anything to displease you, ma'am, but I could not do otherwise than reject him."

"Very prettily said, miss! But where is your consideration for *me*? What a fix you have put me in. I let him run tame in the house, I invited him to all our parties, and now you tell me you do not like him. When I assured him you would receive his proposals with gratitude and pleasure! And so you should have." She sighed. "I do not know what I have done to deserve such ungrateful children, but I do not complain. No one shall know what I have suffered, for those who are silent receive no commiseration!"

Caroline said nothing, knowing that whatever she said would only serve to irritate her mother further. At the door to her room, Lady Wentworth delivered, in trembling accents, her final remarks. "I do not know what will become of us over the diamonds. But I must tell *you* that if you never get a husband I shall not be able to keep you. What poor Wentworth would say I cannot imagine! You will have to live on your aunt's charity, or your sister's, and then I hope you may be sorry you did not heed your mother's counsels."

"Mama—" Caroline began.

"No, do not speak to me. I have no patience left. I am quite overcome. You must look to yourself. I wash my hands of it!"

14

COMING DOWN the stairs in a state of considerable agitation, with the note to be sent round to Mr. Lambert's, Caroline was greeted with the surprising but unwelcome intelligence that Mr. Neville had called, and was awaiting her in the Egyptian saloon.

"I informed Mr. Neville that Miss Julia has taken ill and her ladyship is resting, but he begged just a few minutes audience with you, miss, and I didn't like to send him away, not knowing what you and her ladyship would wish," said Fenwick regally. "If you would like me to, I can tell him you are not receiving today," he added, noting that she did not look in very good point herself.

"No, no, I had better see him now," said Caroline distractedly, lamenting the untidy state of her dress and hair. "Oh, if only everything weren't all topsy-turvy! Could you have this carried to Mr. Lambert's office at once? And when he calls, show him into the library and inform me without delay."

"Is her ladyship to be informed as well?" asked Fenwick impassively.

"Oh, no. My mother is—not quite ill, but far too overburdened to see to any business matters at this time. We must all . . . do what we can not to upset her."

"I understand perfectly," replied the butler. "I shall take pains to see that her ladyship is not disturbed."

"Thank you, Fenwick," said Caroline gratefully. "I knew I could count on you."

"I hope you know you may always do so, miss," he said

meaningfully, for he was not impervious to the undercurrents of sentiment flowing throughout the household.

Caroline was conscious of an irrational desire to unburden herself to the old retainer, so she directed her steps to the Egyptian saloon to confront Mr. Neville instead. She entered the room self-consciously, torn between embarrassment and delight, and found him engaged in apparent rapt contemplation of a blue faience bowl of undoubted antiquity. "This is a very fine piece," he said, rising to greet her. "Was your father a collector?"

Caroline smiled at the thought. "No, he—no, he was not. My mother had the room decorated, and a dealer secured the bowl. There were other things too, but nothing so nice as this."

His dark eyes held a sympathetic look, so that she knew he had guessed that they had sold them. She blushed and turned away. The last thing in the world she wanted was for him to pity her.

"Are—are *you* a collector then, sir?" she asked, striving for a normal tone.

He smiled. "I am not an expert, certainly, but I do have a small collection at Chartleigh, which I intend to install at the Priory. Perhaps, if you are interested, you might like to see it some day, and advise me where I might best display the pieces to advantage."

This was uttered in such a warm tone that she almost blushed again. *Stop being goosish,* she abjured herself with a sharp mental shake.

"Miss Wentworth," he said in a quiet voice unlike his usual languid tone, "your butler informs me that your sister is ill. I trust it is nothing serious?"

"I'm afraid it is influenza, though there is every reason to hope it may not be too strong a case. We are waiting for the doctor now."

"Then I must not keep you. I believe your mother has also taken sick?" he asked solicitously.

"Oh, no! That is—she is merely indisposed. She is resting."

Mr. Neville thought he could guess the nature of the indolent Lady Wentworth's indisposition, and foresaw that attendance upon the sickroom would undoubtedly be left to Caroline. He noted her pallor and the shadows beneath her eyes, and experienced a moment of frustrated wrath. "I wish I might not be going away!" he snapped, surprising himself and her.

"Oh, are you leaving town, then?" said Caroline, hoping her disappointment did not show in her voice.

"I go down to Chartleigh, my family's estate, for a few days," said Mr. Neville, recovering. "But if I may be of service to you before I leave . . . ?"

Caroline willed herself not to think of the Wentworth diamonds, which had unaccountably found their way back into Wyndham Priory, and said pleasantly, "That is very kind of you, sir! My mother will feel herself most obliged to you, but I daresay there is nothing that we need. With luck my sister will be herself again in a few days!"

"I certainly hope so. Please convey my compliments to her, and my wishes for her speedy recovery. Shall I have the pleasure of seeing you at least at Lady Northington's ball?"

"I—I cannot say, sir," said Caroline, wondering if, the next time they met, he would turn horrified eyes on her as a member of a family sunk into the deepest disgrace. More likely they would never meet again, because as soon as Julia recovered, Lady Wentworth was determined to carry her off to Bath without delay. The prospect caused her a certain amount of anguish, however much she strove to remind herself that their parting was inevitable in any event. How decidedly uncomfortable all this is, Caroline thought.

"You are troubled," said Mr. Neville, reading her face, "and would like to be with your sister. I will take my leave of you, but before I go I hope you will accept this." He handed her a parcel. "Not even the Prince Regent had a copy before this week."

She opened the paper and pulled out *Emma*. "Oh it is by Miss Austen!" she cried with delight. "How *excessively* kind of you! I shall read it to Julia as soon as she is recovered enough to listen. I am sure we will both enjoy it!"

"It was not in the least kind of me," he said with an enigmatic smile. "I wish you will stop trying to endow me with virtues I am quite sure I do not possess, Miss Wentworth."

"And *I* wish," said Caroline, rallying, "that you would not always prevent me from thanking you when you have gone to so much trouble on our behalf."

"Then we are both destined to disappointment," said Mr. Neville with a disquieting glint in his eyes.

"Not at all," replied Caroline with an answering laugh, "for, if one is to take you at your word, you will allow that one virtue at least must attach itself to your exertions."

His brows rose. "And that is?"

"The virtue of novelty!"

"So it must," he agreed affably. "And I'm delighted to see that coming to points with me has put the roses back into your cheeks."

"Now that is most shabby of you," said Caroline, blushing even more deeply, "when you know perfectly well you all but invited the thrust. Shall I make amends by telling you how much I mean to enjoy your book?"

"I will eagerly await your critical opinion," he said with a warm smile. "And now I really must go." He bent over her hand and kissed it. "Please convey my regards to your mother and sister, and do take care not to get ill yourself."

When the door had closed on him, Caroline went up to her room to dwell without interruption on the surprising nature of this interview. His civility toward herself and her family exceeded anything she had come to expect from him, and his thoughtful behavior in presenting her with a gift she could not but find pleasing lent itself to the most flattering construction. There was nothing today of the hard look about his eyes, and she thought she must be catching a glimpse of the man Lord Wynchwood and the other few friends he allowed to come close knew and admired. The warm tones he had used with her could only suggest that he had forgiven her for her treatment of him, and really did mean to stand her friend. It was an agreeable reflection, one that occupied her, barring the brief interruption of the doctor's visit, until a discreet tap on the door informed her that Mr. Lambert awaited her in the library.

* * *

The Wentworths' man of business had received, with the gravest concern, Caroline's hastily scrawled request that he call on her at his earliest convenience. The management of the family's finances was no longer sufficiently remunerative to justify such consideration, but he knew Caroline to be a level-headed sort of girl, and if she had summoned him urgently she must have a good reason. His sharpened instincts scented scandal, and even as he prepared himself to listen sympathetically to whatever tale might unfold, he was already calculating how he might distance himself and salvage his own interests.

Miss Wentworth's appearance, though poised, did not reassure him. He thought she looked rather harassed, and as if more rather than fewer burdens had been added to her care since her London Season began. The discovery that Lady Wentworth would not be present, while not unwelcome, was further troubling.

"My dear Miss Wentworth, how may I be of service?" he inquired when she had thanked him warmly for calling so promptly. "I apprehend it must be a matter of some importance. I trust your mother is not ill?"

"She is not well, and I'm afraid Julia has caught influenza," she said quietly, wondering how much it would be necessary to tell him. "But—"

"My dear child! It's not—that is, she is expected to *recover*?" he cried, fearing that something worse than financial indiscretions might be involved after all.

"Oh no! The doctor has just been, and has every hope that it is only a mild case. That is not why I asked to see you." She sighed and smoothed her dress. "I—that is, we—require some information of a somewhat delicate nature. And I hope we may rely on your discretion in not mentioning that such an inquiry was ever made."

"I see," said Mr. Lambert warily. "I believe it is safe to say that you may rely on my discretion whether I supply you with this information or not, unless it is a criminal matter." He looked at her closely. "I trust it is *not* a criminal matter?"

Caroline colored and dug her hands into the folds of her skirt, a gesture not lost on Mr. Lambert. "I shouldn't think so. No, no almost certainly not," she said more confidently.

"I think you had better tell me what you wish to know," said Mr. Lambert patiently.

Caroline raised a pair of strained eyes to his face. "We should like to know who bought the Wentworth diamonds," she said simply.

Whatever he had been expecting, it was not that. He looked quite surprised and said mildly, "But I thought we agreed that it was better for both parties that the purchaser remain unknown to you."

"Yes, but now it is a matter of the utmost importance to know the identity of this person."

Mr. Lambert studied his fingernails with some care. "And am I to be permitted to know why?"

Caroline lowered her gaze. "It may be that we shall be forced to reveal more to you in time, but for now I must beg your indulgence. I've no right to ask you to trust me, I know, but I am going to do so."

He studied her in silence for a few moments. "Very well, I will trust you, with the stipulation that if you should encounter anything you can't handle, you will contact me at once, or your solicitor. I am not bound to a confidence, you see; it was simply a matter of my best judgment under the circumstances." He tapped his fingertips together. "The person who bought the Wentworth diamonds was the same gentleman who purchased the Priory, Mr. Robert Neville."

Caroline was taken aback by her own stupidity. The last person she had thought of, when he should have been the first. "Did he buy *all* the jewels?" she asked incredulously, wondering what he could have wanted them for.

"Oh, no; only a few of the best pieces, particularly those associated with the history of the house. I assumed you were inquiring specifically about the diamonds. The rest of the collection was broken up, and pieces were sold here and there. That's quite usual in these cases."

"How very strange," reflected Caroline. "His family

must have scores of jewels that cast the Wentworth diamonds into the shade!"

Mr. Lambert cleared his throat. "Well, I should perhaps mention that in addition to the historical value, Mr. Neville was aware of the—ahem!—distressing circumstances of your family's finances, and he expressed an interest in reducing this burden somewhat. He thought it might make it less painful for you to quit the Priory."

Caroline was so overwhelmed by this unexpected information that she scarcely knew what to say. "And did he—did you hand over the diamonds to him personally?"

"Yes, certainly. In the presence of his man of business."

"And you've heard nothing since then?" she asked cautiously, not wanting to say anything which would suggest to him that the diamonds might be missing.

Mr. Lambert shook his head. "He had the stones examined by a jeweler and pronounced himself quite satisfied, and that brought the matter to an end. We've had no dealings since that day."

Caroline heaved a sigh of relief. There was still every chance that Mr. Neville had not noticed the diamonds were missing. He was unmarried, so they might lie in their case unregarded for many months. Oh, the humiliation of their belonging to the Nonpareil! When their very purchase had been in part an act of kindness toward her family! Only this morning she had imagined how he might change toward her if her family's disgrace were to be uncovered. How much worse it would be now! What would he think of them? If there was any possible way of returning the diamonds before their loss was discovered, it must be done at once.

Caroline considered, and then rejected, the idea of having Mr. Lambert hand them over, as she could not conceive of any plausible explanation for his doing so other than the truth, and anything less would cast doubt on Mr. Lambert himself. In fact, the man of business, however much he began to guess of the true nature of the problem, seemed rather reluctant to acquire more information than was strictly necessary, and showed a sudden but decided lack of curiosity about the matter altogether. It was not until after she had seen him to the door, with profuse expressions of gratitude and the promise that she would advise him if he could be of any further help to her, that she remembered Mr. Neville's remarks about Mrs. Murdoch.

"Oh no!" Caroline cried in a stricken voice. It had occurred to her that Mr. Neville might have had another motive for his seemingly innocent inquiries about Wyndham Priory's housekeeper. What if he had discovered the jewels were missing? Suspicion might naturally fall upon members of the household, whose characters were unknown to him, and if Mrs. Murdoch had given notice of her intention to leave at the end of the year, what else could he be likely to think? She thought of poor Murdy, innocent of anything but a profound attachment to the Priory and its former inhabitants, laboring—for weeks!—under a cloud of mistrust, all because of Julia's impulsive act. She knew the housekeeper was too sensitive not to perceive the change in climate, but, being ignorant of the true cause, what could she think that would not be dreadfully wounding to her self-esteem?

By this time Caroline was quite wild with distress and determination to return the diamonds without further delay. Every moment placed them in the gravest danger of discovery, and the true story would not only destroy her mother and sister's dreams, but possibly her own. But how to do it? She knew better than to depend upon her mother's help in the matter, and Julia was far too ill to be of use. She turned a dozen schemes over in her mind, pacing restlessly around the room with a kind of frantic, irritable energy.

The barest sketch of a plan had just begun to suggest itself when deliverance, in the venerable shape of her ladyship's butler, knocked at the door.

"Mr. Lacey, miss," intoned Fenwick.

"*Bertie!*" cried Caroline, almost dropping the faience bowl she unconsciously clutched in her fingers. "How perfectly *splendid*!"

15

MR. NEVILLE, upon quitting the Wentworths' house in Mount Street, had formed the worthy intention of calling upon his aunt, Lady Buxton, before he went down to Chartleigh. As such a visit was very little likely to give pleasure to either, he had postponed it as long as possible, but the civility owed to an elderly, if not beloved, family member required his fulfillment of his duty. He had long been impervious to his aunt's outrageous comments and eccentric behavior, and even enjoyed an occasional sparring match with her, but her peculiar insistence that she had the right to regulate his personal life was at the moment particularly distasteful.

Mr. Neville was being very careful. His own reputation and the position he occupied had insured that his attentions to the Wentworths had not gone unnoticed. In fact, his approval had had a quite salutary effect on their social careers. He knew the odds-makers at White's favored the Beauty as his latest flirt, and so long as the *on-dit* was no more than that he was content. But he was anxious to shield Caroline from more malicious tongues and the sort of gossip that would arise from the speculation that the merciless Nonpareil had formed a partiality at last. Mr. Neville had no intention of becoming ensnared, but Caroline had roiled the placid waters of his pleasurable existence, and thrown him into a condition of unwelcome doubt. It was just the sort of situation calculated to excite his aunt's interest and disapprobation, and she was perfectly capable of trumpeting, in a wide-ranging and disagreeable fashion, anything she gleaned from him on the town.

Ushered into Lady Buxton's dim morning room, he was not anticipating a comfortable cose. His aunt did not disappoint him. "So you've shown up at last, have you? I had quite given up expecting you to remember your duty," she said, gesturing toward the somber, unfashionable sofa opposite her own.

He ignored it, and took a seat in a hard, uncomfortable chair near the fireplace. Her ladyship's furniture of necessity inspired a short visit, but Mr. Neville thought he would rather not take his chances on the lumps. "But you see I have, ma'am, *at last,*" he said with deceptive meekness. "I go down to Chartleigh today and called in to see whether you have any commission for me."

"Hmph!" articulated the indomitable dowager. "Chartleigh, is it? Thought you'd been spending all your spare time at that run-down hovel the Wentworth woman hoaxed you into buying. Laying out a lot of blunt too, I've no doubt!"

Mr. Neville opened his enameled snuffbox and took a delicate pinch, a habit that never failed to irritate his aunt. "Well, I daresay it has been a trifle expensive to restore," he said meditatively, "but not by any stretch of the imagination is it a hovel. A but-and-ben, perhaps, a shanty even, but a hovel? No."

"Jackanapes!" said Lady Buxton with feeling. "You won't hoax *me* into believing that Wentworth didn't leave it all to pieces when he cocked up his toes. I never knew a man to have so little regard for what was owing to his name and consequence."

"I think it is generally agreed that his character was not very steady," said Mr. Neville mildly. "But were it not for the fact that he left his widow and daughters very sadly off, I should not complain of *that* you know. I am certainly the beneficiary of his profligacy."

"Ha! And I suppose that is why the *on-dit* of the town is that you're making a cake of yourself over Wentworth's daughter? Are you trying to make it up to them for buying the Priory? There is not the least cause for such benevolence, I assure you."

"My dear ma'am, you must know by now that my motives are rarely benevolent."

"No, you are the most selfish creature alive," agreed his aunt. "But if you are not motivated by charity, do you mean to say that you are *seriously* attempting to fix your interest with a pretty miss just out of the schoolroom? A chit with no fortune or consequence, with *that man* for a father? Are you so lost to what is owing to your family?"

"My flirtations have been the *on-dit* of the town for years, Aunt Louisa," said Mr. Neville, attempting to keep a hold on his temper. "I advise you to pay gossip no more heed than I do."

"Do you deny it then?"

"I deny nothing, ma'am, nor do I affirm it. My character, unlike yours, is not everywhere known for its frankness."

"Ungrateful puppy! I only mean you the best, you know."

"I feel quite sure that you believe that, ma'am."

"Impudence! Have I not been urging you for years to marry and set up your nursery?"

"In that case I wonder that you tax me with attempting to fix my interest with an unexceptionable girl," Mr. Neville suggested.

"But a Wentworth! The blood is *tainted*. You could never know what freakish thing might happen. And it would be decidedly uncomfortable to have relations who put one to the blush."

Rather than succumb to a pressing inclination to respond to this in a fashion which, while gratifying, would be lacking in respect to his aunt, Mr. Neville elected to bring his visit to a close. His aunt's enthusiasm for the encounter lasted a little longer, with the result that she favored him with a harangue of several minutes' duration, deprecating all of his schemes for renovating Wyndham Priory.

At length, exasperated, he said incautiously, "Since you take such an interest in the subject, ma'am, perhaps one day you would like to come down and see it for yourself. I've asked Humphrey Repton to do the landscaping, you know, and the interior will be French, in the classical style."

"I don't go for that sort of frippery myself," said her ladyship unnecessarily, "but I daresay you could use my advice. Perhaps I will, one day!"

Mr. Neville, mindful of Lady Buxton's disinclination to leave her house or bestir herself except on the invitation of one of the handful of Dragon Dowagers who constituted her own set, felt himself relatively safe from attack, but, lamenting his momentary lapse of vigilance, nonetheless resolved not to let his temper betray him into such laxity again.

While Mr. Neville was taking leave of his Aunt Buxton, Miss Caroline Wentworth was greeting the announcement of Mr. Bertram Lacey's arrival in Mount Street with an audible cry of pleasure.

Mr. Lacey, whose longstanding friendship and easy terms with the Wentworths did not normally encompass effusions of such enthusiasm upon being admitted to their presence, was immediately suspicious. "Doing it much too brown, Caro," he said when the door had closed on the butler. "What's amiss?"

"Oh, I beg your pardon," said Caroline with a smile, "but I am glad to see you. I need your help."

"Thought that might be it," said Mr. Lacey, studying her critically. "Here, Caro, you're looking a trifle down pin. Doesn't have something to do with that Ridley fellow, does it? Shouldn't like to interfere."

"No, of course it doesn't."

"The thing is," persisted Mr. Lacey, looking a bit embarrassed, "Julia said you were going to marry him. Said he was going to ask you last night. *Are* you going to marry him?"

"I am not," said Caroline definitively.

"Good," said Mr. Lacey, with relief. "Wish you wouldn't. Can't say that I like the fellow above half."

"I'm afraid I find that I agree with you. Oh, Bertie, it's not Lord Ridley. But we are in the basket!" Caroline confessed the whole of the story in a rather disjointed fashion, ending with Julia's influenza and Lady Wentworth's near prostration. "So you see it's all up to me to set things to rights. And you simply must help me!"

"Lord, what a scrape!" cried Mr. Lacey, awestruck. "What the devil made her do such a thing? Must have known she wouldn't get away with it."

"Oh, Bertie, I'm not saying she didn't do very wrong to steal the diamonds, but she didn't *think*," said Caroline hesitantly. "She didn't mean to keep them, and I don't think it really dawned on her what a shocking thing it was until she saw how poor Mama reacted. And she is so *very* sorry now."

"Didn't know it meant that much to her, selling the necklace," said Mr. Lacey. "Ought to have realized."

"You *do* understand," said Caroline warmly. "But you do see why we must give the diamonds back at once, before they are discovered to be missing! If the truth were known now Julia would be utterly discredited, and the family would be disgraced. I don't mind so much for myself," she said ruefully, thinking with a pang of Mr. Neville, "but Mama had such high hopes for Julia, and this will *ruin* her chances."

Mr. Lacey's hand closed convulsively over hers. "Devilish awkward fix," he agreed. "You know you can count on me, Caro, but dashed if I see what's to be done!"

"You must drive me down to the Priory," said Caroline, whose mind had been turning over the possibilities all day. "I can't see any other way. I'm afraid we shall have to say that your mother has been ill or some such thing, and that since Mama and Julia were laid up in London I came myself to pay our respects to Mrs. Lacey. What could be more natural than that I should stop at the Priory, to call on Mrs. Murdoch? While we are there, you must help me contrive to be left alone, so I can slip the diamonds into some place where they are sure to be found." Caroline paused, frowning. "It's a bit thin; Murdy's sure to wonder why *she* hasn't heard of your mother's illness when you and I come down from London. If I have to I'll try to fob her off with some Banbury story."

Mr. Lacey, who was beginning to regret his unqualified

offer of help, declared; "Won't fadge, Caro! You may be able to hoax Murdy with your flummery, but the Nonpareil ain't a slow-top!"

"But that's the beauty of it," replied Caroline, playing her trump card. "Mr. Neville told me this morning that he was going down to Chartleigh for a few days, so there is no chance of his turning up at the Priory."

Mr. Lacey made an inarticulate noise. "Still don't like it. Havey-Cavey. Bound to get out."

"Like Sal Atticus?" Caroline reminded him pointedly.

Mr. Lacey grinned. "Don't have to twist the knife. You know I'll drive you. Just thought you'd like to know there's every chance we won't pull it off."

"Thank you, Bertie," cried Caroline gratefully. "I knew you wouldn't cry off! Can we leave at once?"

"Lord no!" he said in a horrified voice. "Can't drive to Wyndham in a *tilbury*. Have to use the traveling carriage."

"Oh no, we can't involve any *servants*," protested Caroline. "Then we'll never be able to keep it quiet! It's only a few hours from here to the Priory, Bertie; can't we make it there and back in the tilbury?"

"Scandal," suggested Mr. Lacey succinctly.

Caroline laughed. "I think under the circumstances we must be willing to risk it. How if we leave very early tomorrow, before anyone is up? Then we can be back well before dark."

Mr. Lacey, reluctantly acceding to this plan, said that he would come round just before seven. "What will you tell Lady Wentworth?" he asked her.

Caroline paused thoughtfully. "The truth, I think. Or at least that I have gone to restore the jewels to their rightful owner, and she is not to worry. But you had better leave the carriage around the corner, and I will sneak out the back of the house, or we might have some uncomfortable explaining to do. My mother will know how to make everything right with Fenwick."

"Oh Lord, Caro," said Mr. Lacey woefully, "what a bumblebath Julia's landed us in!"

* * *

Caroline awoke to the cumulative effect of two nights' loss of sleep with a splitting headache. She had scarcely dared close her eyes for fear of missing the rendezvous, and when she pushed back the covers and stood up her head swam a little. When I have given back the diamonds, I shall sleep for a week, she told herself, fighting off an overwhelming urge to crawl back into the bed. She dressed herself plainly in a carriage dress of lawn-colored muslin, and put on her oldest pelisse. She did not want to call attention to herself on the road, and she thought her garb looked suitable to one on an urgent errand of mercy to the sickroom. A roll and some fruit carried off from last night's dinner formed her breakfast, and at length, consulting the clock, she picked up her bulging reticule and slipped quietly down the stairs and out into the street.

Mr. Lacey did not fail her. He was holding the horses' heads with a harassed expression and a look, when he saw her, that was a clear mixture of relief and the liveliest dread. "Did you bring them?" he asked in a melodramatic whisper.

She lifted her reticule.

He looked away and shivered. "Nacky," he said without conviction. "Hope we don't meet up with any highwaymen," he added gloomily.

"Nonsense!" said Caroline, rubbing her eyes. "It's far too early."

The two travelers proceeded largely in silence, each in review of his own plans and prospects, and Caroline found some of her brave resolve diminishing in the face of the queer look they received from the ostler when they changed horses at Slough. Even the handsome douceur bestowed on him by Mr. Lacey did not sufficiently alter his impression that the couple were not quite respectable, and his demeanor toward them was punctuated with knowing winks, scarcely less dismaying than his good wife's formidable scowls. Caroline could not help retreating behind the brim of her straw bonnet, though she suspected this made her look guilty. The exertions of the journey in an open carriage had begun to make her feel very tired, and not a little hot.

By the time the carriage pulled into the grounds of Wyndham Priory, she felt near to falling down with exhaustion, and it was an effort to focus on the familiar landmarks. As these were dotted with quite unfamiliar excavations and mounds of earth, she began to wonder if her tired eyes were playing tricks on her. "What's going on here?" she asked Mr. Lacey.

"Mama wrote that Neville's having the place relandscaped," he said grimly. "Didn't want to mention it. Though it might upset you. Shouldn't wonder if the house isn't at sixes and sevens as well," he added, helping her down from the carriage.

Mr. Lacey's prediction did, in fact, prove to be the case, as they were greeted, upon being admitted to the Priory by a butler of awe-inspiring gentility, by the sight of rolled-up rugs, stacked crates, and the unmistakable smell of fresh paint. Somewhere in the recesses of the house a saw could be heard. Caroline, torn between admiration and distress, was astonished. "It's only been a few weeks," she commented wonderingly.

"Do you mind?" asked Mr. Lacey sympathetically.

"I don't know. It makes it seem—I don't know—as if it's been a very long time since we lived here." She gave him a brave smile. "Perhaps that's just as well. I—"

"Miss Caroline! Master Bertram!" cried a respectable-looking woman with tidy gray hair under a starched cap. "Don't ever tell me you've driven all the way from Ilcombe Hall in a *tilbury*. Whatever would her ladyship say, Miss Caroline?"

Caroline laughed and gave the housekeeper a light hug. "Oh, I've grown quite *rackety* since we went up to town. Now don't scold, Murdy, not when Bertie and I have come particularly to see you."

Mrs. Murdoch preened with pleasure, like an ancient cat. "I'm that flattered, miss, but it's no use trying to gammon me that you've become fast in London. Haven't I known you since you were a babe in the nursery? Now come into the saloon, while I tell Philippe there'll be two for nuncheon." She lowered her voice. "French, you know," she said conspiratorially, "but I daresay I can get you something decent to eat."

"Oh no, Murdy, we really can't stay!" cried Caroline involuntarily. Then, seeing Mr. Lacey's dismayed look, she added, "But something cold on a tray would be very nice."

"Not stay!" cried Mrs. Murdoch. "Why, I never heard of such a thing! Why ever not?"

"Mother's not feeling at all the thing," said Mr. Lacey helpfully.

"Why didn't you say so?" asked Mrs. Murdoch when Caroline had amplified this explanation. Nothing would do but that Mrs. Lacey must have her sovereign remedy for a putrid sore throat, as well as assorted gum plasters and other medicaments the housekeeper found indispensable for treating Mrs. Lacey's vaguely described but rather alarming-sounding ailment.

"Now you've done it," said Mr. Lacey when she had bustled off to see to the acquisition of these objects as well as the cold collation. "What happens when she asks my mother how she's feeling?"

"With luck that won't be for days, and by then we'll be safely back in London. We'll think of something to explain it!"

"I say, Caro, why don't you just drop the thing on the mantelpiece and we'll be off? We're getting in deeper every minute we stay here."

"Don't cry craven now, Bertie, we—"

"There, miss, Master Bertram," said Mrs. Murdoch, returning with the tray. "Now tell me all the news that's been going on in London."

Caroline regaled the housekeeper with a suitable version of Julia's triumphs on the town and ended with the news that she was presently suffering from influenza, and that they would all shortly be removing to Bath.

"Wore herself out, I shouldn't wonder," clucked Mrs. Murdoch, "poor little thing. But now Miss Caroline," she added with a twinkle, "what do you think of the house?"

"There seems to be a great deal of work going on," suggested Caroline noncommittally.

"Lord yes! Mr. Neville plans to bring it back to what it was in your grandfather's day! There won't be a house like it in the whole country! Oh, I beg your pardon, miss!" she said, dismayed. "I hadn't ought to have said that."

Caroline smiled. "No, you are quite right to be proud, Murdy. Is Mr. Neville a good master then?"

Mrs. Murdoch blushed like a schoolgirl. "The very best, miss. We were all afraid . . . well, but he's been ever so kind. We are that relieved, I can tell you."

"Excuse me for asking, Murdy, but *do* you mean to stay on past the end of the year?"

"Why, bless you, Miss Caroline, of course I do." She looked guiltily down at the floor. "Mr. Neville mentioned it to you, I expect. I did think I might not stay, and—and Mr. Fenwick was kind enough to offer me the protection of his name and home." She flushed bright red. "But when I saw how things stood here, I told Fenwick he'd have to wait," she said defiantly. "Well, I couldn't leave the master now, not with the house to put to rights. Whatever would people say?" She straightened her cap. "Now, Miss Caroline, finish your tray and I'll show you through the house. I'm sure you'd like to see all the changes."

Caroline, who had been picking at her food with little enthusiasm, said instantly, "I'm afraid I'm not very hungry today, Murdy. Would you mind very much if I went up alone, while Mr. Bertram finishes his nuncheon?" She smiled hesitantly. "I shan't have many opportunities to see the house again."

"No, you go on, Miss Caroline," said Mrs. Murdoch sympathetically. "Of course you'd be wishful of seeing it on your own. Take your time. There's workmen in some of the apartments, but they won't disturb you."

Caroline was delighted to gain access to the upper portions of the house so easily. She began to feel that the venture might be attended with success after all. Mrs. Murdoch's demeanor and enthusiasm was the best possible news; it meant that she had not fallen under suspicion after all, and that in all probability the absence of the diamonds from the cupboard had not yet been discovered. She had precise instructions from Julia, but she felt that for appearance's sake she should feign interest in the other portions of the house as well.

She did not have to pretend to be interested in the changes of the arrangement and furnishing of the rooms for long. She progressed from curiosity to admiration for the taste that had inspired the alterations, and felt a pang of regret that it was not her family who were turning the Priory into a showplace of beauty and style. Mr. Neville's character, as revealed by Mrs. Murdoch, and his cultivation, as displayed in his improvements to her old home, had never been shown in such a favorable light, and each revelation excited a deepening of that warmth of sentiment, so long suppressed, which had contributed so much to her present discomfort and so little to her peace of mind.

Caroline was so absorbed in these reflections that she scarcely noticed, until she was halfway up the stairs, that her legs were displaying a curious reluctance to proceed. She paused to rest, clutching the banister for support, and was almost overcome by dizziness. At length her head cleared, but she could no longer ignore the alarming signs that she was about to be taken ill. Oh please, don't let it be this wretched influenza, she prayed, or at least not till I get back to London. The thought of coming down with a sickness likely to confine her to bed in Mr. Neville's house for many days induced a sort of panic, which propelled her up the stairs and into the ladies' apartments before it was bellows to mend with her.

These apartments, which looked over the same prospect as the library—out onto the lawn and the gardens—were in as much disarray as the rest of the house. Walls had been removed, furnishings changed or covered with sheets, and one particular part of the ceiling, which Caroline remembered as badly stained and cracked by water damage, was missing altogether. Indeed, she could hear masculine voices close by, and concluded that the workmen were laboring in this part of the house. That threw her off balance, because the contents of the cupboard would surely have been emptied before the work commenced. It would be foolish, and dangerous, to replace the diamonds under those circumstances. She continued on through the rooms, clutching the diamonds indecisively, until she came to the cupboard.

She breathed a sigh of relief. This room, which had been her mother's bedchamber, was unchanged, and bore no sign of habitation. She experienced a queer twisting in her heart, and a renewal of a sense of loss more intense than any she had felt since she had left her home. How foolish she had been to pretend to herself that it did not bother her, when now she could scarcely breathe for the pain that was squeezing her chest. And Julia had been here too, and must have felt so! Though she must always condemn her having done so, for the first time since she had learned that her sister had taken the diamonds she thought she could begin to understand why.

A wave of fever engulfed her, and her teeth began to chatter. She felt an urgent need to sit down. Not yet, she told herself determinedly, taking the diamonds out of her reticule and seeking frantically in the recesses of the cupboard for their case. Her fingers fumbled and found it, closing on it gratefully.

"And through here, Mr. Repton, I hope you'll see what I mean about incorporating the prospect into the design of the house." said a voice right behind her. "These will be my wife's rooms someday, and I think they are most elegantly situated."

Caroline whirled, gasping, and the diamonds spilled from her nerveless fingers onto the floor. She stared in dismay at a mild-looking, elderly man in a black coat, and then lifted her eyes to behold, not a workman, but the owner of Wyndham Priory himself.

16

CAROLINE WOULD EVER after remember, in that dreadful moment in which she questioned why Fate had seen fit to visit both the Nonpareil and the influenza on her in such a fashion, that Mr. Neville's first reaction upon seeing her was unmistakable pleasure. For a moment he stood immovable with surprise, and then, taking in the fallen diamonds and the empty case, his countenance changed.

Caroline would rather have endured a thousand years of torment than another such look. His lip curled disdainfully. "Did you wish to see me, Miss Wentworth?" he asked in a voice that froze her marrow.

Mr. Repton cleared his throat. "If you'll excuse me, Mr. Neville, I should like to take another look about the grounds. No need to escort me; I do best poking around by myself. I'll wait for you in the library, shall I?" He sketched a bow to Caroline. "Your servant, ma'am."

"I—I must explain," began Caroline falteringly, breaking out in a cold sweat. She looked around frantically for a chair, but there was none to be found.

"There is no need," Mr. Neville said harshly. He bent to pick up the necklace and case, and then held them up to the light. "The *Wentworth* diamonds, I believe. Someone warned me, quite recently in fact, that *tainted* blood will out, but even your father would have been shamed by such a trick as this. I've been a fool."

Caroline's eyes leapt to his, and she recoiled instinctively from the blaze of anger she saw there. Whatever she told him, she must not expose Julia to the white heat of his wrath. His eyes told her that he would never forgive her, but she could not justify herself without betraying her sister's part in the affair. Still, she could not bear that he should so misjudge her, and she felt she must say something. She tried to speak, and found she had little command over her voice. A black circle began to form around the edges of her vision, and pinpricks of light danced before her eyes. The room began to fade, and she realized with horror that she was about to faint.

"I'm afraid I can't answer you now," she tried to say, but she had no idea if she'd spoken the words aloud. She lurched forward blindly, and the black circle closed in completely. *Cheltenham tragedy*, she thought to herself, in disgust, and then she lost consciousness.

Caroline awoke from the pleasant dream in which she was lying in her old room at the Priory, with something deliciously cool stroking her brow. She opened her eyes, but the dream did not go away. She frowned.

"There, there, Miss Caroline," said Mrs. Murdoch, who was bathing her face with a handkerchief dipped in lavender water, "you drink this laudanum, now, and try to get some sleep. Mr. Neville's gone to fetch Dr. Wheatley."

Caroline wondered vaguely what Mr. Neville should be doing at her home at Wyndham Priory and why the thought of him should so trouble her peace, but she gave up trying to remember and closed her eyes again.

Dr. Wheatley, when he arrived an hour later, spent a long time examining her, and when he came downstairs again he informed a grim Mr. Neville and frantic Mrs. Murdoch that Miss Wentworth was suffering from a rather severe attack of influenza complicated by a high fever, and that she might be expected to wander in her mind. "She's asking for you, Master Bertram," he told Mr. Lacey, whom he had known since before he was in nankeens. "If you're not afraid of exposing yourself, it might be a comfort to her if you were to go on up. I've left her maid to sit with her. But stay well back, mind. I've enough to do without two patients on my hands."

Caroline, opening her eyes on Mr. Lacey's comforting

presence, remembered that there was something she must tell him. What was it? Concentrate, she told herself. "Please leave us, Mary," she said to the maid.

At a nod from Mr. Lacey, the girl left her chair in the corner and went out softly, closing the door. "How are you, Caro?" asked Mr. Lacey worriedly.

"I feel dreadful," said Caroline honestly. "But never mind that. Did you *tell* him?"

"Who? What?" asked Mr. Lacey, confused.

"Mr. Neville," said Caroline urgently. "About Julia. The diamonds."

Mr. Lacey swelled with indignation. "Of course I didn't."

Caroline sank back against the pillows. "Good," she sighed.

"Why the devil would I—oh, Caro," cried Mr. Lacey, putting two and two together, "he never *caught* you?"

Caroline nodded.

"Didn't realize," said Mr. Lacey. "Thought he *looked* mad as fire when he came downstairs after you fainted, but then he was all cold civility. Thought he just didn't like coming home and finding us taking liberties in the house. He's been locked away in the library with that Mr. Repton, who came to landscape the grounds. Some famous chap. Daresay that's why he came back unexpectedly. I say, Caro," he added, as a thought struck him, "if he caught you, we've *got* to tell him the truth. What's he going to think?"

"He thinks I was trying to steal the diamonds," said Caroline faintly.

"The devil he does! I'll soon set him straight about that!"

"Bertie, you mustn't. *Promise* me you won't say anything till I've had a chance to think of something."

"Now see here, Caro—"

"I'm not just being noble. You didn't see his face. He'll ruin Julia if he finds out the truth, and that will kill Mama. Promise me!" she demanded, tossing restlessly on the pillow.

"Well, dash it all, Caro, all right," he agreed, seeing that she was becoming agitated. "But I don't like it. More likely he'll ruin you."

"Very likely," said Caroline, spilling tears into her pillow, "but after this I'm ruined already."

Caroline dozed uneasily for the better part of three days, her mind wandering in and out of delirium, her needs attended to with affectionate solicitude by Mrs. Murdoch. On the fourth day the fever subsided, and the ache in her head and bones abated. She had her first natural sleep in days, and when she awoke the next morning, Mrs. Murdoch announced that Mrs. Lacey was in residence at the Priory, and would like to come up to her if Caroline felt she was up to receiving a visitor. "She was wishful of coming up before," said Mrs. Murdoch, plumping her pillow, "only Dr. Wheatley wouldn't let her, on account of her delicate heart, and her just getting over being sick herself."

"Did you say she's been living here?" asked Caroline, confused.

"Yes, Mr. Neville sent for her to come, so it would be all right and proper for you to say in the house," said Mrs. Murdoch proudly. "Fancy his coming back like that, with no one the wiser," she added wonderingly. "He went back up to town the day you took sick, and says he'll stay there until you're well enough to go home again."

Caroline could well believe it, but nonetheless was amazed at his consideration for one who he had every reason to believe had betrayed, in the most shocking manner imaginable, his trust and his hospitality. "That's—that's very kind of him, to be sure," she stammered. "And Bertie?"

"Gone up to London to give the news to her ladyship that you're better. Your dear mama wanted to come down herself," said Mrs. Murdoch, pursing her lips, "but Miss Julia's still in a tender state and she didn't want to leave her."

"Oh, Murdy, it's quite all right, really. No one could have taken better care of me than you! Will you ask Mrs. Lacey to come up, please? I do so want to thank her!"

Clementina Lacey was a comfortable, steady sort of

woman, and though her son had, with some difficulty, refused to tell her why he and Miss Wentworth had driven to
Wyndham Priory for clandestine purposes in an open carriage, she refrained from censure or blame, and even obligingly went along with Mrs. Murdoch's concerned inquiries
into the state of her health. A little wiser than her husband,
she knew that Bertram's character was in the main reliable
and true, and that while his judgment occasionally faltered,
she could not do better than to accord him a measure of
trust. She had long believed that Miss Caroline Wentworth
was one of the finest young women of her acquaintance,
and she was inclined to believe that if the children were
driven to such desperate measures, they must have a very
good reason. She was sure that if she held her tongue,
Bertie at least would open his budget to her in time, so she
did not tax Caroline for explanations, listened sympathetically, and thereby learned a great deal more than Caroline
realized she was imparting.

In such soothing company, Caroline made steady
progress, and if it were not for the dejection of her spirits,
she might have been said to be making remarkable improvement. She had always heard that influenza left its vic-
tims weak and listless, and now she knew it to be true.
Never had she felt so blue-deviled. Her restless mind end-
lessly reviewed the appalling scene with Mr. Neville, and
cast about in vain for a solution to her dilemma. None presented itself to lift the oppression of her spirits. She was
further afflicted upon receipt of a letter from her mama,
who, in addition to conveying the welcome tidings that
Julia had left her sick bed and was now well enough to receive callers, could not forbear lamenting that Caroline had
taken it upon herself to rectify the family misfortunes, instead of allowing wiser hands to prevail. Lady Wentworth
had pieced together a notion of what had occurred, based
on the letter Caroline had left for her and on Mr. Lacey's
somewhat inarticulate description, and was daily expecting
the axe to fall. No word of reproach would pass her lips,
and she would bear with equanimity whatever sorrows her
daughters' ill-judged actions brought upon her, but she

could not but feel that the family should repair to Bath just as soon as Caroline felt well enough to travel. Meanwhile, she rejoiced in the news of Caroline's improvement, bade her spare no thought for anyone that might interrupt its progress, and remained, as ever, her most affectionate mama.

This remarkable document had the effect of convincing Caroline that nothing would be more contemptible than yielding to the craven temptation of remaining in bed awhile longer, so she allowed Mrs. Murdoch to help her up, and proceeded, on jellied legs, across the floor to the sofa. She did not have sufficient resolution to glance in her looking glass, but when Mary had brushed her hair and arranged her dressing gown she did feel very much more presentable. She was relieved to find that Mr. Lacey, when he came to bring her the news from London, was of the same opinion.

"Not saying you ain't looking hagged, because you are," he said judiciously. "But not quite so done up as before. How do you feel?"

"Cross as a cat! It's enough to make anyone mifty, sitting here day after day with nothing to do but think how helpless I am. Bertie, I must get out of Mr. Neville's house! Every day increases my obligation to him, and when I think what he believes . . . It's no exaggeration to say he must wish me at Jericho!" She looked at him closely. "You haven't *heard* anything? He hasn't . . . he's not . . ."

Mr. Lacey perfectly understood the meaning of this somewhat disjointed inquiry. "If you mean, has he told anyone he caught you red-handed trying to steal his diamonds, *I* haven't heard it," he said frankly. "Dashed queer stories going round about him, though. Goes to his club every night and doesn't come home till all hours. Plays deep. Gave Countless Lieven the cut direct on the street. Devil of a dustup. Said he didn't see her. Hasn't come the ugly, though," he said, shaking his head, "not that I know of."

"Well, that's something I suppose," said Caroline,

"though Mama writes of the axe that is about to fall, and I must say I know just what she means."

Mr. Lacey, who had no cause to indulge in levity on such a subject, nevertheless looked unusually morose, so that finally Caroline was compelled to ask him if anything else was amiss.

He shook his head gloomily. "Shouldn't say," he remarked.

"Come on Bertie, cut line!" said Caroline. "You know you needn't hide your teeth with me."

He raised his head and looked at her. "It's Ridley."

"Oh Lord." It was not precisely fair to say that Caroline had forgotten about the viscount, but in view of the dreadful events which had superseded her rejection of his proposal, it was not wonderful that he had been relegated to the background of her attention. Mr. Lacey's worried expression raised anew the specter of his threats. "What's he done?"

Mr. Lacey transferred his gaze to the lovely springtime scene outside the windows. He cleared his throat. "Pursuing Julia," he said, sounding embarrassed.

"He's *not*! You can't mean it."

He nodded. "Always there. Julia can't go out yet, so he calls. Brings flowers. That sort of thing."

Caroline knew exactly the sort of thing. "Does she encourage him?"

There was an uncomfortable silence. "Yes," he said at length.

Caroline sat thinking. "I'm afraid I'll sound horribly conceited," she said, "but I fear he might be doing it to spite *me*. He promised something of the sort, you see," she added apologetically. "If that's the case, there is no telling what he may do," she said with growing alarm. "Even if he were sincere in his regard for her, his character is *flawed*. Oh Bertie, she musn't encourage him! What if she tells him about the diamonds? I know he wouldn't hesitate to use it against us all. We have to warn her!"

"Tried to," said Mr. Lacey with a sigh. "Wouldn't listen."

"Oh, *why* am I trapped here with this useless, good-for-nothing body," cried Caroline passionately. "I need to *talk* to her. I'm sure she'd listen to me."

Mr. Lacey shook his head. "Won't fadge, Caro. Ten to one she'll think you're just jealous."

Caroline was momentarily taken aback. "You're right, of course. I should have thought of that."

"Said as much to me," said Mr. Lacey mournfully. "Thing is, thinks I'm jealous too."

"Oh, poor Bertie! How perfectly ridiculous!" said Caroline with a smile.

Mr. Lacey did not smile in return. "Don't know what's to be done, Caro. Julia's in high mops about your mama leaving London. Can't say what she may take it into her head to do. And Ridley's grown very particular in his attentions. Julia seems to like him very well. *Beams* at him, if you take my meaning."

Caroline thought she took it well enough. "Yes, he can be very charming," she agreed. "I don't doubt he means mischief."

"If he hurts her, I will call him out," said Mr. Lacey through gritted teeth.

"Bertie!" cried Caroline, shocked. "I cannot think it will come to that. He could not be so lost to all scruple as to be entertaining the idea of entering into more than a *flirtation* with her, and while that is reprehensible enough in the circumstances, it is hardly a matter for pistols."

Mr. Lacey muttered darkly that he hoped it might be so, for Ridley's sake.

Caroline, a little amused at the thought of Mr. Lacey acting Julia's champion, was nonetheless concerned enough to say, "Well, I shall have to write to Mama instead. I shall have to warn her in some way that doesn't make me sound like a cross between an old cat and a dog in the manger. Perhaps she will be able to speak to Julia without making her fly up into the boughs, though I—Yes, Murdy dear, whatever is it?"

"Oh, Miss Caroline, I'm that sorry to disturb you, but there is a lady downstairs who insists on being shown over the house. And when I told her the master was away and you was recovering from the influenza, she demanded to be brought up to you. She says she is the master's aunt!"

"Lady Buxton?" inquired Caroline with deep forboding.

"Yes, that was it. And a very crochety lady she is too, though I shouldn't say so."

Oh, dear," cried Caroline with feeling. "Just when I thought things couldn't possibly get any worse!"

17

CAROLINE HAD SCARCELY given vent to this heartfelt utterance when her ladyship, hard on the heels of the hapless servant selected to convey her up, entered the sickroom. Mr. Lacey, who had not previously made her acquaintance, rose shakily to his feet, his face a study of slack-jawed disbelief. Lady Buxton's imposing figure, rigid posture, and disapproving demeanor reminded him of nothing so much as his earliest governess, a particularly menacing figure of his boyhood whose occasional presence in his nightmares could still cause him considerable distress. He lost his composure completely, and sat back down.

Lady Buxton, much to his relief, seemed to overlook his presence entirely. "Where is my nephew?" she demanded in reply to Caroline's salutation. "And *where* is your sister?"

Caroline was now a little better prepared to encounter her ladyship's manners and murmured in what she hoped was an unruffled fashion that she believed Mr. Neville had gone up to town. "Was he expecting you, ma'am?" she inquired politely.

"Certainly not. I am never abroad. However, he invited me to inspect the changes he is making here at the Priory, and I thought I should stop in on my way to Lady Hatchard." She eyed Caroline with malevolent interest. "When that housekeeper told me a Miss *Wentworth* was in residence, I made sure he was entertaining your sister."

"Your ladyship can have no reason whatsoever to suppose so," said Caroline between slightly clenched teeth. "My sister is also in London, recovering from influenza."

"Hmmph!" ejaculated Lady Buxton. "No doubt they are together there. It is just as I feared! Your sister has trapped my nephew!"

A stifled exclamation from Mr. Lacey caught her ladyship's attention. "Who is that person?" she inquired, raising her glass to look at him.

Caroline made Mr. Lacey known to her.

"Perhaps, sir, you would be good enough to leave me alone with Miss Wentworth?" said Lady Buxton, fixing him with a quelling stare.

Bertram had not encountered such a look since he had broken a pane of the medieval stained glass adorning his family chapel, but he inquired bravely, "Caro?"

"It's all right, Bertie. Perhaps Lady Buxton has something of a particular nature to communicate to me."

"I assure you, ma'am," began Caroline when the door had closed on him, "that you are laboring under a misapprehension which is as unjust to your nephew as it is to my sister. There is absolutely no foundation for such a belief, and it will certainly do little good, and possibly great harm, for such a tale to be circulated." Caroline could only imagine what Mr. Neville's reaction would be if his aunt were to tax him with this story at such a time, so she exerted herself, with what she considered unwarranted restraint, to disabuse his odious relation of such a ridiculous notion as an attachment between a man of the world of two and thirty and a girl not halfway through her first Season.

Lady Buxton, misconstruing civility for weakness, leapt to the attack. "Miss Wentworth, I am not to be trifled with! You cannot believe *I* wish for such a connection! You may deny it, but does not your presence here confirm my suspicions? What else are you about, if my nephew has not invited you and your family?"

Caroline muttered stiffly that her presence at the Priory was entirely accidental, and unrelated in any way to a connection between the two families.

"It may be so, but I insist on being satisfied. I am well acquainted with my nephew. He needn't try to hide his teeth with me, because I know very well he has a *tendre* for your sister!"

"Did he—did he say so, ma'am?" cried Caroline, dismayed.

"Not in so many words," admitted her ladyship, furrowing her brow, "but he used the words 'fine old family' and 'unexceptionable girl,' and when I taxed him with forming an attachment he did not deny it!"

Caroline, who was fairly sure that the Nonpareil had no interest in her sister, experienced a moment of mingled delight and misery in contemplating what these disclosures might really have pointed to, and then decided, upon further reflection, that it was more probable that Mr. Neville was deliberately provoking his aunt. She said as much to her inquisitor.

"Nonsense!" said Lady Buxton, smoothing down the voluminous black folds of her skirt. "He could have no possible reason for doing so." She threw Caroline a shrewd look. "I see you know more than you are telling, miss. I'll wager you are deep within the plot as well. I tell you, it will not do. You cannot expect a Neville to ally himself with such a family, the descendants of a rake-shame like Evelyn Wentworth!"

Caroline turned quite white with fury. "Lady Buxton, you have no reason whatsoever to insult my father."

"Oh, have I not? That man *jilted* me!"

Caroline's anger gave way to astonishment. "M-my father?"

Lady Buxton's wrath was awesome to behold. "I was an heiress and a Neville as well, so you may imagine that I was prey to a good many basket scramblers. But Evelyn knew how to make himself irresistible to a green girl of tender years. I was quite taken in! My family objected, because even then Evelyn had a reputation. And then he—he married your mother!"

"B-but surely, ma'am, if your family prevented him, he could not pay his addresses to you and would be free to look elsewhere," suggested Caroline reasonably.

"What does that signify?" roared Lady Buxton in a voice

which must have penetrated to the cellars below. "I was *mortified*! And I will not countenance a connection with that man's daughter."

"I already have assured your ladyship that such a connection is very unlikely to take place," said Caroline with a sort of bitter weariness.

"And do I have your undertaking that at least on your part you will not seek to bring it about by attempting to insinuate yourself into my nephew's good graces, through pity or some such thing?"

"*Pity?*" cried Caroline, stung. "I will make no undertaking of any sort. You have insulted me and my family in every possible way. I must beg you to grant me the solitude of my room once more. Mrs. Murdstone will attend to your needs, I am sure."

"Obstinate girl! And *this* is to be my reward when I have honored you with a confidence as painful to give as it must be to receive. I give warning to you and your sister that I will stop at nothing to prevent such a match. I will not be overborne. Should my nephew undertake what I feel would be the greatest folly of his life, I should never speak to him again. And let us see what he has to say to *that*!" she concluded triumphantly, as she sailed out of the room.

Caroline, sinking down onto the bed with an oppression of spirits and a return of some of the headache that had marked her bout with the influenza, thought she might very well have been amused by the scene just concluded if her family's well-being were not so likely to be jeopardized by Lady Buxton's ire. The thought of her father in ardent pursuit of the Dragon Dowager threatened to give her a fit of the giggles, but recalling the mischief she was likely to make with Mr. Neville soon sobered her reflections. Caroline was sure the Wentworths could hardly sink any lower in the Nonpareil's estimation, but so far he had not retaliated, and she was desperate that he not be provoked to do so. Frustrated, helpless, and miserable, she gave herself over to the doubtful tonic of a good cry.

*   *   *

No one observing Mr. Neville's *point-de-vice* appearance or languid expression of unconcern would have concluded that there was anything seriously amiss with him. His neck-cloth sported the most pristine arrangement of the Neville knot, his whip hand was as notable as ever, and his demeanor fully capable of depressing the pretensions of the idly curious. Only Lord Wynchwood, who knew that he had been drinking hard and playing deep, guessed that something altogether unusual was troubling his friend. Strolling into Watier's one evening after midnight, his lordship discovered the Nonpareil rising from the faro table, the remains of the night's indulgences at his elbow. He had, to all appearances, just lost a sum of money by no means considered trifling, but the fact did not seem to disturb him unduly.

"No luck, Robert?" Lord Wynchwood asked him.

Mr. Neville looked up at him with a ghost of a smile. "No."

Something in his tone caused his friend to start. "I wish you will walk home with me, then," he said quickly. "I can offer you some rather special eyewater."

Mr. Neville looked at him with a glint in his eye that showed that his intelligence was not after all overshadowed by the prodigious quantity of brandy he had consumed. "My dear Geoffrey, you have only just come in. Besides," he added with a mocking gesture at the dead men on the table, "I am already devilish drunk."

"Walk with me, then," Lord Wynchwood urged. "I'm not in the mood for the Great Go tonight. Got a headache."

"Well, if we walk long enough, I shall doubtless have one too," said Mr. Neville. "Seriously, Geoffrey, I'm not very good company tonight."

"I'm not feeling all the thing myself," said his companion frankly. "It's this damned battle. Now that Boney's joined his Army of the North, it's like waiting for the other shoe to drop. I shouldn't wonder if it comes any day now."

"Stacey's no cloth-head, you know," said Mr. Neville with understanding. "He'll look out for himself."

"Wish you'd tell my mama that," muttered his lordship.

"She's half distracted with worry." He shook his head rue-fully. "Makes me feel quite useless."

Mr. Neville steered his friend out into Piccadilly, where the passage of carriages was at last beginning to thin out for the night. "That," he said with a touch of bitterness, "is a feeling with which I am singularly well acquainted."

Lord Wynchwood, studying the Nonpareil objectively, wondered just how foxed he really was. He walked with unexceptionable balance, and only the slightest slurring of words attended his speech. He knew that Mr. Neville could carry his liquor as well as any man alive, and was inclined to think that the real source of these melancholy spirits was not to be found in a cup. In an attempt to draw him out, he opened his inquiry with a subject which usually found favor with his friend. "How is the restoration of Wyndham Priory proceeding?" he asked amiably. "I heard you had Repton down to design the landscaping. That's quite a coup; Tavistock's supposed to be mad as fire because Repton promised to do *his* place next. How did you get him?"

"Money," said Mr. Neville shortly, nodding to three of their acquaintance who were proceeding in a determined but somewhat erratic fashion down the other side of the street.

Lord Wynchwood sighed. "Well, it helps to be a regular Midas, I suppose."

"How apt," said Mr. Neville with an unpleasant laugh. "He had a rather unfortunate effect on everything he touched."

"I shouldn't call turning things into gold *unfortunate*," commented Lord Wynchwood, thinking of his own peren-nially depleted pockets. "In fact, I—"

His lordship's feelings on this matter were never to be fully discovered, for as he and Mr. Neville neared the Opera House their conversation was interrupted by a sil-very laugh and the sight of a handsome woman, in a di-aphanous silk gown whose lines were strongly suggestive of dampened petticoats and an ostrich feather headdress large enough to support a plumassier for a month, being as-sisted into a stylish barouche. The lady, catching sight of the two gentlemen, paused briefly in her ascent, tossed a triumphant look over her shoulder, and entered the carriage.

"Good God, it's the Venus Mendicant!" cried Lord Wynchwood knowledgeably. "I hadn't heard she was back in town."

"I should imagine the arrival of the emperor flushed her out of Paris," said Mr. Neville laconically. "For all her faults she was never less than patriotic."

The gentleman handing her up into the barouche turned and saw them, nodded briefly, and climbed in after her.

"Coming down in the world," clucked Lord Wynchwood sadly. "Ridley!" He shook his head. "Didn't she used to be under *your* protection?"

"For a brief period which was nevertheless far too long for the comfort of either of us," admitted Mr. Neville.

"Still, she used to be the most fashionable of the Fashionable Impures. Shouldn't wonder at it if she's a bit of a highflier for Ridley. She'll have him rolled up within a month. Damned foolish thing to do when he's courting Julia Wentworth."

Mr. Neville stiffened slightly. "Miss *Caroline* Wentworth, surely?" he said in a tight voice.

"Oh no," replied Lord Wynchwood, happy to indulge in his favorite pastime. "The *on-dit* is that he has been most particular in his attentions to the younger sister while the elder is visiting friends in the country. I thought *you* might know something about that," he added, recollecting that at one time his friend had shown considerable interest in Miss Caroline Wentworth.

His note of inquiry met with an uncommunicative silence.

"I have heard," Lord Wynchwood continued, impelled by a concern for accuracy to amend his statement, "that Ridley did pay his addresses to Miss Wentworth, and she refused him. He made no secret of it. Came the ugly a bit at the Cocoa Club. Felt himself abused."

"I'm not surprised," said Mr. Neville succinctly.

Lord Wynchwood was startled. "There's something havey-cavey about the fellow. I can't quite like him.

Dashed ungentlemanly way to behave, if you ask me." A suspicion of the general, if not the specific, nature of his friend's problem began to occur to him. "Good God, Robert, you ain't in *love*?" he asked suddenly. "No wonder you're hipped!"

Mr. Neville gave him a twisted smile. "My grandmother has always maintained that persons in thrall to the violent emotions are excessively vulgar. I fear I'm inclined to agree with her."

"Humdudgeon!" cried his lordship. "You can't bamboozle me! There isn't a girl in London who isn't tumbling all over herself to catch you, so what's amiss?"

"I can't conceive why you would suppose so, but in any case I do not mean to put it to the test. At the risk of sounding like a dead bore, Geoffrey, I've made a complete cake of myself."

Lord Wynchwood was at some pains to prevent his jaw from dropping. *"No,"* he protested, awestruck.

"Oh yes," said Mr. Neville bitterly. "For ten years I've moved in the first circles without meeting a single female whose attractions have cost me as much as an hour's sleep. I thought—I thought I had, at last. I had always intended to fix up Wyndham Priory and turn it into something I could be proud of, instead of continuing in this ridiculous life." He gave a short laugh. "I hoped I'd found someone who wanted to share it with me. But I found I was . . . shall we say, sadly mistaken in her character. It was quite a scene. I must regret that I was not just in the humor to enjoy it as it deserved. But I fear I must disclose no more, Geoffrey, or you will think me quite as *ungentlemanly* as Lord Ridley."

Lord Wynchwood heard him out in growing wonder and confusion. He had never expected to extract such a confession from his friend, and he could not help wondering who it was who had wounded the heart of the Nonpareil so cruelly. He was inclined to revise his earlier notion that Mr. Neville had conceived a *tendre* for Miss Caroline Wentworth; what he knew of her character did not accord with such behavior. It was more likely that he had lost his head over some silly chit who had been frightened off by his practiced flirtation, or some such misunderstanding. Lord Wynchwood suddenly remembered his friend stiffening at his remark about Lord Ridley, and another idea occurred to him.

They were now almost upon his lordship's doorstep. "See here, Robert," he ventured, "you ain't been dangling after Miss *Julia* Wentworth?" He stopped and lifted the knocker. "Good evening, Brougham," he said to the porter who opened the door. "Would you ask Fielding to send up some cognac, please? Then you may go to bed."

"Do your servants always wait up for you, Geoffrey?" asked Mr. Neville curiously.

"Of course," he said, leading his guest into the library with a lit candle. "Don't yours?"

"I don't encourage anyone to sit up for me, though I own my valet insists on doing so. He lives in the greatest fear that I will try to get round him and attempt to take off my coat myself."

Lord Wynchwood was not deceived. "You didn't answer my question, Robert," he said when Fielding had left the cognac on the table.

Mr. Neville looked at him for a moment. Then he withdrew his snuffbox from his pocket, opened it, and took a delicate pinch between his finger and his thumb. "Oh, did I not?" he said. "I am quite sure I indicated I have begun to find the subject just the slightest bit tedious."

"Just as you like, Robert," said Lord Wynchwood, passing his friend a glass of cognac. "No need to cut up stiff. I daresay I have it all wrong. Your aunt's spreading it abroad, you know. And I just thought that since you had done such a particular kindness for Miss Julia Wentworth—but no, of course it was no such thing!"

Mr. Neville raised his brows. "Where *do* you get these bizarre notions, Geoffrey?" he said in mock astonishment. "The only service I have performed for the Wentworths, and I admit it was scarcely a trifling one, was to remove that disreputable pretender to porcine accomplishment from their midst. And while my aunt has admittedly conceived an idée fixe on the subject of Miss Julia Wentworth, even *she* has not accused me of anything so uncharacteristic as *kindness,*" he said bitterly.

"That's a bag of moonshine, Robert!" protested his lordship. "You're never going to deny you lent Miss Julia the Wentworth diamonds for her presentation?"

Mr. Neville, who had been somewhat aimlessly watching the amber liquid swirl about in the bottom of his glass, found his attention suddenly arrested. *"What?"*

"Well, some people would have it that the diamonds were paste," Lord Wynchwood remarked judiciously, "but Chuffy Clitheroe was at the drawing room with his sister, and he said that if *those* diamonds were paste, so were Her Majesty's."

Mr. Neville had been struck by what could only be called a bolt of illumination. He sat stunned, his glass motionless in his hand.

"Robert, you *did* lend them to her, didn't you?" persisted Lord Wynchwood, concerned.

Mr. Neville roused himself with difficulty. "Yes, yes, of course I did."

"Knew you had," said his lordship with satisfaction. "I can't think why you want to be so modest—here! Where are you going?"

"I've been the biggest fool alive, Geoffrey!" said the Nonpareil, setting his glass on the table decisively and rising to his feet. "I trust you'll forgive my bad manners, but I must see if I can rectify matters before it's too late!"

"What, *now*?" cried Lord Wynchwood.

Mr. Neville consulted his timepiece ruefully. "Well, no, perhaps, not," he admitted. "But I will leave you all the same. I must go down to Wyndham Priory tomorrow, and there are things I should attend to before I go." He was amused to discover that Lord Wynchwood was regarding him with a rather stupefied countenance. "You will oblige me, Geoffrey, if you will endeavor to put the memory of this maudlin evening completely out of your mind. I need not tell you that I am a trifle disguised." He paused. "On second thought, I will amend that. If anyone should be so vulgar as to express curiosity as to the provenance of Miss

Julia Wentworth's diamonds at her presentation, you may indeed confirm that I lent them to her. I can see it will give rise to all sorts of unfortunate tittle-tattle if you do not. No, no, don't see me out. Good-bye, dear friend. I am more indebted to you than you know!"

18

MISS WENTWORTH, who was not privy to Mr. Neville's epiphany in Lord Wynchwood's library, departed from Wyndham Priory in a state of considerable dejection. She was happy enough to remove herself from an obligation as painful to her as it must be distasteful to her host, and she was certainly traveling up to London in greater style and comfort than the journey down in Mr. Lacey's tilbury. The prolonged rest and attentive ministrations of Mrs. Lacey and Mrs. Murdoch, however, had done more to restore her body than her spirits, and she could not help feeling more acutely than ever the pain of parting from her childhood home. She could not imagine any circumstances in which she would ever be welcome there again, and so, when she bade farewell to her dear Murdy at the Priory's gate, it was in the expectation of seeing her seldom in future, and then only in some distant location unfamiliar to both. Ahead of her lay her mother's prostration, Julia in the mops, and the bleakness of Bath and Aunt Needham.

Caroline had always despised foolish, tearful creatures, and she soon pulled herself up short. Her bout with influenza might have left her thin, pale, and heavy-eyed, but she would not succumb to lassitude as well! She determined to banish from her mind the somewhat melancholy nature of her past, present, and future, and direct her thoughts instead to the vexing problem of what she was to say to Julia about Lord Ridley. The issue called for the highest degree of tact and delicacy, and in attempting to form a satisfactory solution to such a tangled puzzle, she was able to occupy herself for the remainder of her journey up to London.

Julia, however, was in no mood for tact or delicacy. "Oh, Caro!" she cried when she had followed her sister up to her room after a scarcely decent interval to allow her to refresh herself after the rigors of the road, "*what* have you been saying to Mama about Lord Ridley?"

Caroline looked assessingly at her younger sister. Her illness had thinned and whitened her face a little, so that her eyes were almost too large for her delicate face, and she looked more sylphlike than ever. The result was far from displeasing. Caroline thought with a pang of the rather hagged vision her mirror cast back at *her*, and indulged in a little sigh of regret.

"Caro!" Julia insisted, recalling her. "It must have been something quite horrid, because Mama has said that for the present he must not call. And we are to go to Bath at once! Tomorrow or the next day! Even before the house is closed up!"

Caroline cleared her throat. "Perhaps that's for the best."

"Oh, how can you say so? You know it will be the most dismal thing in the world, and we shan't see any of our friends!"

Caroline looked at her sister in wonder. "Julia, you do realize that Mr. Neville caught me trying to return the diamonds? I shouldn't be at all surprised if the half of London who didn't see you wearing the necklace at your presentation doesn't think that *I'm* a jewel thief! And not only that, but it cannot be long before Lady Buxton hears something, and she will stop at nothing to use it against us. We're dished."

Julia looked away. "Well, but Mr. Neville hasn't said anything, has he? Perhaps he won't."

Caroline privately thought this was too much to hope for, but was willing to indulge her sister's optimism. "Perhaps not," she said gently. "But there will be rumors, and in a very little time we will begin to see a decline in the civilities paid to us. Mama knows this to be true. Do you want to stay here in London and watch your suitors cut your acquaintance? I'm sure I do not!"

"Lord Ridley would not care!" protested Julia mulishly, flinging herself down onto the settee. "He loves me!"

"Now don't fly up into the boughs, my love," Caroline said in a steady voice, "but doesn't it seem a trifle odd to you that only three weeks ago he was proposing to *me*?"

"Well, but he *explained* that," said Julia radiantly. "Oh, Caro, I don't mean to hurt you, but since you've brought it up, he only paid his addresses because he'd gone so far he couldn't withdraw. Because of the way he once felt about you, you see. But as soon as he met me again he discovered he had mistaken his feelings. But he *couldn't* back out of it then."

"And did he also tell you that he threatened to make me sorry, when I refused him?" asked Caroline, hanging on to her temper.

Julia's face darkened. "What nonsense! Bertie told me something of the sort but I didn't believe him. As if he would pay his addresses to me just to spite *you*. I expect you misunderstood him, or some such thing."

"I did not misunderstand him, Julia," said Caroline quietly. "He threatened me. He was . . . not a gentleman. Whatever you do you must not tell him the truth about the Wentworth diamonds. He will use it against us!"

"I never head such rubbish!" cried Julia angrily. "I must say I did not expect this of you, Caroline. You are not content with rejecting him yourself; no one else must have him either. And now you've won Mama to your side as well! Why must you be so hateful?"

"Julia—" Caroline began in an anguished voice.

Her sister clapped her hands over her ears. "I won't listen to any more! I won't!" she said tearfully. "You and Bertie and Mama may say what you like but you won't stop me from seeing him. And I will never forgive you for this, Caro, never!" She strode angrily to the door and jerked it open. "And you needn't think I have any intention of dwindling into an *ape-leader* in Bath, either!" she cried and slammed it behind her.

Mr. Lacey had been engaged to dine, and Caroline could not but think it would have been far better if he had cried off. In an atmosphere so charged with tension, she would ordinarily have been grateful for his easy presence, but she feared that under the circumstances he would only act as a goad to Julia's irritation. Lady Wentworth, who was nursing a morbid vision of her future as a social pariah, could scarcely be counted upon to rouse herself to make the evening a success. Still, when Mr. Lacey was announced and shown up to the saloon, she was surprised to see him looking quite pale, and unusually solemn.

"Why, Bertie, what is it?" she asked at once.

Mr. Lacey swallowed visibly. "Rumors," he said after a pause.

Caroline and Lady Wentworth exchanged stricken looks. Julia stared fixedly at the carpet.

Mr. Lacey cleared his throat, rather loudly in the sudden silence. "It's war," he said at last, "and we may have lost it."

Caroline would later remember with shame that her first reaction to this news was to let out her breath in relief. "Oh, Bertie," she said, recovering, "that's terrible! What have you heard?"

"It's started," Mr. Lacey replied gloomily. "Boney's cut up the Prussians under Blucher. Refugees pouring into Antwerp and Ghent."

"And Wellington?" Caroline asked, distressed.

Mr. Lacey's shrug was eloquent of ignorance rather than disrespect. "Fallen back, or so they say. Somewhere just outside of Brussels."

"Is it in the newspapers?"

"Not yet," admitted Mr. Lacey.

"Then it's too early to know anything for sure," she suggested firmly. "We'll just have to wait and see."

"Mama," said Julia in a tone whose sweetness might have aroused suspicion in a more powerful mind than Lady Wentworth's, "this is *dreadful* news. Surely we must delay our departure to Bath until the outcome is decided one way or the other. It would be positively unpatriotic to leave now!"

"Dearest," said Lady Wentworth in tones of pained reproof, "how can you suggest such a thing? London will be *filled* with quite vulgar demonstrations, whatever the outcome. I assure you that no time could be more propitious for our departure, when people's minds will be occupied with other things!"

"But, Mama—"

"My mind is quite made up, my love," said her ladyship placidly.

The effect of this conversation on Miss Julia Wentworth's disposition was so far from happy as to cast a pall over the rest of the evening. It would not, in any case, have been a lively gathering, as all of the participants harbored their own reasons for lack of cheer, and the cataclysmic events of the outside world provided the topic of most of the dinner table's desultory conversation. Rumors, however, were a poor basis for an exchange of information and inquiry, and very soon even this subject was exhausted. The last part of the meal, which Caroline believed must rival the most tedious punishments of purgatory, was a hedgehog made with cream, eggs, sugar, orange water, and canary, molded and stuck with almond quills. Caroline pushed it feebly around her plate, and it glared at her with malevolent currant eyes.

Caroline passed a restless night, dreaming of slamming doors and whispered voices in the corridor. Occasionally she awoke to the vague feeling that something was amiss, but the disturbing element eluded her until she realized that the streets were unnaturally quiet. It's the battle, she told herself, thinking of all the people throughout the country who must be waiting for news of sons, brothers, husbands. In the small hours of the morning, a nightmare-ridden sleep overcame her at last, and when her maid drew back the curtains and she awoke, she felt more tired and less refreshed than when she had taken to her bed.

Julia did not come down for breakfast, but as Caroline had very little appetite for her toast and eggs herself she could not be surprised. There was a great deal to do; the servants would close up the house after their departure, but the personal effects they would require in Bath must be packed now. The earliest hours of the morning had already passed off when Lady Wentworth entered her bedroom, dragging a tearful, and obviously frightened Betty.

Caroline had seen her mother on the point of swooning, in the throes of a spasm, and rendered nearly insensible by any of a host of the maladies that prey on those with exquisite sensibility, but she had never seen her in such real distress. Anger and shock made her nearly speechless, but her pallor and the death-grip she had on the hapless maid filled Caroline with immediate apprehension. "Good God, ma'am, what is it?" she cried, dropping the spencer she had been folding.

The terrified girl, eyes almost starting out of her head with fear, began to gabble that she hadn't meant to do it, and in any case Miss Julia had made her *promise,* and how could she have known what she had in mind?

Caroline stared at the maid in bewilderment. Her mother released her hold and the girl sank to the floor, sobbing. "This ungrateful wretch carried a message last night, from Julia to Lord Ridley," said Lady Wentworth in a hoarse voice. "And this morning Julia is missing, along with her portmanteau, some of her clothing, her brushes, and tooth powder!" she added in awful accents.

The implication of this dreadful news was not lost on Betty, who, her teeth chattering, began to gasp out assurances that nothing could exceed her devotion to her ladyship and the Misses Wentworth, and that if she had known Miss Julia meant to elope she would have died before she'd have carried any messages to his lordship. "Only she was that sad, you see," said the maid tearfully, "on account of leaving London and maybe never seeing Lord Ridley again. She said she only wanted to say good-bye to him. But I never knew more than that, ma'am, I swear it! She made me *promise* not to tell. But when her ladyship asked me where Miss Julia was," she said to Caroline by way of explanation, "I had to tell what I knew, didn't I?"

Caroline, hearing herself addressed, made a resolute effort to pull herself together. Shock had held her immobile for what seemed like an eternity, and she felt quite as unequal to dealing with the situation as her mother, who had, after her initial blaze of rage, sunk into an armchair in pathetic resignation to her unspeakable doom. Still, if any attempt were to be made to salvage the situation, it would be necessary to rely on Betty's discretion, and in that case the sooner she was soothed out of her hysterics the better.

"Stop crying," she said firmly, handing the girl one of her own handkerchiefs. "Of course it was your duty to inform her ladyship of what has occurred. It's a pity you didn't recollect it earlier, but I am persuaded you never meant to do anything that would bring harm to Miss Julia. We know nothing for certain yet, but if you have assisted her in an elopement you will have done her a very ill turn. What happens next will depend in part on your conduct now."

Betty observed contritely that she would do anything Miss Wentworth required, up to and including offering herself as a burnt sacrifice, a fodder for wild beasts, and a candidate for the hangman's noose if it would help set matters to rights.

Caroline, who had begun to imagine how easily the hapless maid had succumbed to her sister's romantic schemes, said more sympathetically, "Well, I shouldn't think any of that will be necessary. We must see what is to be done, and perhaps no one need know what we fear has taken place today. In any case you will not speak of this to *anyone*. Do you understand me? Now go downstairs and tell Fenwick I wish to have a hackney brought round as soon as may be. At once, if you please!"

"To think of having a daughter married over the anvil," moaned Lady Wentworth piteously when Betty had gone. "The scandal! How could she do it?"

Caroline, who was assailed by guilt for not having succeeded in making the true nature of Lord Ridley's character plain to her sister, had no answer for this. Still less did she feel able to confide to her mother her suspicions that if

Julia and Ridley were in fact en route to Gretna Green they might count themselves relatively fortunate. She feared that his lordship might harbor less honorable intentions toward her sister, but her mother was already prostrate with anxiety and there was little point in alarming her further until the ineffable worst was known. She began to gather up her pelisse and her gloves, and tied her bonnet strings under her chin.

Lady Wentworth roused herself from her misery enough to inquire where she thought she was going.

"I fear you won't like it, Mama, but I am going round to see Bertie. He can help me make inquiries on the Great North Road, and then we will see what is to be done. Perhaps we may even overtake them, and I can bring her back. I don't count on it, but it might be possible. I'm sorry," she finished lamely, "but I don't see what else I can do."

"But you can't go careering off through the countryside with Bertram Lacey," gasped her mother in horror. "It isn't proper! Let him go by himself!"

"Someone must be there to take care of Julia," said Caroline firmly. "Bertie can't do it by himself. If—if we should need you to—to lend respectability, will you come if I send for you, ma'am? I don't like to ask it but—"

"Of course I shall," replied her mother with a sudden resolve which took Caroline aback. "I'm sorry to be so useless. Of course you must do as you think best; it is far too late to worry about anything else. Please thank Bertram for me."

Caroline assured her that she would, and prepared to hurry downstairs to the waiting hackney. "Caro!" cried her mother, calling her back.

"Ma'am?"

"I—I must apologize before you go," Lady Wentworth said in a faltering voice. "When I think how I urged you to accept Ridley, against your wishes! Only I didn't know he would be capable of *this*! Can you ever forgive me?"

Caroline knelt beside her mother's slumped form. "Oh, dearest ma'am, I beg you won't consider it! I am as much at fault as anyone! If I had made his character known to

Julia earlier this would never have happened. But it is too late now to repine. I had much better go after her at once!"

"Caroline," said her mother in such a small voice that Caroline had to strain to hear, "if . . . if you should find that they do not intend . . . they have not . . ." Lady Wentworth raised her eyes from her lap. "I beg you will bring her home at all events."

"Oh yes, Mama!" cried Caroline, embracing her quickly. "I must go!"

19

THE HACKNEY was a large and run-down vehicle, with a slightly listing body and upholstery redolent of antiquity and a variety of encounters with passengers of less than exalted ton. It was scarcely the carriage of choice for persons aspiring to Fashion, but it was the best Fenwick could do on short notice and in the face of an alacrity a chastened Betty had urged upon him. Whatever the redoubtable butler thought of these proceedings he kept to himself, for which Caroline bestowed on him a grateful smile. She might have known she could rely on his discretion.

The jarvey appeared to be of the same vintage as the hackney, and his only reply to her earnest request that the sluggish pace of the horses might be stepped up a bit in order to reach Mr. Lacey's before nightfall was an unencouraging grunt. The streets were rather empty and quiet, but Caroline found the slow clop-clopping of the horses' hooves frustrating, and several times considered descending from the coach and attempting to hire another. She was conscious that every passing minute put her farther behind Lord Ridley and Julia, and soon all hope of overtaking them must be irreparably lost. She slogged along, tormented by apprehension and doubt, until the hackney drove beside Green Park, and prepared to turn down St. James's.

An unmistakable roar met her ears, one growing in intensity every moment. "Oh stop!" she ordered the jarvey as the coach swung into the street. Too late, the driver tried to pull up the team. A tide of humanity was sweeping down on them, blocking their path. The shouts were deafening. The horses shied, and the jarvey, cursing, sprang to their heads.

Caroline, looking out, saw gentlemen leave their clubs and come into the street, pounding each other on the backs and exclaiming. "Oh, what is it?" she called to a young urchin in a cap as he swept by the carriage.

He flashed her a gap-tooth grin. "Victory, ma'am! Old Boney's beat to flinders!"

"Thank God," said Caroline fervently, enjoying a moment of exultation. The celebrations in the street had taken on a wilder character, and the coach was effectively blocked on all sides by dancing, huzzaing crowds. Some of the revelers had broken out the champagne, and one of these leered into the window at her. Startled, Caroline tried to get the jarvey's attention, and soon discovered that he had disappeared.

The irritating effect of this news on Caroline's peace of mind can scarcely be underrated. Her plans to rescue her sister were in ruins, and she was more than likely to need rescuing herself. St. James's Street was not the proper locale for unescorted females, and the unwelcome attentions she was increasingly receiving from slightly inebriated gentlemen confirmed her impression that a hasty departure was devoutly to be desired. Even if the driver had not deserted her, however, it would have been impossible to move the hackney more than a few feet, much less turn it around. Seething with frustration, she had just determined to risk descending into the unruly crowd and make her way through the streets on foot when a large, brutish face appeared at the hackney window. Its possessor, appearing to like what he saw, reached in to open the door and admit himself to the coach's interior. Caroline abandoned any attempt at civility and let out a scream. The face, momentarily shaken, held an expression that was no less determined than it was puzzled. Caroline screamed again, a heavy hand fell upon the face's shoulder, and he disappeared from view with a muffled grunt and a thud. In a moment the hackney door opened and a languid voice said, "May I be of assistance, Miss Wentworth?"

Caroline, finding herself looking into Mr. Neville's penetrating dark eyes, burst into tears.

He climbed in at once and took her hands between his. "He didn't hurt you?" he asked after a moment.

Caroline shook her head. "N-no. He frightened me, that's all. Thank you! He's not—he's not *dead*?"

Mr. Neville smiled grimly. "Not even half. Though I daresay he'll have a sore head tomorrow and more besides. Something to remember the victory by!"

"It's quite true, then?" Caroline asked. "Wellington's won?"

"Oh yes. A very large battle, just outside Brussels. It will be a day or two yet before they begin to count the costs."

"The c-costs?"

"It lasted twelve hours, Miss Wentworth. The losses must have been enormous." He saw that she was still dazed, and her hands in his were cold. He released them, and said gently, "You know, I can't but feel that we will both be a great deal more comfortable if you allow me to lead you out of here. There is something I particularly wish to say to you, but I scarcely think this is the time or the place."

Caroline sat up with a start. "Oh, how *could* I be such a goose? We must go at once! Would you be so good as to escort me to Mr. Lacey's residence? I only hope it is not too late!" She stopped, and a wave of embarrassment washed over her. She had forgotten, in the turmoil of events, about her last meeting with Mr. Neville, but now a painful consciousness brought her up short. "That is . . . I . . ."

"With the greatest of pleasure," said Mr. Neville with an odd smile, helping her down from the carriage, "if that is what you wish. But may I venture to suggest that you accept *my* services instead. My curricle and four are waiting nearby."

Caroline was forced by circumstances to take his arm as he pulled her along through the crowd, but she could not look into his face. "You could not wish . . . you do not know . . ."

"No, I don't *know*," he said judiciously in a low tone, "but I suspect you are attempting to rescue your sister from an elopement. Is it Ridley?"

Caroline's mouth fell open. "How did you guess?"

"I am no mind reader, Miss Wentworth," said Mr. Neville, bearing her into a quiet side street at the end of which stood his curricle and four, and his very fidgety groom, "but when I called at Mount Street your butler informed me that your mama was quite unwell, and that you had departed rather hastily in a hackney whose nature seemed to outrage his sensibilities in the extreme. It wasn't too difficult to guess what the matter might be, nor to track you here. As to the identity of your sister's suitor, I am indebted to Lord Wynchwood for a scrap of information he let fall. I hope it does not distress you, but I assure you you may rely upon my saying nothing." He did not add that the redoubtable Fenwick had let rather more drop than was strictly proper to one in his position, and had urged Mr. Neville to render whatever assistance he could to the valiant Miss Wentworth.

Caroline felt as if her mind were not quite awake. "You c-called?" she stammered, confused.

"Did I not tell you I had something I particularly want to discuss with you?" he suggested helpfully. "Here, Fawkes, I won't need you anymore today," he said to the astonished groom. "You may walk home, or join the celebrations, whichever you wish."

Fawkes, who had hitherto had little reason to regard his master as an eccentric, looked considerably disappointed, but accepted with a degree of composure the handsome inducement which accompanied his dismissal.

"Now then," said Mr. Neville when he had assisted Caroline up into the curricle, "what is it to be? Shall I take you to Mr. Lacey? I should perhaps mention that I am prepared to drive you to Finchley or perhaps Barnet to make inquiries, but if we should find no trace of them there I'm very much afraid further pursuit will be useless!"

Caroline found that, despite everything that had passed between them, her instincts still urged her to trust him. "Oh, if you will be so good as to conduct me there, it would be the greatest kindness! And I'm sure we will get there much faster than Bertie could!" she added, admiring the fine set of matched grays pulling the curricle.

Mr. Neville, apparently occupied with the engrossing task of maneuvering his team at a rather clipping speed through the crowded streets of London, said little until they departed Moorgate, and Caroline was left to her own thoughts. She was quite unnerved by Mr. Neville's kindness and forbearance, and cudgeled her brain to think of some way to apologize to him without revealing the truth about the diamonds. Jostling along with this impossible conundrum was her very real fear that it might be—indeed it must be—too late to intercept Julia and Ridley, even assuming they had undertaken the journey to Gretna Green. She knew that her sister's embarrassment and humiliation over the diamonds had as much to do with her flight as her impulsive attachment to the viscount, and she lamented, for perhaps the thousandth time, the bitter stroke of fate which had brought Mr. Neville into her presence at the precise moment of her attempt to dispose of the necklace.

Mr. Neville, who had been studying her profile in silence for some time, noticed her anguished expression. "You can always make the best of it, you know," he said thoughtfully. "I don't deny that to be married in such a way is not quite what one would wish, but if they contrive to live quietly for a time the scandal will soon die down. They certainly won't be the first!"

Caroline shook her head in misery. "You don't understand!"

"I see," he said, a grim look settling over his face. "Did he mean as much to you as that?" Caroline started and colored up, and he added, "Forgive me! I had no right to ask you such a question."

"Oh, *no!*" Caroline cried in horror. "Did you think I—it's no such thing! I'd as soon be married to—to a viper! Julia doesn't know . . . I very much fear that his character is such that his intentions toward her may not be honorable. She has no father, and no fortune, nothing that would induce him to offer for her! And she has thrown herself on his protection without realizing that he is seriously flawed. She will be ruined whether she marries him or not!"

Mr. Neville handed her a handkerchief to dry her dampened cheeks. "I'm quite sure you're mistaken. Ridley would not be so lost to worldly considerations as to dishonor a girl of birth and breeding," he said in a voice of quiet authority. "You are scarcely without connections, Miss Wentworth. No respectable house in London would receive him if he were to do such a thing."

An odd gleam in his eye escaped Caroline's attention, as she was busy blowing her nose. "I hope you may be right," she said with a watery smile. "Indeed, when you put it like that I'm sure you must be."

Mr. Neville, his gaze focused down the road along which he was fairly springing his horses, said in a distant voice quite unlike his own, "If I'm not deceived, Miss Wentworth, this is not the first time you have undertaken to rescue your sister from a bumblebath of her own making!"

Caroline's eyes flew to his face. What she saw there, while not precisely *reassuring,* made her gasp. "You *know*?"

"Let us say that until very lately I have been laboring under a grave misapprehension," he said grimly. "Accept my apologies, Miss Wentworth. I wish I had cut out my tongue before I suggested such a dreadful thing when I found you with the diamonds."

"Well, you can scarcely be blamed for thinking I was trying to steal them," Caroline said dispassionately. "And I must say it was very handsome of you not to spread the tale all over town. It seems to me that you have nothing whatever to apologize for. Oh, if you only knew what a relief this is!" she cried. "When I have been *longing* to explain it to you, but I couldn't think how!"

Nothing but the unassailable inadvisability of dropping the reins at that particular moment kept him from taking her in his arms and ruthlessly kissing her, but he said warmly, "My dearest pea-goose! Could you not have trusted me?"

"Well," she said meditatively, "I did consider it, but since you have just apologized for not trusting *me* I feel sure you will understand. You might have ruined Julia. You mustn't think the worst of her; when she found the diamonds she didn't know you had bought them. She thought they must have been left at the Priory by mistake, and she had some vague notion of returning them after her presentation. Of course it was very wrong of her but . . . Oh!" she cried as an unpleasant notion occurred to her. "However did you find out the truth?"

"Lord Wynchwood heard that she was wearing the necklace at Court. It wasn't difficult to puzzle out the rest."

"Then it must be all over town," said Caroline sadly. "Julia's ruined in any event."

"Not at all. If I know Wynchwood, at this very moment he's spreading the news that it was I who lent the diamonds to your sister for her presentation."

"Why should he do that?" asked Caroline, looking up at him.

"Because I told him I had," he said simply.

Caroline with difficulty suppressed a desire to snatch up his hand and kiss it. "Oh, how kind! How good you are! We can never thank you enough. My mama—Julia—"

"I have told you often enough I don't want your gratitude," said Mr. Neville with a slight smile, "but if you will persist in ignoring my wishes, let it be for yourself alone. Whatever I might have done for your sister, I did for your sake."

Caroline, cast into an agreeable confusion, looked down at her lap.

"Do you know why I bought Wyndham Priory?" he asked after a short pause. He took her silence for encouragement, and continued, "My grandfather brought me down in your grandfather's day. I was just a boy, and I believe your father was away at school. I thought I had never seen such a beautiful place. Even then, it was looking a trifle the worse for wear, but you could see what it had been. I promised myself my home would be like that someday." He sighed. "My grandmama left me an immense fortune, which I came into far too early. I've led an indolent, pointless life, but until I learned that the Priory was for sale I never had the slightest inclination to change it."

"I thought you bought it because you were *bored*," Caroline protested involuntarily.

"And so I was," agreed Mr. Neville equably. "Bored with what my life has been up till now. I want a real home, and someone to share it. Miss Wentworth, will you do me the honor—"

"Oh, *stop*!" cried Caroline in sudden anguish. "That's Ridley's carriage, and it's *overturned*!"

20

MR. NEVILLE, pulling up his team, alighted at once to inspect the traveling carriage lying on its side next to the road, and discovered that it did indeed bear the viscount's coat of arms. The horses had already been cut from the traces and removed, and there was no sign of the occupants or the groom. Rapid inquiries of the assembled persons who, prior to his arrival, had apparently been attempting to carry away any parts of the vehicle not specifically bolted down, elicited the information that the passengers had suffered some (possibly grave) injuries, and had been conducted to a nearby inn. He returned to the curricle with such a drawn look that Caroline had no need to ask what he had discovered. She clutched at her shawl, and sat tight-lipped while the team, the sweetest of sweet-goers, fairly flew over the ground.

The inn, an establishment of unprepossessing appearance and modest hopes, came into view at last, and Mr. Neville, handing off the reins to an astonished stable boy, led Caroline into the front door without the ceremonious overtures necessary to soothe the feathers of suspicious landladies. No such person being in attendance, however, a chambermaid directed them to a private parlor, which, without bothering to knock, they entered without further ado.

Julia was sitting on a rather rustic sofa, her dress disheveled, and a streak of dirt marring the perfection of her unblemished face. A half-empty glass of burgundy sat on the table in front of her, and she looked as if she had been crying. "Caro!" she cried, getting to her feet.

Caroline, relieved to see that she was welcomed joyfully,

enfolded her in her arms. "Are you all right?" she asked, inspecting her. "Where's Lord Ridley?"

Julia's face darkened. "Upstairs. The doctor's with him. Oh Caro, it was so *awful*!"

"Hush, love. I'm sure he will be all right. It he—is he very badly injured?"

"I'm sure I don't know," said Julia stiffly. "I am only waiting for the doctor to tell me he is not dead, and then I hope I may never see him again!"

Caroline exchanged glances with Mr. Neville over her sister's head, an act which caused Julia to take note of the Nonpareil's presence for the first time. The effect was remarkable. She put a hand to her tumbled curls, and then preened coquettishly. "Oh, sir, I didn't see you," she said with a dazzling smile. "Did you come to rescue me?"

"No, you abominable brat, I did not. I came to bear your sister company, but as long as I'm here I may as well try to disentangle you from the dreadful coil you've landed in. Now out with it girl, what happened?"

Julia, submitting to the voice of authority, said sulkily, "I *tried* to get him to take me home, but he wouldn't. I—I couldn't go through with it. Not when I saw the dreadful way the ostler looked at us when we stopped to change the horses, as if he *knew*. . . . Oh, Caro, I wanted to run away from—from everything, but I *couldn't*. I couldn't do it to Mama. And I told Ridley, and he was *horrid*. He said I'd led him on, just like you. He said if I didn't marry him he'd tell—he'd tell—" She stopped, and looked at Mr. Neville in wide-eyed horror.

Caroline, interpreting this look correctly, said soothingly, "About the diamonds. It's all right, Mr. Neville knows everything."

"Does he?" asked Julia wonderingly. "You warned me not to tell Ridley, Caro, but I never thought—" She broke off, choking back a sob.

"Of course you didn't. What happened then?"

"He wouldn't stop the carriage, so I jumped out."

"Good God," said Mr. Neville.

"Julia, you might have been killed!" cried Caroline.

"Well, I must say I didn't think it would be going quite, so fast, but I landed on some grass, you see. Only it frightened the horses, and they reared up and hit something in the road, and the next thing I knew the carriage had overturned. So it's a good thing I wasn't in it," she said decisively.

"Good God," said Mr. Neville again.

A knock, not at all timid, sounded at the parlor door, and Julia shrank behind her sister. "It's the landlady," she said in a terrified whisper. "She's been nosing out a scandal since we arrived, and she is most *odiously* top-lofty. I couldn't think what to say to her!"

This formidable personage, a Mrs. Chickley by name, did enter the room with a rather militant gleam in her eye and a determination to get to the bottom of matters which had contributed to the death of one husband and the disquietude of two. Such intentions were checked, however, by the discovery that the disheveled young miss, whom she firmly suspected of being involved in some sort of havey-cavey elopement, had been joined by two members of the Quality. One of them, a gentleman dressed with an elegance not usually seen in the parlors of insignificant inns along the Great North Road, was regarding her in such a quelling fashion through his quizzing glass that she was compelled to abandon her martial attitude and drop him an unwilling curtsy, an event that would have greatly heartened Mr. Chickley, had he been privileged to witness it. "Dr. Ross," she announced, in accents which managed to convey the information that this hapless individual did not enjoy her wholehearted approval.

Dr. Ross, a benign, intelligent-looking man of middle years, was less discomposed than Mrs. Chickley at finding the company increased. "How do you do?" he asked mildly. "I take it you are friends of his lordship and Miss Wentworth?"

Caroline did not betray by any alteration of manner her dismay at learning that Julia had not thought to supply Mrs. Chickley with a false name. "I am Miss Wentworth's sister," she said in a gentle voice, "and this is Mr. Neville. We are indeed friends of Lord Ridley and are grateful to you for attending him. And to you, ma'am," she said to the landlady in a slightly cooler tone. "I fear you are being put to a great deal of trouble. But pray tell us how his lordship is getting on!"

"Oh, it's not as bad as I feared! He's broken his arm and collarbone, and received a thumping knock on the head, but with rest and healing he should be all right in time. Not that he isn't badly wracked up, and in pain. And I wouldn't advise you to move him, not for some days yet, if you were planning to carry him away with you."

Julia and Caroline looked at each other in dismay. "Lord Ridley was kind enough," said Mr. Neville, helping himself to a pinch of snuff with an elegant deliberation that seemed to fascinate the landlady, "to offer to escort Miss Julia Wentworth to my family's estate at Chartleigh. As her sister and I are on our way there now, we will be able to conduct her there ourselves. His lordship, alas, had business in the north and could not make up one of the party. He will no doubt wish to continue there as soon as he is able. I should like to arrange for his comfort here, however, if I may." He bowed gracefully to Mrs. Chickley. "I wonder if you would be so good as to let the unfortunate viscount lodge with you a bit longer? Naturally," he said, extracting some notes from his pocket, "I would expect to compensate you for your trouble."

The mention of Chartleigh exercised quite as powerful an effect on Mrs. Chickley as the spires of Byzantium on some befuddled Crusader. The mantle of protection Mr. Neville had thrown over the young lady and gentleman involved cast a new light on previously suspicious circumstances, and she could only stammer that it was no trouble at all, and, tucking the notes into her ample bosom, declare that her house would be quite honored to house his lordship as long as he cared to stay.

"Good, that's settled then," said Dr. Ross with an amused expression. "I'll call in a few days to make sure he's getting along all right, and that it's safe for him to travel. Mrs. Chickley knows where to reach me if I'm needed. If you want to go up to him now, by all means do so, but don't stay too long. He needs his rest." The doctor had his own theory about why such an invitation should cause the Misses Wentworth to regard him with consternation, but he held his peace. "Right, I'll be off then," he said pleasantly. "Mrs. Chickley, a word with you about what sort of care our patient needs!"

When the door had closed on them, Julia's expression, which had been one of awed admiration for Mr. Neville's fabrications, changed to one of dismay. "Oh, *must* I go up and see him?"

"Well," said Mr. Neville meditatively, "it will look very odd if you don't."

Caroline, who was scarcely less eager for this confrontation than her sister, said bravely, "Mr. Neville's right, Julia. We must try and scotch the scandal, if we can."

"All right," agreed Julia reluctantly, "but if he says anything *horrid* I shall run out."

"If you run out, you silly chit, I will leave you here to abide by the consequences," replied Mr. Neville calmly. "I think, however, that you may safely leave this matter to me."

"I am *not* a silly chit," said Julia, stiffening her spine.

"Good," replied the Nonpareil, fortifying himself with another pinch of snuff.

"Thank you," said Caroline warmly, laying a tentative hand on his arm.

He patted it reassuringly and conducted them upstairs to the viscount's room.

Despite the rather uncharitable sentiments Caroline was harboring toward his lordship, she was forced to admit that he really was a pathetic sight, and could not help allowing a trickle of compassion to seep into her feelings for him. His face was puffy and bruised, and one eye had swelled half shut. His bandaged arm hung awkwardly at his side, and he looked to be in a considerable amount of pain.

His expression, when he saw them, was one of surprise, followed by deep dejection. "Come to gloat?" he asked bitterly, looking at Caroline.

"Don't be a dead bore, Ridley," said Mr. Neville calmly,

brushing an imperceptible piece of lint off the sleeve of his coat. "We've come to ascertain for ourselves the state of your health, and to discover whether there is anything we can do for you."

"Much you care," muttered his lordship darkly.

"Well, perhaps you are right," admitted Mr. Neville complacently, "but I should very much like to put a period to any unfortunate gossip this ridiculous escapade might give rise to, and to that end I am prepared to go to some lengths to establish that we are all on amicable terms. I have given the landlady a deposit toward your lodging, and I will be happy to send for your valet, if you have not already done so."

"Damn it, I don't *want* your help," cried Lord Ridley furiously. "And you may do your possible to scotch the scandal, but you must be bacon-brained if you expect me to protect either one of these she-devils. I don't know what your part in this is, Neville, but if you think I am going to keep quiet about the diamonds Julia stole from you, you are a great deal more caper-witted than you look!"

"Charles!" cried Caroline in anguish.

"I should not do that if I were you," said Mr. Neville in a quiet voice that nonetheless sent shivers up the spines of his audience. "I think you will find that Society will believe that I lent the jewels to Miss Wentworth for her presentation, and your credit is not sufficient to convince them otherwise."

"And why should you do that?" his lordship asked with a sneer. His eyes traveled to Caroline's face. "Well, one explanation does present itself. What is the most notable flirt in London doing escorting Miss Caroline Wentworth, *unaccompanied*, along the Great North Road? I wonder if *your* credit is sufficient to carry that off, my dear Caro!"

"I feel I should make it known to you," said Mr. Neville in a very controlled voice, "that Miss Caroline Wentworth and I are betrothed, and that—"

"Gammon!" scoffed his lordship, noting, even through his clouded vision, Caroline's astonished expression.

"I do assure you," said Mr. Neville with a dangerous

calm that penetrated even the viscount's fevered rage. "And if I should discover that you are spreading any sort of rumor at all about my affianced wife, her sister, or any member of her family, I shall take the greatest pleasure in calling you to account. In fact," he said judiciously," it is only your rather pitiful condition that prevents me from arranging a meeting with you now."

The viscount, rendered speechless at last, glared at him balefully.

"We are going," said Mr. Neville in the same deliberate tone, "to continue on to Chartleigh, where we will have a family party to celebrate Miss Wentworth's and my betrothal. I have told the landlady that you were escorting Miss Julia Wentworth there on your way north on business. I should not advise you to attempt to contradict this story; I intend to send a report to that effect to the *Gazette*. In fact, while I should not presume to dictate what you must do, I think it would answer very well if you were to remove yourself from London Society for a time—say, for a year or two. I feel quite sure you will perceive the advantage of such a plan." He turned to Julia. "Miss Wentworth, have you anything to say to Lord Ridley before we leave?"

Julia shook her head, reconsidered, and said shakily. "Only that—in spite of everything—I'm sorry."

Caroline remained silent, knowing that her pity would be harder for him to bear than her contempt.

"Oh, *famous!*" cried Julia when they were descending the stairs again. "What a splendid Banbury tale! Caro," she added, noting that her sister looked quite uncomfortable, "you're not going to turn *missish*? Mr. Neville has rescued us completely. Poor Ridley was at a standstill. I must say it was a stroke of genius to say you were engaged to Caro, because it makes everything all right! Although I don't quite see," she said thoughtfully, "how it is all to work out in the end. And *are* we to go up to Chartleigh? I should like it above all things. I daresay," she said to her sister kindly, "that it will be a trifle awkward for you to cry off from the 'engagement,' but I can't think of any story that would have answered half so well."

Caroline was in an agony of mortification but was powerless to silence her voluble sister. Mr. Neville, scarcely less conscious but considerably more amused, said equably, "Thank you. I'm quite overcome. But—"

Mr. Neville's observations on such an interesting topic were forcibly postponed by the sound of a slamming door and the progress of heavy footfalls across the hall and up the stairs. The newest arrival, demonstrably out of breath, nearly collided with them where they stood on the landing.

"I say, Julia," said Mr. Bertram Lacey in a voice of considerable relief, "are you all right?"

Miss Wentworth's reply to this was to launch herself into his arms with a glad cry. "Oh, Bertie! I *knew* you'd come!"

21

"STEADY ON, OLD GIRL," said Mr. Lacey, patting her absently on the back as she clung determinedly to the lapels of his coat. "No need to cry. Only me."

"Bertie!" exclaimed Caroline in amazement. "How in the world did you know we were here?"

"Didn't," said Mr. Lacey, "that is, not all of you. Julia left me a note. Asked me to inform her ladyship. Hen-witted! Didn't like it above half, so thought I'd come after her myself. Would have been here sooner but I got caught in the victory celebrations."

"Julia, you *never* left Bertie a note instead of poor Mama. What an infamous thing to do to him!" said Caroline.

Mr. Neville, to whom the import of this information was rather clearer than it was to Julia's outraged sister, smiled suddenly. "Might I suggest," he said mildly, "that we continue this discussion in the parlor? I have the greatest reluctance to encounter Mrs. Chickley again, or to put her in possession of any more of the facts than is strictly necessary."

This prudent suggestion meeting with approbation, the assembled party withdrew to the shabby parlor where Julia, reviving, recounted her adventures on the road to Mr. Lacey, whose countenance, by the end of her recitation, had lightened considerably. "Oh, Bertie," she said, clasping his hand between both of hers, "I know it was very wrong of me, and I never would have consented to run away if I'd had the smallest notion how it would be! Only I was so very *miserable*!"

"Know that," said Mr. Lacey soothingly. "Not going to pinch at you."

"You are a great deal too kind to me. But you don't know the half. Mr. Neville has had to tell the most incredible *bouncer* and say he was engaged to Caro! And he told Ridley that he *gave* me the diamonds to wear, and that we are all going up to Chartleigh to celebrate the betrothal. And while I must say I think it was very clever of him, and handsome too, I do see how it might be a trifle awkward, and . . . oh, Bertie, I'm so very sorry!"

"No use apologizing to me," said Mr. Lacey, observing without surprise the rather unsettling effect this disclosure was apparently having on Caroline. "Don't need to tell you you're dashed indebted to Neville here! And Caro too! Don't suppose you bothered to apologize for nabbing his jewels while you were at it?"

"Oh no!" cried Julia with a stricken look. "I . . . I forgot. Oh, sir," she said, turning an impassioned gaze on Mr. Neville, "can you ever forgive me? I behaved so dreadfully, but I didn't *mean* to!"

"I am quite sure that you did not," said Mr. Neville calmly. "As a matter of fact, I have every reason to be grateful to you. If you had not, ah, borrowed the diamonds, I would not have had occasion to discover my own mind on a predicament which I have every hope of resolving shortly in a particularly felicitous manner. And the next time you want to borrow the Wentworth diamonds, you outrageous brat, just ask me, and I will be happy to lend them to you!"

"You *will*?" cried Julia, who had scarcely understood anything from this speech other than that she was apparently forgiven.

"We're very grateful to you, sir," said Mr. Lacey, his earlier suspicion confirmed by Caroline's unnatural silence and the blush overspreading her cheeks, "but what's to be done now?"

Mr. Neville smiled. "I must confess to a desire to remove myself from these premises as soon as may be. As I have been at some pains to establish that we are all going up to Chartleigh, I think that must be the best plan. If your uncle can spare you, Mr. Lacey, I would be honored if you would form one of the party."

Mr. Lacey, perfectly well aware of what that gentleman would say about his accepting an invitation to one of the most illustrious establishments in the land, replied that he was quite sure that his uncle could spare him, and that he was delighted to accept.

"Excellent," said Mr. Neville. He turned to Caroline. "If I send a message to Lady Wentworth, might she be prevailed upon to join us there? Her presence is rather necessary to our plan, you know."

Caroline, remembering her last interview with her mother, replied with conviction that Lady Wentworth might be relied upon to do everything in her power to scotch the scandal.

"Then, if we are agreed, I wonder if you would be so good as to return to the posting house in Barnet, Mr. Lacey, and hire a post-chaise for the trip? I think it would be inadvisable for the ladies to travel so far in open carriages."

"With pleasure, sir!" agreed Mr. Lacey. "Shan't be a trice," he said to Julia, who was pulling at his coat again.

"Mr. Lacey!" cried Mr. Neville, recalling him.

"Sir?"

"I think it would be an excellent idea if you were to take Miss Julia Wentworth with you."

"Oh, but—" began Julia, who had had quite enough of odious posting houses and knowing ostlers for the day.

"Come along, Julia," said Mr. Lacey with a grin. "Shall we meet you there, sir?"

"We shall be along presently," agreed Mr. Neville, amiably shutting the parlor door on Mr. Lacey and a submissive Julia. "*Now* then," he said with satisfaction, turning back to Caroline.

"I must say," she said thoughtfully, "it was very *chivalrous* of Bertie to come haring after Julia like that. Whoever would have thought it?"

"My dear girl, you must see that he's in love with her!" offered Mr. Neville, amused.

"*Is* he?" she asked, her eyes wide. Her brow wrinkled.

"Yes, I suppose he must be. How odd that I hadn't noticed it." She paused, startled. "Does she love *him,* do you think?"

He shrugged slightly. "More than halfway there, at a guess. Why else would she leave him the note, if she didn't secretly hope he'd come after her?"

Caroline, thunderstruck, was silent.

Mr. Neville possessed himself of her hands. "Do you dislike the idea very much?"

"Oh, no, I . . . it's just so unexpected, after all this time. But I'm afraid Bertie's father may not like it. He hopes for a more . . . eligible connection for him."

"Then Mrs. Lacey, whom I have reason to believe to be a woman of excellent understanding, will persuade him to accept it. Besides, I hope to be allowed to make a handsome settlement on your sister when she marries."

" Mr. Neville . . . ," murmured Caroline, suddenly shy.

"Miss Wentworth, will you do me the honor of becoming my wife?"

She found herself unable to meet his eyes and attempted, without success, to draw her hands away. "You cannot wish to marry me," she said unhappily.

"You must know that I do."

"But," she said, giving voice to the thought that had tormented her ever since she had begun to suspect he meant to pay her his addresses, "you know that we are quite done up. Everyone would say that I only married you for Wyndham Priory, and your fortune."

"My dearest goose, I have been an indolent idler, a wicked flirt, and, as you have cause to know, a strutting coxcomb. I have a great deal to repent, but I swear to you I have never cared a pin for what Society thinks."

"Yes, b-but even your family might think so. Lady Buxton certainly will."

"Aunt Louisa will say what she pleases in any case. You will have to comfort yourself with the knowledge that she could scarcely abuse your character any worse than she has mine. Besides, she quite thrives on being crossed, you know! And in any case you would have me to support you through the ordeal."

"She called my father a 'basket-scrambler'!" suggested Caroline with a little laugh.

"My dear, she has nursed a *tendre* for him for forty years. And only think how relieved she will be when she learns I am not dangling after your sister!"

"She will say I trapped you with my arts and allurements, because I am on the catch for a rich husband," said Caroline frankly. "And how do you know it isn't *true*?"

"Caroline!"

She lifted her eyes reluctantly to his face. He leaned over very close to her, his dark eyes fixed on hers. "*Is* it true?"

"N-no," she replied mistily.

"Of course it is not," he said with a laugh. "If I remember correctly, you seemed to have taken me in dislike from the very first, and did not hesitate to give me a set-down. If you were casting out lures for a rich husband, that was scarcely the best way to proceed."

"Oh, pray don't remind me of my impertinence toward you," said Caroline, blushing. "It was quite unforgivable."

"What did you say I did not deserve? After you heard me say such abominable things to Lord Wynchwood, you were quite within your rights!"

"You *knew* that?"

"Not then, no. But I soon guessed, when Wynchwood reminded me of my ill-chosen remarks. How insufferable you must have thought me!"

"I'm afraid we both behaved rather badly," admitted Caroline, "but like the diamond affair, perhaps it would be just as well not to quarrel for the greater share of the blame."

"I can't allow that," he said, holding her hands more tightly between his. "*Your* behavior there was entirely blameless; you only acted—quite resourcefully too—to try to save your sister. Can you forgive me for what I thought? I had come to love you already, and I couldn't bear to think I had been mistaken when I thought I'd finally found a girl I wanted to make my wife. And then when I discovered my error, I was so afraid I'd killed any regard you might have felt for me." He smiled. "It was Mrs. Lacey who encouraged me to hope that your heart might not have hardened against me after all."

"Mrs. Lacey?" cried Caroline in surprise. "I never said a word to her about my feelings for you."

"Well, I don't know how it may be, but she seemed to feel my case would not be hopeless. And then, when Aunt Louisa told me you would not give her an undertaking never to form a connection with our family, I thought it might be that you could one day forgive me. Caroline, my little love, *are* you going to marry me? I have never in my life wanted anything more than to marry you as soon as may be! Now whatever have I said to make you shed tears?"

"Nothing. I don't know. Only I *never* disliked you . . . well, only at the beginning, perhaps. . . . But I didn't expect to be so *happy*."

In response, Mr. Neville took her in his arms and kissed her, which she was delighted to discover was an even more agreeable sensation than she had imagined in her dark bedchamber, her face on a damp pillow. "Mr. Neville," she said, at length, when he had loosened his hold on her enough for her to catch her breath.

"Robert," he corrected.

"Robert," she agreed. "Are you quite *sure* you wish to marry me? I feel I should just mention that I am not likely to be a very *biddable* sort of wife, and it would be so shocking if we were to fall out."

"And so unusual!" said Mr. Neville, and kissed her again.